LET'S
GET BACK
TO THE
PARTY

LET'S
GET BACK
TO THE
PARTY

a novel by

ZAK SALIH

ALGONQUIN BOOKS OF CHAPEL HILL 2021

Published by
ALGONQUIN BOOKS OF CHAPEL HILL
Post Office Box 2225
Chapel Hill, North Carolina 27515-2225

a division of
WORKMAN PUBLISHING
225 Varick Street
New York, New York 10014
© 2021 by Zak Salih.

LIBRARY OF CONGRESS CATALOGING-IN-PUBLICATION DATA

Names: Salih, Zak, [date]– author.
Title: Let's get back to the party / a novel by Zak Salih.
Other titles: Let us get back to the party
Description: Chapel Hill, North Carolina : Algonquin Books of Chapel Hill, 2021. |
Summary: "Estranged childhood friends Oscar and Sebastian—both too
young to have a personal relationship with the AIDS crisis but too old to
have enjoyed the freedom of an out adolescence—spend a year grappling
with cultural identity, generational change, and what they see in,
and owe to, each other"—Provided by publisher.
Identifiers: LCCN 2020034507 | ISBN 9781616209575 (hardcover) |
ISBN 9781643751146 (ebook)
Classification: LCC PS3619.A4377 L48 2021 | DDC 813/.6—dc23
LC record available at https://lccn.loc.gov/2020034507

10 9 8 7 6 5 4 3 2 1
First Edition

For Scott

"I'm getting sick of crowds," Bill said one night at a particularly noisy gathering. "Let's take a walk." After ten minutes on the moonlit road, none of the lights from the school were visible to interfere with the vast, heavy, velvety blackness of the sky, nor did sounds of laughter and music penetrate the almost terrifying hush. We stood still, enveloped by the awesome multiplicity of the stars. "Let's get back to the party," said Bill. "The universe gives me the creeps."

— ELAINE DE KOONING
"de Kooning Memories"
Vogue (December 1983)

LET'S
GET BACK
TO THE
PARTY

⟆

ONE

Ecce Homo

Sebastian

He arrived at the wedding dressed for a funeral. Sharp black suit, shiny black shirt, skinny black tie, polished black boots. Black hair cresting over black sunglasses in a Hokusai wave. I turned away from the grooms and watched him tiptoe to an empty back pew on the opposite side of the aisle. Oscar Burnham. I hadn't seen him in ten years, but underneath that violent head of hair—bowl-cut when we'd first met as children, shorn in rebellion when we'd last met as undergraduates— was the same slim boy, slipping inside the ceremony like a snake. Would he remember me? Probably not.

After the service, I stepped out of the church into the haze of another high Washington summer. I searched the crowd for Oscar but couldn't find him. As if he'd just floated in and out of the wedding, briefly, like an errant leaf. Or a ghost.

At the foot of the church steps, under a full tree draped in white ribbon, someone laughed. I heard a photographer attack the wedding party, back inside. Loving it, the photographer said. Give me more.

Cocktail hour. I lingered outside with a beer. Guests milled around the back lawn and garden of the Georgetown estate. Bar tables swaddled in white cloth and crowned with swollen floral arrangements dotted the clipped grass; beyond that, in a brilliant patch of sunlight, the grooms posed for more photographs. Smiling. Hugging. Kissing. Whispering. Chucking their chins. Nuzzling their noses. I'd been watching them for the past several minutes, forcing my face into a look of fondness so the other guests wouldn't realize I knew absolutely no one here. Dani, my date for the evening, had abandoned me for the restroom and a fresh glass of wine. There was nothing for me to do but stand there and sip, smiling at the people who passed by, at the couple out on the lawn. Trying, unsuccessfully, not to dwell on my own recent uncoupling.

There! Oscar's long black shape, slicing through the space between wedding guests. It paused at the opposite end of the massive stone porch, leaned against a wrought-iron balustrade, watched the grooms. No, he was no phantom. He was here, occupying physical space. To look at him, you'd think Oscar was in danger of being blown off the porch by the slightest breeze, he was so slender. He reminded me of something by Egon Schiele. Tall, lanky, otherworldly. With his eyes hidden behind those sunglasses, Oscar's gaze was mysterious, unreadable. He was all body, no expression.

Across the lawn, the photographer signed a countdown from five. The wedding party, now regrouped, held hands and leapt in the air. The photographer, checking her camera, said, That's great. Let's try it again. A groomsman said, Christ, I need a drink.

Fragile grandparents, beer-bellied college buddies, nieces and nephews dolled up in flower dresses and loafers. Someone passed by me and whispered to his companion how great it was to finally be part of a gay wedding. The woman (I assume his wife) said, It's about time those two wild dogs settled down.

Dani returned, holding her glass against her green summer dress, as energetic and ebullient as she was every Monday through Friday at Douglas Mortimer Secondary School. I had no idea how she pulled off such joie de vivre. It had been three years since the staff meeting where she'd seen me, the new guy, and patted the empty chair next to her. Since then, she'd become a friend and colleague, a sounding board for my administrative gripes—and my personal ones. She was the first person I called when, only a month ago, Jake left me for a job in San Francisco. Dani, ever the optimist, had a simple solution for my despondency: Throw myself back out there. Go on the hunt. But I was no hunter. I relied on the forwardness of others, their generosity of time, their curiosity. First moves, final moves; I was terrible at both. Where I flourished: the middle, where everything was comfortable. Where I felt I'd finally checked that box off my existential to-do list—Find A Boyfriend— and could get back to more serious matters. I thought I'd had it checked off, but now the check mark had been erased, recklessly, and without the distraction of work, summer was proving difficult. Last weekend, I'd found myself, like an idiot, staring at our four-poster bed, built for two but home now to one, and sobbing without shame in big, sucking intakes of breath. Thinking what a fool I was to have believed a life out here was something Jake actually wanted, that I was more than just a caretaker supporting him through the traumas of failed relationships from which he still couldn't completely extricate himself. Thinking of all the times he told me how safe he felt with me, of all the times he didn't say how happy he felt with me. Calmed by three glasses of wine, I'd called Dani. After listening patiently, she'd extended an invitation to be her plus-one at a friend's wedding the following weekend. A bit late, I'd said. She'd told me her original date had to leave town. Aunt's funeral, she'd said. I was just going to go alone, but I think this'll be good for you. At the very least, it's free drinks. On the drive into Georgetown, I'd received a text from Dani. *FYI: Lee's husband invited single friends. Come prepared to meet people.* At a stoplight on M Street, I'd written back: *You're joking.*

I turned to tell Dani I knew the guy standing over there on the opposite porch, then saw she had someone with her. Sebastian, she said, I want you to meet John. He's one of Lee's friends. John, this is my friend Sebastian Mote. The art history teacher. I shook John's hand politely and smiled. I love art, John said. He was soft: in speech, in body, in manner. Like me. He wore rolled-up shirt-sleeves (past his elbows—Jake's definition of gauche) and a loosely knotted cotton tie. Like me. Dani took several steps back, watching us as if awaiting the result of a strange experiment. I forced myself to be considerate. I was, after all, a guest at a wedding. Not just any wedding. A Gay Wedding, one painstakingly designed to strike traditional notes despite its untraditional participants. The escorting of the grooms down the aisle by their mothers. The biblical readings that sidestepped any mention of Iron Age gender roles. The vows, the exchange of rings, the precarious lighting of a unity candle. The kiss, long and slow and deep and just a touch inappropriate. Everyone at the wedding, from Patrick's dying grandmother to Lee's three-year-old niece, on a collective high from last month's Supreme Court decision. According to Dani's pre-ceremony brief on the front steps of the church, the wedding had been planned almost a year ago with the verdict already in mind. (I avoided asking what would have happened had the morning of June 26, 2015, led instead to an embarrassing kink in the arc of social justice.) Then there was me: heartbroken and struggling to see this day as a capstone to all the years I'd spent in college volunteering with the campus queer student organization, the months I spent canvassing for gay marriage outside suburban Metro stations and grocery stores. (Have a moment for gay rights? Not today? Thanks for your time.) All this—the back lawn of the estate, the strings of paper lanterns, the massive marble planters boiling over with vegetation straight out of a Fragonard—was what I'd done my infinitesimally small part to bring about. It was what I'd wanted for all of us. For myself.

I looked over John's shoulder at Oscar, peering Narcissus-like into his phone, oblivious to my glances, as stone-stiff as I remembered from those three childhood years we spent as neighbors on Cinnamon Road, when he practically lived at my house because his own was a den of strict rules and passive-aggressive silences. The last time I'd seen him, he'd been surrounded by a pack of college friends, moving through a party with preternatural ease, half-drunk on peach schnapps. So free of the constraints of his past life that, when I'd gone up to him, expecting him to pull me into an embrace, he stared at me, unable to recall my face, having abandoned it with the rest of his childhood, until I reminded him and he said, Ah, drawing the sound out from behind his red plastic cup. How nice, I'd thought, to be so free of the past.

You enjoy teaching? I turned away from the grooms, from Oscar, to see John smiling around red cheeks. I do, I said. My father's a professor. It runs in the family. There, I thought. The ice had cracked. Now there was an awkward pause. We both sipped our drinks until I realized what was expected of me and I asked John what he did for a living. I work on the Hill, he said, relieved. He gave me the name of a Vermont politician who wasn't Bernie Sanders. I asked if he enjoyed it. Mm, he said. Very much so. I waited for him to take a sip of his drink, then threw my eyes across the balcony again. Oscar was gone. John asked which of the grooms I knew. Neither, I said, nodding to Dani taking pictures of the wedding decorations with her phone. I'm her plus-one. Oh, John said. I see. So you live in the city? Not anymore, I said, and left it at that. I stared at Dani in resentment, feeling duped. It was too soon. It was much too soon. I extended a hand to John, said it was a pleasure meeting him. Dani shot me a stern look. I excused myself to go inside.

Down in the garden, two best maids wedged themselves under the grooms' arms and strained upward to kiss their extended cheeks. The photographer cooed and said, That's going to look so cute.

I wandered through the ground floor of the colonial-style manor, with its Byzantine tapestries and glass cases of Pre-Colombian sculpture, its high ceilings and broad spaces that diminished the size of a wedding crowd that, earlier in the small church, had seemed like a teeming mass, as if the whole world had been there to watch Lee and Patrick become man and man. Everywhere were pictures of the grooms in frames and collages. Lee and Patrick holding hands in front of Caracalla's massive stone baths. Lee and Patrick kissing in kayaks in the Florida Keys. Lee and Patrick running hands along the ragged walls of an ancient Thai temple. Lee and Patrick at corporate holiday dinners, at family picnics, at bed-and-breakfasts. Lee and Patrick as infants, as toddlers, as teenagers, as college students, as working adults. In front of a staircase blocked off with velvet rope, a string quartet played the familiar air from Bach's Orchestral Suite No. 3. I stood and listened to the music, thinking of the first time I'd heard the piece, as a child in the living room of a friend's house. I kept my eyes open for a glimpse of a slender, slippery shape among the guests. The quartet finished the piece and began a slow, strange arrangement of Dusty Springfield's "I Only Want to Be with You" that soothed my resentment toward Dani and, invariably, drew my mind like a donkey on a well-worth path back to Jake.

That spring, I'd asked him to move with me out of D.C. and into a rambler on the outskirts of northern Virginia. The rambler's owner: my father, Dr. Malcolm Mote, Professor of American History, invited for a two-year teaching stint at his alma mater in western North Carolina. Facing rising rent and on the outs with a roommate (and former lover), Jake agreed to the impulsive move. Let's give it a shot, he said. (Had I only paid proper attention to what he said next: What's the worst that could happen?) So this is it, I thought. It's happening! This is where life starts! A month later, however, that life began to soften and buckle. While

I unpacked and arranged and organized, Jake sat in chairs and played with his phone, a great white shark forced into mindless circumnavigations in a cramped aquarium. For a few weeks, I deluded myself into thinking the wild animal I'd captured would adapt, that he'd realize how much easier it was out here away from the urban scene. That he'd realize he didn't need all the parties he went to (without me), all the complex social circles through which he rotated (without me). And then the bed arrived, a mammoth four-poster piece we'd found on a weekend drive through the valley towns along Interstate 81. We had a horrible time getting it into the house, spent hours unscrewing, carrying, reassembling, both of us sweating despite the crisp March air. That evening, I came into the bedroom anticipating sex. Instead, I found Jake flung across the flannel sheets like a troubled Fuseli dreamer. We never did break in that bed properly. Instead, we argued more frequently over more trivial matters: refrigerated tomatoes, the origins of a pubic hair stuck to the side of the tub. Petty things that didn't seem to carry any weight when I complained about them to Dani. Still, I convinced myself, Jake and I had a history. We had three years of dinner dates, of three-day weekends in Pittsburgh and Boston, of countless nights when I consoled him, as if he were one of my students, over the unnecessary social drama he couldn't seem to pull himself away from. I thought that was enough. I really did. So I was dumbfounded when Jake came to me one evening in May and said he was going nowhere doing temp work and had accepted a marketing manager position with a San Francisco start-up. That's all the way out in California, I said like a moron. The next thing I did, admittedly, was the last thing I wanted to do. Jake turned from my tears but kept a limp hand on my shoulder, which made it worse. I excused myself to the bathroom, where

I punched a hole in the drywall above the toilet. I wasn't sure if Jake heard me. I didn't care. I felt something twist in my shoulder, but I didn't care about that either. The job was just pretext. The truth, I knew, had less to do with his career and more to do with our experiment in domesticity, with his decision to slum it out in the suburbs. He wasn't leaving me because of a job. He was leaving because he'd panicked. After more wine, Jake elaborated on his decision. I thought this was what I wanted, he said. I asked if he really didn't want it, or if he just thought he didn't deserve it. Incensed by the backyard psychoanalysis, Jake said, Maybe I'm just not happy with you. Later, in bed, lying board-stiff next to one another, I stared up at the popcorn ceiling in a rage while Jake snored as if it were just another night. The next day, he left to stay with friends back in the city. Three days later, he came back with a rental van, packed up his barely unpacked boxes, and was gone.

In the hall, the wedding party lined up to enter the dining room. Lee's father, plump and drunk and ready to be painted by Frans Hals, beckoned the guests inside with scoops of his arm. Dani came in from outside. There you are, she said to me. We're Table Six. John was with her. Me too, he said. We walked into the dining room and took our seats, mine next to Dani's, John's next to mine. Two tables over, against the eastern side of the dining room, Oscar sat among several other men in slim khakis and pastel bowties. He was looking down at his phone and smiling.

Behold, the grooms! Here they came, striding hand in hand into the reception hall, on display for the family members, the friends, the co-workers, the ex-lovers. They stopped in the center of the dining room, padded over with a layer of faux wood flooring in anticipation of the evening's dancing, and waved to everyone. The emcee (Patrick's cousin, Dani said) stepped back from the grooms as if in deference to the sheer physical force of their union. The photographer returned, flapping around the men to capture them from every possible perspective. Patrick and Lee raised their arms in triumph. The wedding guests raised bottles of beer, glasses of wine. A hard-fought battle, finally won. Here, now, were the victorious soldiers, returned from the field of war and prepared to live happily ever after, their armor not blood-crusted chainmail but matching gray suits with white carnations affixed to their left lapels. At one point in their revolutions, Lee smiled and waved at me. It took me a moment to realize he was actually waving at Dani, who shouted her congratulations. Patrick beamed a smile and pointed a finger in Oscar's direction. I watched Oscar give a limp wave and lean back in his chair with a toothless smile, arms folded against his chest, elbows stuck out like tiny wings. Lee and Patrick began to slow dance while the string quartet, now installed in a corner, played a rendition of "At Last." This is so much cuteness I can't handle it, someone at Table Six said. I knew Lee would take Patrick's last name, Dani said to John. A waiter asked if I wanted red or white. John turned to look at me as the waiter came by to pour his wine and gave me another bashful smile. I returned the smile, reluctantly, then tilted my eyes to get another glimpse of Oscar on his phone. The strings began their final, sweet descent, and the couple ended their dance with another long kiss. There was a resurgence of applause, of sparse drunken cheers from Table Eight (Lee's teammates from the gay rowing club, Dani said). The grooms continued to hold hands as they walked to the wedding party banquette, a Last Supper tableau with paper lanterns and an arbor of waxy white flowers.

Muted conversation. Clinking glassware. Then the minister, tow-headed and red-cheeked, took the microphone from Patrick's cousin. I'm sure you've heard quite enough from me already, he said. But before we sit down to eat with these two fine men, I'd like to start with a brief invocation. Don't panic. The Bible's staying back at the church where it belongs. The room laughed. Instead, I want to open up this wonderful evening with words I'm sure most of us here, if not all, are already familiar with. The minister unfolded a piece of paper, cleared his throat, and started to read: No union is more profound than marriage, for it embodies the highest ideals of love, fidelity, devotion, sacrifice, and family. In forming a marital union, two people become something greater than they once were. It would misunderstand these men and women to say they disrespect the idea of marriage. Their plea is that they do respect it, respect it so deeply that they seek to find its fulfillment in themselves. Their hope is not to be condemned to live in loneliness, excluded from one of civilization's oldest institutions. They ask for equal dignity in the eyes of the law. The Constitution grants them that right. The minister put away the paper. The room was silent. Let us bow our heads in prayer and thanks, he said.

Plates came and went. Dani told Table Six about her math classes at Mortimer, her Arab background. I was wondering where all that beautiful skin came from, Will, one of Lee's real estate colleagues, said. John talked politics with Will's boyfriend, Tom. I kept quiet until Dani noticed and, with the same tone I'd heard her use around shy students, volunteered information on my behalf. Sebastian's Arab, too, she said. Well, half. His mom's side. You've got nice skin too, Will said to me. I saw John frown over his shrimp salad as if the words had been plucked from his mouth. Everyone around the table looked at me, and I realized I was expected to explain. My mother came here in the seventies for college, I said. She met my father, fell in love, stayed. Dani raised a salad fork. Seduced by the white man, she said. His mother was a lot less pious than mine. Table Six chuckled, and I felt pressured to continue. I didn't even get an Arab name, I said. She didn't want anything to do with that part of her. I just got the skin. And the dark hair. It's so full, John said. Tom asked how my mom handled my sexuality. I shrugged. She doesn't care, I said. She's dead. Table Six went quiet. Dani frowned at me, aware of what I was trying to do, and I felt gleefully malevolent. It was a long time ago, she said to break the silence. Back in college, right, Sebastian? I took a long draught of wine. That's right, I said. She was no model Muslim. She married a white Christian against her parents' wishes, she never covered her hair. She smoked pot. Supposedly. She made pork chops for us once a week, which she loved and I hated. Sometimes, I'd see her drinking scotch in the living room while my father rubbed her feet. So no, I don't think she'd have minded too much that her son sucked dick. I added the childish noun for levity, to steer Table Six away from the cloud cover of death and to turn the conversation away from me. Then Dani said, The dogs. Tell them about how your mom loved dogs. Reluctantly, I told Table Six about the dogs my late mother had sheltered in our Fairfax home from as early as I could remember. Not young dogs. Not puppies. The old and infirm. I mentioned Snoopy, the black lab frosted white with age, who padded awkwardly around the house from an irremovable tumor in his lower back. I told them about Spencer, the blind beagle a childhood friend and I would take for painfully long walks up to the elementary school. (I shot a glance across the room at Oscar, as if the story would somehow draw his gaze toward me instead of at his plate of shrimp, which he was picking at in obvious disgust.) I didn't tell the table about Emma, the basset hound who'd been en route to a vet appointment when my mother's vehicle had its fateful encounter with a harried early-evening driver. John asked if I ever thought about getting a senior dog. One day, I said. Maybe, I thought, I'll name it Jake, take care of it just like I took care of him. And when it dies, I can bury it in dad's backyard and finally be ready to start over again. Growing up with dying dogs, Will said. That's fucked up. Tom slapped his arm. Sorry, Will said.

Midway through a best maid's speech, a flash of black drew my attention to Table Nine, where Oscar summoned a waiter for more wine. I remembered clearly the evening I'd once held that tender, thin limb in my grip. A minute later, Oscar pulled out his phone, smiled, and headed toward the restroom on those impossibly long legs of his, past caterers bringing out trays of beef medallions and chicken piccata. I watched him until he disappeared behind a heavy wood door, then turned to see John watching me expectantly. Sorry, I said to him. What was that?

The grooms arrived at Table Six. They loomed over Dani, over me. My co-worker, Dani said. He teaches at Mortimer with me. Nice to meet you, the couple said. We shook hands. Hope you're enjoying yourself, Lee said. I am, I said. There was a flash of light as the photographer took our picture, a candid shot destined for some handmade wedding album. I imagined myself immortalized behind adhesive plastic, looking dumbstruck up at Lee and Patrick. There's Dani, Lee would say decades later. We used to be close.

Not sure who that guy with her is, though. Patrick turned to grab a flitting shadow and pulled it into a hug. Oscar, he said. Glad you made it. Patrick introduced him to the table. A friend, and one of my senior graphic designers, he said. Been with us for eight years now. Nine, Oscar said, surveying the table. Hey, he said to John. Hello there, he said to Tom. Hey, he said to me. Hi, Oscar, I said. Hey, he said to Dani. I waited for Oscar to do a double take, to come back to my face. I wanted to borrow words from the grieving ghost in *Hamlet* (which my honors English students would be reading in the fall): Remember me. But there was no recognition I could see. Patrick plucked at Oscar's jacket, said, You know this is a wedding, right? It was all I had, Oscar said. Lee, not hiding his displeasure at their funereal guest, tugged Patrick's hand. Mom wants us to take a picture with Nana, he said. I watched the grooms move to where Nana, drowning in a blue tulle dress, waited patiently for what could be one of the last photographs of her life. When I turned around, Oscar was back at his table.

The dancing began. Avoiding John's longing look, I got up and left the reception hall, stepping out onto the back porch and into warm evening air. I watched several guests mill around the gardens, inspecting flowers, watching planes breach the clouds from their takeoffs at National. Perhaps it was the weight I'd gained in the intervening decade, the softening around my face and middle, that made me just another anonymous wedding guest instead of an old friend. For professional reasons, I avoided social media, so I had little inkling of Oscar's public life other than what I conjured in my imagination. So what was holding me from marching back inside, from going over to Oscar's table, tapping him on the shoulder, and telling him exactly who I was? Standing in the night, away from the party, I realized it was a fear that had already been halfway confirmed: Once again, he'd forgotten me.

Despite the heft of its architecture, the estate couldn't contain the music coming from inside, where the string quartet had been supplanted by the Beach Boys singing "Wouldn't It Be Nice." I moved away from the music toward the edge of the back porch. I counted fireflies for what felt like forever until I heard someone step outside. I turned around. There he was. He was looking intently at his phone and so I walked over, stood in front of him with my arms outspread (not too wide) and said, It's me. Oscar looked up and smiled, hesitantly. Then I saw the beautiful recognition. Wait, he said. Sebastian? Yes, I said. I pulled him into my arms and he hugged me back, delicately, the way you'd cup a chick in your palm. He smelled of sharp cologne and hair gel. I felt an emptiness as he pulled back and picked up the glass of wine he'd set down. Wow, he said. The last time I saw you was—. College, I said, committed to doing his remembering for him. The lawn party at Jefferson. Yeah, Oscar said. Yeah, that's right. Wow. He put his phone in his pocket and picked up his drink. We clinked glasses. Nice out here, he said. I said, Isn't it? I needed some air. And I hate dancing. Oscar smiled. I opened my mouth to ask the first of my many questions, then Oscar clutched his right thigh as if in pain. He pulled out his phone and looked at the screen. He grinned. Have to take this, he said. Okay, I said. See you back inside.

The wedding cake was a four-tiered affair, vaguely Venetian, topped by two tuxedoed men set shoulder to shoulder. Oscar and I stood next to one another, me with a refreshed wine glass, he with his cell phone. We watched the grooms feed each other, first with their hands and then, to the ribald delight of the younger guests, mouth to mouth. Oscar groaned, tapped at his phone. Someone handed me a slice of white cake lacerated with raspberry icing. Oscar put his phone away to receive his plate of cake. He watched me take the first bite. He asked, So? It's wedding cake, I said through the corner of my mouth. They spent more time on the outside than the inside. No, Oscar said. So how have you been? What's new? And after ten years, all I could say in that moment, cake in my mouth, was, Good. Nothing much. Oscar asked if I was going out with the others after the reception. I didn't know there was something going on, I said. After party for the guests, Oscar said. I think I heard it was happening at Empire. I'm sure the ladies are excited. Even Nana will be there. Oscar took an angry bite of cake and set it down on a nearby table. I asked if he was going, wondering to myself if I could tolerate the crowds and noise to spend just a little more time in his company. No, he said. Don't think so. Been Cruzing back and forth all evening with this college kid. So fresh out of the closet he's got mothballs sticking to his shoulders. Still, pics look promising. Here. Oscar opened up Cruze on his phone and I watched the logo—which, depending on your mood or luck, was either a carnival mask or a death's-head—pulse purple against a gold background. Then the screen divided into the familiar series of tiled images: faces, torsos, buttocks, eyes, biceps. I imagined Jake, who'd never been able to delete the app from his phone while we were together, out on the West Coast with a small digital square of his own. The thought made me ill, so I declined to pass judgment on any pictures, turning away from Oscar's phone and looking instead at the mass of shifting bodies on the dance floor. I saw the grooms pose for a selfie with Dani and John. I wanted all these people to disappear, one by one, until it was just Oscar and me, away from the crowds and the noise, back in the hush of my childhood basement where we'd spent so much time together. Oscar put his phone back in his pocket. So, he said, when are you going to be the main event at one of these? I drained my wine. Excuse me, I said.

They were playing "Just Like Heaven" when I returned from the bathroom. I moved around a table of coffee-sippers and sec-ond-slice cake eaters, back to Oscar's side, feeling like space junk pulled inexorably into the orbit of some massive dark planet. I opened my mouth to ask Oscar where he lived now, how his par-ents were, but he cut me off. Deal sealed, he said. Drinks at 11:30 at the Attic. Hey, you majored in English, right? I beamed with pleasure that he remembered. So this guy says he's an English stu-dent at American. Give me the name of some books I can impress him with. I was too drained to be witty, so I said I'd have to think about it. No worries, Oscar said. You think about it and text me some titles and I'll drop them into our conversation. We exchanged numbers with little ceremony, with no promise of meeting up.

Dani emerged from the dance floor glazed in sweat to tell me the wedding was winding down and some people were heading over to Empire. You're coming, right? I looked at the floor. I felt Dani looking at me. I felt Oscar looking at me. Then I said, No. No, I don't think so. Come on, Dani said. You won't do yourself any good going home and brooding. You do brood, Oscar said. That I definitely remember. I looked up at Oscar, thinking how a few moments ago I'd wanted to hug him and now I wanted to hit him. He just got out of a bad relationship, Dani said to Oscar. I'm try-ing to get him to come out and have fun. Help me out here. Oscar raised his hands in mock surrender. Staying out of this, he said. On the dance floor, couples swayed in various stages of inebriation while Nat King Cole crooned about love and sentimentality. Dani went back to find John. So, Oscar said. Single.

We stood outside the front doors of the estate in two facing rows, me wedged between Dani and John, Oscar on his phone down at the end of the opposite row. Someone handed us sparklers. Someone else dropped small steel tins of flame intermittently along each line of guests. The whole moment, despite the revelry, despite the yawns and stumbles, had the air of a solemn sacrifice. Then they came, into the sparkling archway of light, into the warm night. Everyone cheered, yelled, hollered as the grooms ducked into a waiting car and waved goodbye.

Inside, staff were already gathering plates, stacking chairs, unhooking paper lanterns, disassembling tables. I looked for Dani to tell her thank you and goodbye, saw her with John and several other people. Then I saw Oscar, clutching his black jacket and stealing off into the night. Without thinking, I began to follow him out of the estate and east down the cobblestone sidewalk, hardly getting closer than half a block. (Those swift legs! Even as a child, I'd had a hard time keeping up with them!) I tripped on the uneven bricks of the sidewalk and caught myself against a tree, where I watched Oscar get into a compact car with its hazards blinking. I thought about calling out to him, offering to give him a ride to the Attic, but he'd already shut the passenger door. As the car drove past, I cringed against the tree as if playing one of the games of flashlight tag that had occupied our childhood summers. Don't see me! Please, please don't see me! Then, once again, Oscar was gone.

Oscar

Fuck, I'm glad that's over.

I've got thirty minutes to meet A., who says his name is Aaron, at the Attic. Just enough time to get home, change out of this suit, clear my head, drink some water, and take a massive shit. Already, I can feel my bowels seizing in the back of this car share that smells like ginger and patchouli. These Judas gays with their undercooked shrimp on neat square toasts.

But I did it. I suffered through the wedding and now it's over. I'd never have shown up if my job hadn't, in some way, depended on it. I mean, imagine what my next employee review would have been like. It's not just that Patrick's my boss, you see. I knew Patrick long before he sold out, back when we were just dumb twenty-somethings spending epic evenings hopping like frogs from bar to club to bar to bar to someone's bedroom. (Or, if not someone's bedroom, McDonald's.) I knew him long before Lee gelded him, dragged him into the same sad life of every other boring breeder. And now? Now Patrick's a stranger to me. Another one of the lost.

Christ, what's happening to us? This summer, more than ever, it seems like all the young gay men in this city are dropping like flies. It's an epidemic, for sure. (No, not that one.) It's been going on for months, years even. Only now, thanks to Saint Obergefell, can I see the pattern, the gravity of it all. Like an infestation. First you spot a single ant crawling on your kitchen floor, and you think nothing of it. Then you see five ants, and you begin to get annoyed. Then, finally, the entire swarm reveals itself, crawling along your baseboards and behind your trash can, and you start to feel hopeless. You start to feel like *you're* the invasive species, not them.

The stories are everywhere. I hear them doing the late-night rounds at Empire, at Curio, at Captain Dave's. I read the announcements in the overlooked back pages of our two dueling gay rags, the *Lance* and the *Dagger*. I see the status updates on my social media feeds, get the text messages on my phone, all of them emoji'd to hell and back. I hear snippets of news reports on public radio, in breaking-news email alerts. It's happening to celebrities and unknowns alike. Wherever I go, it's rubbed in my face. Once, I even saw an announcement taped to a bathroom stall, papering over magic-marker cocks. Trust me: They'll start unfurling banners from the tops of mid-rise condos and chartering private planes to spread messages in exhaust across the skies. Can you imagine?

Some of my friends and acquaintances, admittedly, go discreetly. Others—like Patrick—depart with triumphant fanfare, like Viking corpses set out to sea on flaming biers. One week, I'm sharing an awkward hello as I pass an old hookup on Seventeenth Street or in the crowded corner of once-gay bars now packed with straight women. Then I see him less and less, until finally I don't see him at all. Unanswered texts, unanswered emails, un-liked Facebook comments, un-loved tweets, unacknowledged selfies. Then you get the news. He's gone. Vanished to another plane of existence, never to return. The latest one to pass up the mantle of proud queer, to leave me behind.

Take Bart. Two years deep into a relationship with Jackson, a man I introduced him to, no less. Bart. My soldier-in-arms, my wingman. He'll cave soon, too. Just wait. It's only a matter of time before I'm stuffed, once again, into a church pew listening to those god-awful words, "Dearly beloved, we are gathered here today . . ."

Everyone's a victim of marriage fever now, you see. Everyone's conforming, shacking up instead of hooking up. Everyone's feeling, as of this warm July 11, 2015, like they've reached the summit of some impossible mountain.

And here's the worst part: Everyone's so fucking thrilled about it all.

A BLOCK AWAY from Fourteenth and N, I get a message on Cruze from A.

Hey.

Hey, I write. *See you at 11:30. Need to stop off at home.*

The car pulls up next to the bus shelter outside my apartment building.

See? This is what I'm talking about.

On one of the walls, inside protective plastic, is a stock image, hardly doctored, of two men (one black, one white), both handsome in that safe, demographically pleasant way, foreheads pressed together, eyes closed, scripted type compelling the viewer to MAKE HIM YOURS FOREVER. Below this, in the blur of the lovers' upper bodies, is a logo for a high-end jeweler with locations in Georgetown and Chevy Chase. I can't remember when this ad first appeared. It must have been months ago. And every time I walk out the lobby doors of the Beardsley, there it is, ready to smack me in the face. I think about the young men who pass by this bus shelter at night, on their way up into the gayborhood, longing not for fun but for the opportunity to follow in the same sluggish, knuckle-dragging footsteps of their parents and their parents before them. I think of the legions of gays to come who'll see this ad, or another like it, and think: Yes! That's what I want! That's what I need! That's what I have to have! Storybook love! Domestic bliss! Forget the beautiful grit and grime and rebellion; forget the sheer faggotry of it all. Power-wash that rust into the sewers! We want something shiny and polished! We want something tame!

Sometimes I have fantasies of creeping out in the early-morning hours and kicking at the plastic of the bus shelter until it cracks, until there's enough room for me to tear out the ad and drag it to the ground and spit on it.

It's a perilous three-minute wait for the only working elevator (I'm on floor nine of ten), but I make it to the toilet just in time for the great release, the crack and splatter of half-digested shrimp and asparagus. Sitting there and enjoying the blessed emptying of my gut, I take my phone and scroll again through A.'s Cruze profile. Round-faced, almond-eyed, head heavy with dark brown curls. Twenty-one years old. (Phew.) Versatile. (Read: bottom.) A little short, but a decent height-to-weight ratio, and I don't mind a little belly. Location, curiously, turned off, so that he could be anywhere in the world right now. Something cute and earnest and mysterious about him, intriguing enough for me to pay attention when I received his first message earlier this afternoon on my way to the church (late, as usual).

Nice pics. How's it going?

During the reception, we kept messaging one another. I spoke about my current social imprisonment in Georgetown, he of his freshman year at American. I told him about my work in advertising and branding, to which he responded with a shirtless picture of himself. Then a shot of plump buttocks swaddled in bright green Skyler Mountain briefs, a triptych of his cock in stages of excitement.

Then: *Your turn.*

How awkward my cock must have looked in the opulence of that Georgetown bathroom. There was no response for a while and I wondered, Size queen? Then, just when I'd stepped out on the back porch and started talking to Sebastian—Sebastian! After all these years!—I got a response.

Free later?

Was I free later? Of course I was free. And after all, what better way to toast the evening's conformity than with an empty, casual fuck.

He wanted to meet in public first. I said I certainly wasn't traveling all the way up to Tenleytown. He said he was at the Kennedy Center for a show, he could meet somewhere in Georgetown. I said, *No gay bars in Georgetown. Let's do the Attic.* He asked me where that was, and I was excited by his innocence.

Dupont, I wrote. *Old townhouse.*

I gave him the address.

Okay.

Nothing left in me now but air, I drop our message history and its attendant amateur shots into my Cruze archive. Five minutes later, after changing into a plain white T-shirt, jeans, and boat shoes, and after readjusting the gelled swell of my hair in the bathroom mirror, I head back out into the night.

THE ATTIC, NO surprise, is dead.

Built into the shell of two adjacent rowhomes east of Dupont Circle, the once-popular institution is now just a sad husk, left like snakeskin in the dust of the bigger, more brazen bars to the east (where I really should be tonight). What business the Attic gets now rests on the backs of the old gays who come here out of obligation, chained to their past, or the new gays who know they should be somewhere else but prefer to toe the water first. I was that new gay once; now, walking up the front stone steps and sharing a meaningless smile with three old smoking queens, I wonder if I'm not already that old gay bracing himself for the sad, half-conscious looks from boys yet to be born.

The doorman, more mascara than muscle, checks my ID. I move into the dark and up the narrow staircase with its walls painted deep purple, thinking of the ghosts of the rich mid-century breeders who used to climb up and down these same stairs. I pass the second floor with its wave of loud Eighties music—Naked Eyes, "Always Something There to Remind Me"—and its strobe lights moving lazily across a sparsely populated dance floor. At the bar, several women laugh and flirt with the shirtless young bartender who's handsome in that chiseled, well-oiled way that helps sell drinks and earn tips. Now, however, he's simply an animal on display for the tipsy bachelorettes, one of whom—the bride-to-be, I imagine—wears a headband crowned with tiny glittered cocks bobbing on springs. As I pass, the bartender and I share a brief look of commiseration.

It's quieter on the top floor of the Attic, the music from below a dull beat you can easily tune out. It's also, I see, been redesigned. The far wall is now a gallery of gay icons trapped in haphazard frames of cheap wood, metal, and plastic. Rock Hudson, dripping with pool water. Alan Turing, with his slightly extraterrestrial stare. Walt Whitman with his proud wizard's beard. Divine, with her drag-queen ferocity that never fails to unnerve me. A legion of gay artists, actors, performers, and politicians. On another wall, the divas. Madonna, Gaga, and Kylie. Babs and Britney and Cher. Betty and Bea and Rue. Around them, a veritable art museum of publicity stills, amateur paintings, movie posters, old photographs, album covers. Intestines of glittery garland and string lights coiled around exposed pipes and ductwork. Red plastic booths lining the opposite wall, an older man sitting alone in the far booth under a massive print of Banksy's embracing bobbies. On a widescreen television, those two old Bouvier biddies shambling through their vermin-infested Hamptons mansion. Over the long bar, above a skyline of liquor bottles, several framed copies of the front page of *The Washington Post* from two Saturdays ago. GAYS' RIGHT TO WED AFFIRMED. By a pair of bay windows, a small pack of bears pass judgment on the Seventeenth Street foot traffic.

At the bar, I order a vodka soda, then I turn around and look for a college-age boy trembling with fear in this near-empty space.

No one.

I check Cruze.

Nothing.

I take my drink to the nearest booth and sit down. My stomach shudders again, but it's not the shrimp. It's because I think I know how this is going to turn out. Still. I'll give it twenty minutes. Wouldn't be the first time a hookup flaked, and God knows I'm just as guilty. Guess I won't be texting Sebastian for book titles after all. He's probably long since tucked himself into his sub-urban bed, anyway. Probably already dreaming of his own nup-tials. God, Sebastian! Just as straight-laced, just as proper, just as responsible, just as brooding as he was in elementary school. Now playing the role of the broken-hearted, envious single man at a wedding. No surprise he's another sellout, though I suppose in his case, it comes from having a halfway decent family to raise you.

The vodka-soda's tasteless, but it settles my stomach. I stretch my legs along the red plastic, flex my feet, think of the crush of bodies several blocks east at Empire. I feel another surge of panic, a low-lying terror that I'm not where I'm supposed to be. Two minutes later, the vodka-soda's gone, and I start chewing ice. Another drink? Home? I text Bart to see what he's up to, but I doubt he'll answer. Somewhere with Jackson, most likely. I think about texting other people, sending out a high-range S.O.S. so I don't have to be alone, when my phone seizes on the table and I hear that familiar bullfrog call that's impossible for me to ignore.

A new Cruze message.

But not from A.

You look worried.

The profile attached to the yellow text bubble is just a gray silhouette. No face pic, not even the awkward courtesy of a cock. No age, no description of needs or wants. Not even a real name. Tiber. Distance: 15 feet.

I look up and around. Over by the window, a bear points at something (more likely someone) and laughs in a high staccato that doesn't register with the barrel swell of his belly. The bartender's cleaning glasses. Two men I don't remember coming in hunch over the bar and flip through free copies of the *Dagger*.

My phone croaks again.

Your left.

Of course. The old man under the Banksy. What, late sixties? Sinewy, swaddled in a white button-up shirt that's puffed around the waist, so he looks like a snowman in mid-melt. The first two buttons of his shirt are open, revealing a thicket of gray that matches the bristled military cut on his head and the goatee framing a thin-lipped mouth. He looks at me from under arched eyebrows, intent, focused. Then he smiles.

To be polite, I smile back.

Then I text A.

You coming or what?

There's no more ice left in my glass to chew. Shit. Separated from this stranger by three lonely red booths, ignorance is impossible. I've got no choice but to respond to this man who's been a Cruze member since—great. Since earlier this evening. A two-for-one-special on newbies tonight.

No, not worried. Just waiting for someone.

How long?

That's forward.

No. How long have you been waiting.

A while.

He's not coming.

Yeah?

Yeah. If he wanted to be here, he'd be here.

Movement from behind me and I think, It's A., hiding all this time in the restroom and finally coming to save me, like some inexperienced knight, from the hypnotic eyes of this ancient dragon. But it's just the bartender on his way over to Tiber's booth. They talk for a moment (I can't hear their voices), then the bartender leaves, smiling at me as he passes.

I look at my phone, at the television, at the entrance to the third floor. Anything to avoid eye contact. The bartender returns to the man's table a moment later with two glasses of amber and ice. He puts one in front of Tiber and, on his way back to the bar, the other in front of me.

"For you," he says.

Tiber raises his glass to me in a not-so-distant toast. I raise mine back and think, Ketamine? I take a sip.

Jesus.

Not ketamine. Worse.

Scotch.

Over by the door, three young men come upstairs with their drinks, take a look around, then, clearly disappointed at the clientele, turn and walk back downstairs. Wait, I want to scream. Come back! Take me with you!

My phone croaks.

Come sit. I don't bite. If your lover shows up, I'll say I'm your uncle.

I check, one last time, for a message from A. Nothing. I get up and walk over to where the old man sits, regally, one arm stretched along the back of his booth. He releases his drink and swallows my outstretched hand in a grip that's tight and cold and wet.

"Sean," he says.

"Oscar," I say, hoping the plastic seat doesn't fart when I sit. (It does.)

"Any relation?" Sean points behind me with his knob of a chin. I turn and look at an old blown-up photograph of Oscar Wilde perched next to some nineteenth-century twink who looks like he'd rather be anywhere else.

"God no. No, no, no. My mother named me after the Muppet. Apparently I was a colicky baby. Prone to fits of unexplained anger. I never wanted to be left alone."

"A drama queen." Sean smiles. Strange, I think, how a face so lined could be so disarming so quickly.

"Yeah. A drama queen." I point to Sean's phone lying on the table between us. "How's your new toy?"

"Hate it." Sean laughs. "But I'm from out of town, and I'm bored. Not good at being by myself, even after all these years." He stares at me and smirks. "How do you even tolerate this? There's too much going on. This isn't cruising. It's not even spelled right. This is ordering pizza."

"I guess colored handkerchiefs just became too much."

Sean laughs again, louder this time. I can't tell if he's drunk.

I take another painful sip, then ask where he's visiting from.

"New York City," he says.

"Ah, an old New York fag." He's a bit taken aback by the noun, clearly hasn't realized we've reclaimed those three letters for ourselves.

"Something against it?"

"Overrated," I say. "I'm quite happy here in diet Manhattan. Even with these embarrassing height restrictions on our buildings."

"I've noticed that. There's a lot more sky here. Not as many people, though. Don't you get sick of seeing the same men over and over again? Not very suited for casual sex, is it?"

"I'll give you that. You've got the sheer numbers. But don't underestimate our turnover rate. Every election cycle it's like the shelves are restocked with new goods."

"Funny. Martin says the same thing."

"Let me guess. Husband."

"Oh, no. An old journalist friend. I'm staying with him up in Kalorama for the weekend."

"And he recommended this place? Some friend."

"I was out earlier, but I didn't want to go home. So I walked around. Had a late dinner. I was reading one of those free papers I see everywhere in this neighborhood and saw a silly ad, so I came here for a nightcap. Which has now become two."

"The ad. Guy had a mohawk, right? Dyed rainbow colors? Holding a champagne flute and a sausage link on a fork."

"A friend of yours?"

"Stock image. I added the colors and the champagne and the sausage." And it's true. It was a lazy, half-assed project I did on the side for the Attic early last year when they decided to get in, five years too late, on the weekend brunch scene. A former bartender in the first-floor restaurant asked, after sex, if I could help them sell a new bottomless brunch. So I gave him something admittedly derivative. Management loved it.

"An ad man," Sean says.

"Just a designer. A mid-level grunt. I freelance, too. Websites, posters, fliers, shirts, branding, social media. That sort of thing."

"Just now getting off work?"

I share the brief sad story of my afternoon and evening, describing the entire event as its own artfully manicured, branded ad campaign for marriage equality. "I ran into an old friend of mine there," I say. "Guy I haven't seen since college. It's funny, we used to be close in elementary school. So strange."

"How romantic. Is that who you're waiting for?"

"God no."

Sean leans back, ignoring the plastic flatulence. Is he appraising me? I've been looked at this way before by older chicken hawks than him. And yet there's nothing pervy about the way he eyes me over his scotch glass, completely at ease with the quiet between us. It's something else. Recognition? Impossible. I've never seen this man in my life. Politician, maybe? No. Lobbyist, probably. And so, to solve the mystery, I ask that eternal D.C. question.

"What do you do?"

"I'm a writer."

Oh. A writer.

"I'm not much of a reader," I say.

"I was giving a reading earlier this evening."

"New book?"

"Yes. No."

Sean lifts up the gray blazer on the space next to him, opens a battered brown messenger bag, takes out a bent paperback. "Reader's copy," he says, as if apologizing for the damage. He hands me the book. The author photo takes up the entire back cover. In it, Sean looks easily thirty years younger. The goatee is still there, the hair still close-cropped, the body still roughly hewn. He's sitting in a jean jacket open over a white shirt and jeans on the front stoop of what has to be some New York side street, hands clasped between outspread legs. At his feet is the upper half of a monstrous Great Dane, gray with age. The two of them—young man, old dog—look ready to eat me.

"It's a reprint," Sean says. "So the old photo seemed appropriate."

I flip the book over. On a plain white background are black words: *Ecce Homo* and *Sean Stokes*.

"First major piece of writing I published," Sean says. He sounds as if he may as well be reminiscing with himself, alone. "Juvenile and polemical, of course, as first books usually are. All the subtlety of a scream in an empty canyon. What else do you expect from a frustrated boy from small-town Ohio? Anyway, my current publisher acquired the rights to the book, so they're reprinting it along with the new one. *Tiberius at the Villa*."

"Haven't heard of it."

"Of course not. It isn't doing well."

"But I have heard of small-town Ohio. Spent my adolescence outside Cleveland. Yoder."

"Ah, Yoder. So you know what it feels like to escape that."

"I do."

I finish the rest of my scotch and wait for the burning to pass. I look away from Sean to the bay window and notice the bears at some point have left the room. The bartender is on his phone. The digital clock above his head, next to a photo of Harvey Milk picking up dog shit, reads 12:13. I look back at Sean, realizing we've now arrived at that awful point in which we've run out of things to say. It always makes me anxious. Sean leans forward and looks at me as if I've got something on my face. I check my nose and lips for any embarrassing crust. It's like he's aware of something I'm not; something in the swoop of my hair, perhaps, or the white T-shirt clinging to my stick of a body. (Praying mantis, the boys of Yoder called me. Among other words.) He's looking at me the same way Sebastian looked at me hours earlier.

He says, "Do you believe in metempsychosis?"

I say, "Excuse me?"

"No. Me neither."

I look again at the digital clock, and he notices.

"You have to go," he says.

"I have to work tomorrow morning."

"Of course."

"It's true," I say insistently.

"I believe you, Oscar."

He digs a pen out of his messenger bag and opens *Ecce Homo* to the title page. Mouth open in child-like concentration, he scribbles something below his printed name. He caps the pen, takes a look at what he's written, hands the book to me. His signature. Below that, bracketed by the bottom halves of two baroque S's, an email address.

"Take it," he says. "Read it. Let me know what you think."

"Don't you need this?"

"Tour's over. This was the last stop. Back home tomorrow afternoon to figure out what I'm going to do with the rest of my life."

"Write another book?"

"I'm starting to think people have heard enough from me."

Another pause. The distant echo of more Eighties music from one floor down. Sean looks at me with sympathy, then reaches across the space between us and pats the back of my hand, which rests on his book.

"Sorry about your trick," he says. "Happens to the best of us."

We rise from the booth in mirrored movements. Sean opens his arms for a hug, and I let him envelop me. I move to rest my chin against a shoulder. He kisses me on the cheek, firm, as if stamping a letter. His hands on my back are polite; they don't wander. We hold one another for a few seconds, as if in solidarity against strange forces amassed against us. We let go. Sean brushes my chin with a knobby fist.

"Be well," he says. "Stay in touch."

With a final wave, I turn and leave. I don't look back to see if Sean's watching me go. What's the use? Eyes forward, Oscar. Eyes forward.

I take the stairs down past the dull thump of music on the second floor, past a sloppy make-out session on the landing, past an equally sloppy breakup on the front stoop. Rolled up in my front pocket, Sean's copy of *Ecce Homo*—my copy now—rests against my hip like some proud Tom of Finland tumor.

THE CRAMPS ARE back. My stomach goes through cycles of clenching, like a fist trying to produce a vein. I get up and go outside, hoping the night air will calm things down.

I'm never eating shrimp again.

Sitting in an old plastic chair, I open up Cruze and see the familiar grid: the faces, eyes, and torsos; the abdomens both firm and plump, the flash of a cotton-swaddled bulge resting against a hairy inner thigh. I think about all the early-morning assignations happening right now throughout the city, of gays at play, and feel the biting sting of envy. A. is nowhere to be found. I debate leaving him some kind of snarky message, a teachable moment for the budding young gay, but sitting here outside, several hours before dawn, it just doesn't seem worth it.

Below me, a stretch of Fourteenth Street rises for a block before being cut off by the corner of a postwar co-op building housing the elderly and infirm. (Every morning, it seems, I leave my apartment for work and watch an ambulance outside the building give birth to a sheeted gurney.) Across the street, in clear sight from my ninth-floor perch, is an empty plot paddocked with fencing whose deep blue tarp flaps and cracks on windy nights, keeping me awake. A banner wrapping one side of the fence proclaims the promise of ULTRA-MODERN URBAN LIVING. Blown-up images celebrate the projected future of the Echo with beautiful men in various states of domestic play: cooking dinner with school-age children over stainless-steel appliances; lounging on duvet covers with basset hounds in light-filled bedrooms; entertaining out-of-town family with holiday cocktails in living rooms ringed with exposed brick. One of the photoshopped revelers has a sharp part in his hair, left to right, just like Sebastian.

Sebastian.

Has it really been a decade since I last saw him? The boy I lived near as a kid, the grown man I saw for one brief evening in college. A man whose mystery is all the more palpable for the fact that he doesn't exist on social media (I checked in the car ride back from the wedding). May as well be a ghost. Still handsome, I suppose, if a bit fleshy. Those hooded eyes, that eternally parted black hair. It comes back to me now, that hair. I remember those frequent weekend trips to the community pool, remember how, even plastered wet with pool water, that smooth, clean part would stay there. I'd often reach over to disturb it, which would make Sebastian so angry so easily. He never understood that was how I said thank you for rescuing me from the quiet monotony of life with my father, Harrison Burnham.

Should I text him? *Hey, good running into you at the wedding. So my hookup never showed, but guess who I met instead?*

The knot in my gut strains tighter.

Maybe later.

I get up and start pacing, hoping that the longer I move, the quieter my insides will get. I see, on the small table by my front door, the curled copy of *Ecce Homo*. I take the book and pore over Sean's signature and email address as if they hold some secret knowledge. I walk from one side of my apartment to the other, holding the book like a club. I try to stop thinking about my spiteful guts and think, instead, as I always do, about men. The one I didn't meet. The one I just met. The one I met again.

TWO

A Boyhood

⚡

Sebastian

I f my students could rebuild their lives every school year, surely I could, too. And to start rebuilding, you had to tear everything down. Look closely at the foundation. If the foundation wasn't stable, the structure wouldn't be either. Principle of architecture, from Phidias to Philip Johnson.

It would start, I decided, with my classroom. On a Sunday morning in late August, I took several large plastic tubs of books and papers and posters out to my car and drove to Mortimer Secondary School. I'd be teaching in a trailer this year. Possibly next year as well. In response to an influx of new students, renovations had started on the school two days after graduation. First would come expanded hallways, then work to replace the school's early-Eighties exterior, a carapace of brick and concrete. It would be a facelift for the twenty-first century. Construction was starting on the western edge of the school and moving east, which meant my classroom for the last three years was one of the first to go. I and several other teachers had been unceremoniously reassigned to trailers parked like placid cows along the school's blacktop. Siberia, we called it.

The sky that morning was cloudless, nothing to give it weight save for several distant airplanes unzipping the day with their white contrails. Two miles before the turnoff to Douglas Mortimer Road, traffic stalled. What should have been a simple, ten-minute drive became a forty-minute crawl. Idling past the scene of the accident, I saw a horse trailer, detached from a nearby truck and upside down in the small ditch that ran parallel to the road. Off in the grass, where the lawn ended in a tangle of underbrush, a giant shape lay blanketed in a blue tarp. Two women stood next to it, arms folded, crying and gesturing to a police officer. I found myself, like everyone else, stopping to stare. I thought about dogs. I thought about my mother. Then, urged by two irate honks behind me, I continued on my way to school.

My trailer, T-5, sat in the shadow of two basketball hoops. Its thin door creaked open onto a room with threadbare gray carpeting. The overhead lights did little to improve the gloom. As I walked around the space, I noticed how tender the ground underneath was, imagined at some point during the school year a student dropping thigh-deep through the floor. I put my boxes on the empty teacher's desk (my computer was scheduled to arrive next week) and began to rearrange the scattered tables and stacked chairs so they faced me and, behind me, the whiteboard. I thought of my own school days: the dated clack of rotating slides in my own AP Art History class, a Gothic church or Botticelli fantasia sometimes appearing upside down to titters from those students still awake. Now I pulled everything up on a computer screen; a slideshow I could build and edit right from my desk. Still. I couldn't give up the laminated exhibit posters I'd picked up at thrift stores or the paintings I'd printed on stock paper my first year of teaching, inspired by a high school teacher who'd collaged his entire classroom with writing from students who'd long since graduated (some of whom could very well have already been dead). I wondered if the thin defenses of this roughshod kingdom could handle so many prints and posters, was surprised the television suspended from the ceiling hadn't already brought about the trailer's collapse.

And the books. I always saved the books for last. Art books and exhibit catalogs—my own, my father's—collected over the years from secondhand shops, from museum discount piles and library sales. Books on Renoir, Degas, Cassatt, Picasso, Hiroshige, O'Keefe, Trumbull, Turner, Monet. Special exhibits on Goya and Remington, on illuminated manuscripts, on printmaking, on the Ashcan School. Academic studies of Raphael and Gauguin, of Egyptian deities and Byzantine angels. A paperback of Vasari's *The Lives*. Poems by Michelangelo, letters by Van Gogh, essays by Ruskin. Multiple editions of textbooks by Janson and Stokstad warping the straight edge of an entire shelf. These I unpacked ceremonially, one by one, to the sound of jackhammers and the beep of reversing construction vehicles from outside. I sat in my desk chair, flipping through the glossy pages, thinking back on childhood days when I used some of these very same art catalogs and monographs to explore (always in secret, always in shame) their nude male bodies in marble, in oil, in charcoal and pen. Those dumb, silly days when I was naïve enough to believe I was the only person in the world who lived with the deep dread of dreaming about other boys' penises, lips, stomachs, buttocks. At sleepovers with friends (the small group I'd managed to cobble together after Oscar disappeared the summer before seventh grade), while other guys crept into computer rooms and waited impatiently in the dark for nude women to appear line by pixelated line, I'd long to be back home, in my bedroom, staring into the soft face of the young Joseph Mallord William Turner in his self-portrait from 1799. The enormous eyes, the dark bubble of his lower lip, the handsome Roman nose, the parted forelocks. Imagine: an entire gallery crammed like some nineteenth-century European museum with Turner's self-portrait and countless other works curated over the years, below each an ekphrasis with which the marginally curious could piece together the boyhood of a late-twentieth-century suburban homosexual named Sebastian Allan Mote.

Watson and the Shark. **John Singleton Copley**. 1788. I'm on a field trip with my third-grade class to the National Gallery of Art. My mother is a chaperone, keeping up the rear behind a group of eight kids who follow the docent through the galleries. We find ourselves in front of an enormous oil painting. That doesn't look like a shark, someone says. That's because it was invented by Mr. Copley, the docent explains. Someone asks: Why is that man naked? I think it's a girl, someone else says. Look at her long hair. A new kid, Oscar Burnham, asks: Did he die? No, the docent says. The young man was rescued. He lived a long, happy life. Later, during lunch on the grass outside the museum, I see the new kid sitting alone. He looks lonely, my mother says. Go over and talk to him. I take my lunch and sit next to the new kid, the two of us at a slight remove from the rest of the group. You just moved near my house, I say. I know, the new kid says. I see you playing outside from my bedroom. Come out next time, I say. The new kid just has carrots with his ham sandwich, so I share my grape fruit rollups. We spend the rest of lunch pressing small squares of dried fruit into the roofs of our mouths. We attach small strips to our tongues and pretend we're lizard people.

Mortimer's LGBT social group started not with me but with a fourteen-year-old boy named Thomas Pitt. On April 26, two days after Jake and I brought the first of our boxes into my father's vacant house (when I first began to suspect bringing Jake out here was a mistake, that I wouldn't be able to fit him into the domestic plans I had for my future), Thomas Pitt asked his World History teacher for a bathroom pass. He walked down the main hallway, past the bathroom, out the front doors, through the crowded faculty parking lot, and around the side of the building, where a small footpath cut through the tree line separating the school grounds from Lake Mortimer Road. He followed the asphalt path along the road for a quarter mile, turned right, and walked down a steep incline until the path flattened out again around a small lake ringed with townhomes. He stopped by one of the recycled plastic benches and unlaced his sneakers. He tugged off his shoes and socks, his shirt, his jeans. He typed the word *GOODBYE* into his phone and put it, screen-up, on the bench. He walked into the water.

The Shaft Scene. Unknown. 17,000 B.C.E. I'm ten years old, in my father's basement with Oscar. I'm sitting in an old wingback chair, flipping through an enormous book on the history of Western art, trying to stay busy while waiting for my turn on my Game Boy. I toss the thick pages, working my way to the end of the book and back to the beginning. I think the more I concentrate, the more I absorb in my mind what's directly in front of me, the faster time will pass until our agreed-upon, ten-minute rotation. I come across reproductions of primitive paintings on the rock walls of some old French cave. I stare at the galloping herds, trace the curve of a cow's brown back with a finger. I turn the page and see a crude illustration of a bull knocking over what looks like a man. It reminds me of drawings on the blacktop at Cardinal Elementary: the flowers and suns and salamanders in colored chalk, the cuss words and boobs and boners in black magic marker. There's a slash above the man's stick-figure legs that looks like a dick. Below the image is a caption: "Photograph of Walls in the Shaft of the Dead Man at Lascaux Cave." I look up at the back of Oscar's head, the neck poking out from his sweater, the hair like the fuzz on my father's tomato plants. I ask, Is it my turn yet? No, Oscar says. I haven't died. Possessed by an uncanny, inexplicable compulsion (the same one, perhaps, that must have propelled these ancient cave people to decorate their ancient cave walls), I want to reach over and place my hand on Oscar's neck, to touch each individual hair, to feel that secret warmth. I want to fall in Oscar's lap and curl up, kittenlike, in those long arms. Considering how much time we spend together, how often Oscar's at my house on weeknights and weekends, it makes a strange sort of sense to me. I'm going to piss, I say. Whatever, Oscar says. I rise from my father's chair, then pretend to trip on the hassock. I drop the art book on the carpet and throw myself, awkwardly, onto Oscar's back. Shit, Sebastian, he says. My game. I know I can't stay here for long. It's dangerous. This isn't what two boys are supposed to do. Maybe brothers. Certainly not friends. Pushing up against Oscar's shoulder blades, I brush my lips against the back of Oscar's neck, feel the tickle of near-invisible hair. Oscar stiffens, then he shoves me off. Stop that, he says. Then: Weirdo. He reaches for the Game Boy and resumes playing. We spend the rest of the afternoon in silence. Oscar's ten minutes on my Game Boy are up, but I let him keep playing, hoping my generosity will make him forget what just happened. I sit in the chair with the art book and think how stupid and strange I am. Will he tell his parents, or someone in class? Sebastian tried to kiss me. *Blech.* Then I think of how often Oscar tells me he doesn't like his parents, doesn't like the other kids at school, and I feel a little relief. Think what you like, Sebastian, but keep it to yourself. Don't ever do that again. Looking at Oscar hunched over the Game Boy, I daydream of empty caves and echoing wind, of holding someone close by primal firelight. Then my father calls us up for dinner.

For months, apparently, someone had been slipping folded sheets of paper into the metal gills of Thomas Pitt's locker. Typed notes. Crude illustrations. It could have been anyone. It could have been everyone. The school closed for a day. There were emergency meetings with faculty and staff, with district administrators and grief counselors, that extended into the weekend. While Jake spent the following Saturday and Sunday in D.C. with his friends, I spent those days in little theaters and conference rooms and administrative offices. Statements were prepared and shared with students and parents. Ideas were thrown out for a memorial fund, for a mathematics scholarship in Thomas's memory. Someone suggested a club for LGBT students, to keep them connected, to keep them safe. Principal Jones sat down with some of us, asked if any-one was interested in sponsoring the group. The other teachers stared into the middle distance. I looked at each of them in turn. I thought of Thomas Pitt floating like driftwood in his underwear. I thought about myself after college, on a family cruise and contem-plating the possibility of my own death by water. I thought about how a group like this might have changed my youth, made me stronger, made me more confident, made a little more bearable the bloodless violence of my high school hallways. I raised my hand. I'll do it, I said. I came home that evening and told Jake about my day. I told him this could be my great moment of activism. Leaving the city, joining the massive human herd—this was the true front line of the struggle. This was where rainbow flags could still be a political statement, not just a decoration. This is where, maybe, I could make a difference. Then a dangerous sentence: It might be good practice for raising our own kids one day. Jake scoffed, propped his feet on an unopened box, went back to his phone.

Portrait of Henry VIII. **Hans Holbein the Younger. 1536–1537.** It's one of the rare nights I'm at Oscar's house. The family eats dinner with the television on. Oscar's father, full-figured, lordly, sits at the head of the glass table through which I can see our pairs of crossed legs. Pass those potatoes, Oscar's father says in his tyrannical voice. The roast bleeds on its platter. Oscar swings his feet and eats in silence. Upstairs in his small bedroom or out in his side yard, we can't stop talking. We reflect, in excruciating detail, on the smell of Nick's retainer every time he takes it out of his mouth in class. We debate whether the metal in Wolverine's claws is pronounced "adamantium" or "anatidium." We recite bawdy lines and reenact bawdy scenes from *Ren and Stimpy* episodes. We

create a new lexicon of sounds with our action figures: *badapang,*
screesh, schmoof. We take bets on which of my mother's dogs is
going to die first. We imagine what we'd do to Michael's face with
our fists if we could get away with it. At the Burnham dinner table,
however, we're always silent. I hate these meals. I wish Oscar and
I could take our plates and eat somewhere else. Sometimes, seeing
him around his parents, he reminds me of one of my mother's
blind dogs, disoriented in a potentially dangerous environment.
It's okay, Oscar, I think. I'm your friend. I'll take care of you.
With every bite of red meat, every sip of soda, I look up at Oscar's
father, watch the brute's powerful jaw muscles masticate under a
heavy beard, watch the kitchen light bounce off his forehead. A
baby's forehead, I think. On the evening news, a reporter interviews a man about palliative care for AIDS patients. Faggots,
Oscar's father says. He shakes his head. It'll be another five years
before I begin to associate that word with myself, or rather with
someone inside myself, living in my skin and operating my brain
and body. Oscar's mother looks up from her dinner. Harry, she
says. Please. I look over at Oscar, see him shrink in his seat.

The student body quickly adapted to the loss of one of its own, like
a school of fish instinctively filling in the gap left behind by a lost
comrade and pushing onward in glittery revolutions through the
sea. A tiny death soon forgotten, even by the queer students who
continued to walk the halls of Mortimer, many of whom arrived in
seventh grade with their sexualities already discovered, who were
taking same-sex dates to homecoming dances, to proms. Who
were living the adolescent life I never did, a life without shame.
Nevertheless, I threw myself into the work. I adapted the idea
from the same social group I'd joined my final year at Jefferson,

from similar initiatives in neighboring, more forward-thinking school districts. (It didn't surprise me that Mortimer was behind the times. The school was named for a Confederate general, and most of us on staff figured it was just a matter of time before the name had to go.) There would be posters put up during the opening week of school with the slogan I'd devised: WE HELP EACH OTHER HERE. There would be email blasts to parents and teachers. There would be elections for a president, a secretary, an entire micro-bureaucracy. As uncertain as I was about the plan, the project kept me busy through July. It kept my mind off Jake. The legacy of a failed three-year relationship replaced by the legacy of a fourteen-year-old's suicide. And here I was, having never even planned to become a high school teacher. I'd studied art history because I'd been taught by my mother—the lapsed Muslim, the guardian of elderly canines—that there was no shame in obsessing over something you loved. I graduated from Jefferson with a double major in art history and English literature, then (because what other real choice did I have if I wanted to make a living?) took an additional year for an accreditation in education. I moved up to D.C. and taught English at charter schools for the next six years while working some evenings and weekends at an independent bookstore in upper Northwest. It was there I met Jake. He'd come in and asked for my help. I just joined a gay book club, he said. I'm looking for *A Boyhood* by Sean Stokes. Staring intently into my eyes. I can help you, I said. Together, we scoured the Literature section, then the Gay and Lesbian section, until we finally found the book on the discount tables in the back. I remember the cover: a sepia-toned photograph of a young boy who couldn't have been more than fifteen, crouched in the grass of some flat Midwestern lawn in imitation of a football player preparing to charge. There, against the parti-colored rows of books, Jake goaded me into more conversation. No, I said, I'd never read the book or anything else by Sean Stokes. I hadn't done much dating in recent years, so I was particularly baffled. People still met this way? In bookstores, searching for books? Ringing up Jake's purchase, I agreed to meet him in an hour for coffee downstairs. A week later, we were spending nights at one another's apartment. Several months after that, I followed up on a colleague's email about a job posting fifty miles south of the city. A school district was looking for an English teacher who would also be required to take on a unit of AP Art History. It felt fated. A month before the start of the school year, I got the job. Two years later, exhausted by my commute, ready for something different, I finally convinced Jake to move out to Virginia with me.

Number 1, 1950 (Lavender Mist). **Jackson Pollock. 1950.** That's in the middle of the country, I say. It's late spring of 1994. Oscar and I are out on the driveway of my house, pitching my father's racquetballs against the closed garage door. Yeah, Oscar says. Dad's got a new job. We throw the blue balls for another few minutes. Wow, I say. Ohio. It sounds like the name of another galaxy. I throw my racquetball harder against the garage door, want to see if I can punch a hole through the painted wood. Then I say, I'm going to miss you. What I don't say: Who'll take care of you now? You'll come visit us, Oscar says. My mom says you're invited. There's another minute of silence. I know this will never happen. I can tell Oscar's already cutting ties, already starting to forget about me. Then, because I fear I'll have no other opportunity, I lean in and whisper. Hey, remember what we did that one time a few months ago? What one time? That one sleepover. When we, you know.

I remember the moment vividly but don't have the right words to express what we did or the deadly concern I feel about it, so I take my two index fingers and swat them back and forth against one another. I'm embarrassed to just do that much, but I'm also hoping Oscar feels the same secret shame, that it'll coil around us and keep us connected despite our impending distance. That of all our boyhood adventures, both normal and clandestine, this will be the one he remembers most. Oscar looks away. Yeah, he says. I remember. Strangely relieved, I say, You can't get AIDS from that, can you? No, Oscar says. I don't know. He turns to chase his errant racquetball as it rolls across the street. He comes back, hands it to me. Anyway, he says, I should go home. I watch Oscar dash across our neighboring yards and know I've just experienced an irrevocable moment. Life could have been one way, but now it will only be this way. I stay outside and continue to throw the racquetballs against the garage door, harder and harder. From inside, one of my mother's dogs bays, an incredible sound that might as well have come from my mouth. An upstairs window opens and my father yells through the screen for me to stop. Suddenly, I turn away from the garage door and throw up a splatter of green and gray onto the driveway. The racquetballs bounce into the street. I feel my mouth yield to the movements of my stomach, I shudder with the realization that vomiting always brings: that your body, not you, is in control. If your body wants you to throw up, you'll throw up. If your body wants you to rub dicks with your friend in the early-morning hours of a sleepover, you'll rub dicks with your friend in the early-morning hours of a sleepover. I feel at the mercy of something I can't rein in, let alone understand. I feel, for the first time in my life, truly hollowed out. I step back from the mess on the concrete, the sloppy sick sight of it, the strands of vomit mingling with tendrils from old motor oil leaks and blades of mown grass and flecks of compacted minerals. That's enough, I tell myself. You just threw up. That's it. My father calls from upstairs: You alright? I'm fine, I say. Why don't you come back inside? Okay, I say. Before you do though, Sebastian, just take the hose and spray that mess out into the street, will you?

I looked up from one of the open books on my desk to see the afternoon light already beginning to fade. Strange, how time passed in an empty classroom. In a few weeks, with bodies piling in and out of the trailer, it would pass much slower. I closed the book—*Jackson Pollock and His Times*—and took it over to the shelves, where it would remain until my students began their assignment. Once in the fall and once in the spring, I sent them to these books. They were to pick one, read it over two quarters, and come back with three pages of their impressions. And remember, I'd say as I sent them up to the shelves in random order, I've read all of these. All of them. So I'll know if you haven't. In the two years since I started this assignment, my students had gone diligently about the task. Most plucked at the familiar names, the titans of Western art. Those who went last ended up with what they probably thought of as the dregs: Hubert Robert, Artemisia Gentileschi, Berthe Morisot, French court painting. I loved the idea of my students immersed in books that belonged to me, imagined each book going off into a separate home, a separate life. If only the books could report on what they'd seen.

Ulysses Deriding Polyphemus. **J.M.W. Turner. 1829.** I wait for weeks. I wait for months. No phone call, no letter. He's probably just busy getting settled in, my father says. No, I think. He's disappeared. As seventh grade begins, my sadness turns to indignation. How could our three years together mean so much to me and so little to him? Slowly, cautiously, I make new friends. At night, I think of Oscar, talking to other boys at cafeteria tables and on school buses. Still no phone call. Still no letter. As time passes, the anger, the sadness, dissipates into more pressing matters: my mutating body, growing hairier and smellier; my secret desires, which frighten me because the older I get, the more urgent they become; my academics, the only arena in which I perform as well as the high school athletes whose bodies I browse as my school bus pulls away from the parking lot. Still. Every so often, taking the dogs for a walk after dinner, I stop at the end of the driveway, older now than I was on the hot morning Oscar moved away. If I focus my mind, I can see the navy blue Chevy Blazer growing smaller as it moves down Cinnamon Lane. I can see myself, twelve years old again, waiting for a waving arm to emerge, for Oscar to press himself against the back window. But there's nothing. The car continues on, pauses briefly at a stop sign, turns right, and heads in the direction of the highway. And then he's finally, truly gone. Off to new adventures with new people, leaving me here abandoned. Humiliated. Enraged.

It had been more than a month since the wedding, and nothing from Oscar. I'd resigned myself to another disappearance, had even thought about deleting his number from my phone. I'd forgotten about Oscar before, and I could do it again. But he was everywhere in these books. In the Pollock, the Turner—in the paperback of Modigliani portraits I found lying forgotten in the bottom of my last box. Here he was, recast on the cover as the 1918 portrait of Leopold Zborowski, with the same long neck, the same nonexistent shoulders. The gray vacancy of the figure's close-set eyes, as if there was nothing behind the face but smooth stone. The impression the painting gave was of a man who, despite the beard, was still very much a boy. I stared at the portrait for another few minutes, then put it on the shelf where it belonged. I went over to my desk, took my phone out of my bag, and called Oscar Burnham.

Oscar

Follow me!

Down the boardwalk, past the taffy shops and noisy arcades, the jewelers, the stalls hawking fried chicken, fried crab, fried potatoes, fried dough. Past crowds of families plodding along wooden slats in bare feet and sandals, past seagulls dive-bombing for shards of waffle cone, past beaches thick with reddening flesh. Past forests of umbrellas, past the smell of baked-on sunscreen and salt-crusted hair, past the great, noisy churn of human activity and commerce. South along the boardwalk, to where it ends, appropriately enough, at Prospect Street. Over small hills of sand to a small patch of earth where dogs run off-leash, where there are no lifeguards to frown over your cigarettes and alcohol—or to save you from drowning. To a quiet strip of Delaware shore with music, with seaside strolls, with private dance parties and lemonade ices, with hamburger patties sizzling on a coffin-length charcoal grill. To a sliver of respite from the chaos of Rehoboth to our north and Dewey to our south. To Poodle Beach, our summer grounds, where we D.C. gays come to be left in peace.

This year, alas, I'm late.

It's the second weekend of September, the only time (thanks to poor planning) we were all able to get together for our annual beach trip. There are ten of us at the house this weekend, the same one Marcus rents every year. You can see it there, sitting back behind us, beyond that scrim of beach grass and that sagging picket fence, marked out with an enormous rainbow flag like something you'd see hanging off a battleship. Of course, we're all on the shore now. We sit in a semicircle facing the water, having secured the best positions for sun, for shade, for vantage points from which to watch the tragically few handsome shoreline strollers with their tiny swimsuits, their bulges like pastel Easter eggs. I'm out in front of the pack on a blanket, rotating every fifteen minutes in a futile attempt to brown my pale skin. Bart's next to me in a chair, eyes hidden behind sunglasses, sharing a red solo cup with Jackson, so slim he shivers every time the sun slips behind a cloud. I've got sunglasses on, too, not because the September sun is intense but because it's easier for me to cruise and gape and gawk. To admire. To judge. Unfortunately, the sunglasses make it difficult to read.

Yes, that's right.

I'm reading.

Trying to, anyway. Instead, I'm transfixed by what's happening to my left, just a few feet away from our seaside commune. How is anyone else not watching this? Why can no one else see what's happening here?

He's no older than five, the kid, armed with a yellow plastic bucket and shovel. For the past half hour, he's been mindlessly stuffing wet sand into the bucket, dumping it out, stuffing it back in again, happy with his endless chore. Chubby tyke, probably on a diet of fast food and prepackaged dinners. Down by the shoreline, his father helps an equally pudgy daughter build what looks like a step pyramid in the sand.

Wondering what a child is doing here, on Poodle Beach, in our space?

I'll tell you: They're building settlements.

The breeders wanted us to leave their families in peace, didn't want us drooling like wolves over their young sons. So we left. We were happy to. We could make this part of the world in our own image, not theirs. And now? Now that it's popular again? They want it back. The straight hordes are coming for us, and right here, right next to me, is one of their new colonists, sloppy with wet sand, oblivious to the mess he's making.

I can't stop staring at this kid. I just can't. I want to load a pile of sand on my left foot and flip it over at him. Something to make him cry and scamper off. His father and sister are busy at work on their temple. They'd never know it was me. It would be the boy's word against mine. And I've got a book in my hand: the perfect alibi.

The little monster emits some sort of alien gurgle, pleased with his work. I turn to Bart, who's zipped himself up in a purple hoodie and sits with folded arms. I ask if he's seeing this.

"Yeah," he says. "Adorable, isn't he?"

"No, I mean what's going on here. This entire weekend, the last few summers. All these families. Kids." I flip over onto my stomach. I can't watch this anymore. "They're getting closer and closer, you know. They're coming for us. It's a classic pincer move-ment. They're driving us into the sea like rats." I laugh, to give the impression I'm not as concerned as I really am.

"Would you feel better if I told you that man was one of us? That he was raising those two kids with another man? Because I know for a fact that's the case. I saw the four of them earlier up on the boardwalk."

"That makes it worse."

Now the boy's digging a trench. In my direction. He's preparing to settle in for a long winter of warfare.

Bart leans over, tips his sunglasses down the bridge of his nose, and looks at me in a way that confirms the nagging thought I've had in recent months: that in this body of friends, I'm the vestigial limb.

"You're insufferable," he says. "All weekend. I wasn't going to say anything, and I don't want to sound like your father because we all know how you feel about him. But your attitude. And you're spending a lot of time in the house, alone. You're either always on your phone or you're reading."

"I'm reading at the beach. That's what people do."

"I'm just saying." Bart pushes his sunglasses back up his nose, pats my forearm, then settles back into his chair and reaches out for Jackson's hand.

Oh, Bart. You've already forgotten, haven't you? The rough-and-tumble days when it was just you and me. No scene left unexplored, no event unattended. Have you forgotten the bar tabs, the trips to leather conventions? Have you forgotten the summer you and I went to London and we both hung out our hotel window trying to get enough reception to hook up with Englishmen on Cruze? Have you forgotten that drunken threesome with the visiting Argentinian? Have you forgotten when you had two hands to live your life with instead of one?

I roll onto my back again and quietly pick crystals of sand out of my chest hair. Next to me, above the peak of my open paperback copy of *A Boyhood*, the little kid's trench gets wider. Deeper.

Despite its brilliant opening line—*I vow, henceforth, to live by cock alone.*—and the frankness with which Sean speaks of his desire to live his queer life outside the shadows, I didn't care that much for *Ecce Homo*, found it too bogged down by obscure references to someone named Corydon. Way too intellectual for me. I told Sean as much in the first email I sent him, several weeks after we met at the Attic. I didn't expect him to respond; it felt good just to write a long letter to a stranger. But he did respond, a week later, and suggested I try the novels instead.

If it's sex you're after, Oscar, it's all in those books. That's what people wanted. That's what got me attention. At least, it used to.

He instructed me to go chronologically, said it would make the most sense that way. He also demanded I get the books from a bookstore, not the library.

Support your poor, starving gay authors.

So I went, dutifully, to a Dupont Circle bookstore in search of Sean Stokes. I was directed by a bookseller to the new annex next door, purchased in 2008 from the owner of a queer bookstore who heard the call of retirement. I found the LGBT ISSUES section in a back corner, between CULTURAL STUDIES and MILITARY HISTORY. I browsed an alphabetical listing of literary erotica and theoretical criticism, of personal memoirs and sociological studies, of paint-by-numbers coming-out tales and mass-market paperback quests for Mr. Right. The gays mixed with the lesbians mixed with the spare, slim volumes on transgendered people.

I found *A Boyhood*—the "novel" of Sean's sexually graphic adolescence in Ohio—next to several copies of *Tiberius at the Villa*. There were some of his other novels, as well. *A Manhood*, the sequel, published three years after *A Boyhood* and following Sean's barely fictional hero as he fucks his way east across the United States to claim sanctuary among a small group of gay Manhattan writers and critics. *Skin Dreams*, from 1980: nothing more than a catalog of Sean's sexual conquests during the disco era, a ribald laundry list of the men and boys he slept with when he wasn't teaching literature at New York University or trashing other novelists in *The Village Voice*. A shrink-wrapped copy of 1983's *1001 Nights*, in which Sean and his friend Cal (and their cameras) visit North Africa for months of sex with Algerians, Libyans, Egyptians, and Nubians. *The Little Deaths*, a doorstop of a book from 1994 whose chapters, ranging from several paragraphs to several pages, cover the deaths of Sean's friends and lovers during the AIDS years.

I'm curious to know what you think of that one, Oscar. It's not sexy, but it's the one I'm proudest of.

I wrote back: *Maybe later. Seven hundred pages is a big ask, Sean. Twenty-first-century attention spans and all. Anyway, is it true? Did you really sleep with 300 people in 1978? Where did you find the time?*

HALFWAY THROUGH A hot scene in *A Boyhood*—high school bleachers, blow job—someone screams.

We look up from our phones, our books, our red plastic cups. I think for a moment, God, I did it. I kicked sand in that little boy's face and now they're coming to get me. But no. The screams are coming from farther down Poodle Beach.

Look. See him? In his bright red speedo, scampering into the wild surf up to his calves, kept at heel by the waves. Arms are raised as if he's trying to pull down the sky. He cries out to the water, and I wait for a body to appear facedown from behind the swell of a wave.

But it's not a body.

It's a small motorboat, puttering in parallel to the shore and fighting the waves, one of those vessels you see throughout the day with their small marquees advertising happy hours, surf-and-turf buffets, the occasional stern commandment from our Lord and Savior. This one's carrying a message I've never seen before: JOSHUA CHIN MARRY ME. And this must be the eponymous Joshua Chin by the shore. He's not screaming, I realize, but calling out his response back to his pack of friends. Behind him, the groom-to-be waddles down to the shoreline. The two men press their bodies together in a long embrace while freezing waves crash against their legs. Someone from their group comes up to them and takes their photograph. The groom-to-be pulls Joshua Chin up toward dry sand, then gets down on one knee. From inside the pocket of his floral swim trunks, he pulls out a small box. Joshua Chin squeals and presses his hands together. A moment later, properly tagged, Joshua Chin and his future husband amble back up the beach where two girls rush to give them towels.

Energized by the public proposal, the people on the beach become restless, like a flock of birds rustling in anticipation of an earthquake. There's polite applause, several hollers. A seagull plunges past me, plucks something from the sand near the shoreline, takes off for the boardwalk. The motorboat continues to grumble north to load its next message (which, if there's any irony left in the universe, will be a passage from Leviticus).

"Da!"

A voice too soft, too new to this world, to be one of ours. I turn around, see the little trespasser still in the sand.

"One sec," his father calls back.

I take off my sunglasses and lean toward the boy. He looks up at me, surprised to discover I've been sitting here all this time. We stare at each other. I can't stop looking at that tiny monkey fist gripping the plastic shovel like a cudgel.

"Hey," I say. "Listen to this." I pick up *A Boyhood* and start to read. "'I loved the feeling of his young beard, like pinpricks on my body. He smoked my hardness like the cigarettes I'd watched him smoke earlier in the parking lot, taking long, hard pulls. I couldn't hold it anymore. I exploded into his mouth. He groaned in gratitude at my gift. He'd been starving for it. Now, he'd been fed.'"

The boy continues to stare at me, bewildered. Then he tosses his shovel, clambers to his feet, and scampers toward his father and sister, shamelessly tugging his swimsuit away from the crabapples of his ass cheeks.

"You're awful," Bart says. He takes a pack of cigarettes out of his beach bag, lights one, blows the smoke with relief into the air. Jackson, still shivering, asks Bart how many cigarettes he's had so far today. Bart groans and stubs the cigarette out in the sand. Vindicated, I roll back onto my stomach and continue to read.

I'M STILL READING later that afternoon, lying on the bed in the room I share with Bart and Jackson and air-drying after a shower, distracted occasionally by the gleefully childish sight of every single wet hair on my body lying flat and straight. (Is this what being one-dimensional feels like? Fuck you for saying that the other day, Bart. Even if you were just joking.) Then I put my book down and write another quick email to Sean—my second this week.

While I told my friends about my encounter with him on the top floor of the Attic (Bart: "Who's that?"), none of them know about the emails we fire off at one another like flares over a massive battlefield. Let them be my unshared, unspoiled secret. Besides, I don't think they'd understand.

> *Going out again this evening. It's all there is to do here. There's a strip of gay bars up off the main drag. Certainly nothing like what you're used to. (Bart's boyfriend, Jackson, says we're not supposed to call them gay bars anymore. Just bars.) It's our usual routine: Café Rico for cocktails. Maurice's for dinner. Drinks and dancing across the street at the Beachcomber. I think there's a drag show tonight.*

Then, because I always end with a question for fear of unintentionally signaling the conclusion of our correspondence: *Think this would make a good setting for your next book?*

I send the email, then do what I've been doing a lot of lately: living my life through Sean's photos—or what few there are on the Internet. Here's the original dust jacket of *Skin Dreams*, featuring a shirtless Sean at twenty-five, leaning against an iron fence in some lower Manhattan park, showing off decent pectoral muscles and twists of armpit hair, his jeaned bulge announcing itself as the book's true protagonist. Here's Sean at a series of bars and nightclubs with the obligatory seventies moustache, caterpillar-thick and suggestive of the countless cocks it's tickled. Here's Sean with several lovers at a writer's colony in upstate New York. Here's Sean, with the same goatee I'd seen him sporting at the Attic (a little blacker, a little fuller), in the background of an early-Eighties Halloween party, dressed as Dracula, hands down someone's pants. Every icon, however posed or candid, gives off a pride, a rebelliousness I don't see in the sterility around me. This isn't a placid homosexual. This is a faggot, triumphant. What a life! Age may have softened that body (and his book sales—he often writes of his disappointment with the reception of *Tiberius at the Villa*, the poorly attended readings, the dismissive capsule reviews), but surely he still has within him that beautiful ferocity. That rebel captured in a simple string of eight words.

I vow, henceforth, to live by cock alone.

Wouldn't that look great tattooed along my lower back?

From downstairs, Bart yells for me to hurry up. I get dressed— torn jean shorts, boat shoes, pink V-neck—and decide what to do with my hair for the evening. Flatten it like a gangster? Raise it up in a small band of stegosaur spikes?

Wait.

I take some gel and force my hair into an unnatural part, left to right.

There. Like the sort of good old boy you'd want to bring home to a mother and father who actually loved you.

Like Sebastian Mote.

I recall his voicemail, still unanswered, telling me he'd been feeling nostalgic about our childhood, how he'd driven past our old homes on Cinnamon Lane, how he'd like to get together some- time soon. Text messages are easy to ignore, but a voicemail? I should call him back at some point for an hour or so of "Remember when?" but I suppose I have no real desire to reminisce over those days. I can't think about Sebastian and not think about the boy- hood that came with him; the fun times, yes, but always, with those fun times, the home I'd eventually have to go back to. The vacant mother, the irate father. I should be an adult and pick up the phone to return Sebastian's call, but every time I do, I end up Googling Sean or writing him another email instead.

"Oscar!" This time it's Jackson. "Let's go, girl!"

I take one last look at this ugly part in my hair, then destroy it with my fingers, massaging the thickness until I reach a satisfactory display of artfully constructed chaos.

AT CAFÉ RICO, we stand around one another in a tight circle, lost in the separate realities of our phones. The place isn't nearly as packed as it would have been a month ago, at the apex of the summer season. The patio crowds, drinking and talking and texting underneath pennants advertising beach beers? Sparse. The exciting push of the throng that normally piles out onto the sidewalk? Gone. What few people are here absentmindedly tuck their toes into trucked-in sand or pluck the skin on their necks. The music pumping out into the evening air from inside feels forced, sad. Even the banner hanging over the door leading inside and selling a lemon shandy—HAVE ONE LAST SUMMER FLING—seems in on the game.

After dinner, we move on to the Beachcomber, which is a little more crowded, but not much. Not the way it used to be. From speakers around the room, Rihanna begs us not to stop the music. To make up for my nagging insistence on leaving Maurice's, loud with families, I buy everyone a shot of Fireball. Then, after ten minutes of eye games between bodies, a short redhead charges toward me like a fireball of his own and says his name is Paul.

Yes, we're all drunk. But he's really drunk. In minutes, he's unpacking his emotional baggage, throwing his arms around in sync with his complaints. At one point, I catch his hand before it swipes someone across the face, and he smiles at me.

The music stops. A tired voice trying not to sound tired announces the final summer performance of Madame Pamplemousse. I finger the straw in my vodka soda, search the room for my friends. Marcus is still here. Drew's still here. Bart and Jackson, it seems, have gone back to the house.

Enter from stage right Madame Pamplemousse, in a glittery cocktail dress, her ample bosom complimented by a collar of fat white plastic pearls. She curtsies, and the modest crowd cheers. The loudest calls come from the back. I turn away from Paul mid-conversation and see—oh God, no—a group of women blocking off a corner of the bar. One of them, a brunette showing signs of what's either a stroke in progress or three martinis too many, screams with excitement. Madame Pamplemousse waves to the girls, and I think, Traitor. Then her song begins, in French, ushered in on plinking strings and supported by an electronic beat added sometime in the last several years. My high-school French classes aren't much of a help. Something about boys and girls holding hands, making future plans. Something about walking through streets alone, in pain.

Madame Pamplemousse looks harried, exhausted. Defeated. I feel like this is the last place on earth she wants to be, and listening to the catcalls of these women behind me, I sympathize.

"—just didn't understand. If I sent him a text, I shouldn't have to wait forever for a response. He can't seriously tell me he didn't see it. He stares at his phone all the time. I'm not an idiot. He thinks—"

"Let me get you another drink," I say to Paul. "Rum and diet?"

Paul nods, smiles, brushes his hand against my bare arm. I leave him in thrall to Madame Pamplemousse, who's stolen an unsuspecting old man from the crowd and is crooning into the top of his bald head.

Following that natural current you often find at small bars, I arrive at the corner opposite the one bartender on duty, next to the pack of women drinking and clapping at Madame Pamplemousse. A bro wearing an ugly boardwalk T-shirt (I POOPED TODAY!) nibbles on his girlfriend's ear. Another woman, in a short black dress better suited for a cocktail lounge than a beach bar, whistles as Madame Pamplemousse rocks her bosom. The bartender arrives and takes my order just as the brunette closest to me screams in laughter. He and I share knowing glances, and he shrugs as if to say, That's life. I turn back to look at Paul, who quickly turns away to look at the stage.

"Hilarious," the brunette says, putting down a half-empty martini glass and clapping in wild applause as Madame Pamplemousse curtsies, rubs her hands along the old man's bald head, and helps him back into the audience. The girl takes another sip of her martini, turns to her friend, and says, "God, I love my gays."

And that does it.

Emboldened by steady hours of drinking, by the promise of sex just across the room, by my rising anger, by the reckless life of a young Sean Stokes, I take the Becky's glass from off the bar and drain the rest of her drink.

Fuck.

Gin.

Serves me right.

"Whoa," she says, as if slowing down a galloping horse. "That wasn't yours."

I give her a flick of a rubbery wrist. "Oh, thorry."

"Excuse me."

"Look. I think it's time you and your girlfriends left. And the frat boy too."

"Excuse me?"

"Get the fuck out. You're not as welcome here as you think you are."

"You're joking."

"No. No, I'm not. You think this is part of the show? That we're all going to strip and flap our soft junk in your face? I'm not joking at all. I see people like you here all the time in these places. All. The. Time. You're everywhere now."

"People like me."

"Look. Just go somewhere else. Please. They all belong to you anyway. This place belongs to us. Let us at least have that much."

"I'm pretty sure this is a public place." The bartender returns with my drinks, and she catches his eye. "He'll be adding a gin martini to his order."

"Fucking Becky."

"You've had a lot to drink, sir. I can smell it on you. You're disgusting. And sad."

She turns away. I reach out and pull her back by the shoulder, imagining Sean at my side, impressed. I'm not done yet.

"What is it about places like this you love so much? Really. I really want to know. Is it the men? The drag queens? The drinks, the music?"

"Don't touch me."

I hand my cash to the bartender, tell him to cancel that martini. Then I lean in close to the Becky's face. I think I might be growling.

"No. I know the reason you're here. It's because you can be around men without feeling threatened. Isn't it? You think we're just a bunch of harmless fags. You think you're safe here." I grab her by the waist and pull her to me so she feels the pressure of my crotch. "But you're not."

There's a wet *crack,* and the right side of my face explodes. For a second, I think I've been shot.

"Hey," the bartender says. "Cut it out."

The woman, wild-eyed, has a palm raised for a second strike. I let the pain echo along my check, the top of my jaw, the base of my ear. My eyes start to water.

Don't, Oscar. Don't give her that satisfaction.

"Fucking Becky," I say.

She swipes again at my face, but I'm already gone, over to where Paul stands perplexed in a far corner by the door. I grab his arm and tug him outside. He stumbles, but doesn't resist.

I KNOW WHAT to do next because I read about it in *A Manhood.*

Sean, freshly arrived in New York City, joins a group of gay Midwestern expats for a jaunt to Fire Island. Some of them go off cock hunting along the Meat Rack, but Sean decides to walk over to a quieter part of the beach with a college student.

> *I could feel the tension in the air, the nervous fear of this young stud as I guided him over the crest of the dunes and down to the water. We held hands like young lovers. We were hard, our erections guiding the way like divining rods to the site of our coupling.*

And yes, Paul and I are holding hands as I lead him toward the beach, the crowds of families and kids long gone. The moon plays a coy game of peekaboo from behind heavy clouds. We sidestep spilled ice cream, kick off our sandals, walk into the cold sand.

Ahead, in the darkness, the surf crashes. I lead Paul to a deserted lifeguard stand and, before he can say anything else, press his body against the white, salt-beaten wood with mine.

> *We were hungry for one another. We groaned with lust. If we could have, we would have ground our crotches to dust with all our gyrating. From up the beach came the laughter of a group of boys. I wasn't sure if they were laughing at us. I didn't care. I didn't care what anyone thought about my desires. With a quick tug, I pulled the boy's swim shorts, still damp from our swim, down to his ankles. His erection slapped against his stomach.*

Between kisses, I guide Paul into the hollow underneath the splintery lifeguard station, toss aside a half-moon of paper plate, pull him down onto the sand with me. Our wet mouths meet again, our breath freshened (and sterilized) by rounds of vodka and rum. I'm spurred on by anger as much as lust. Four days here, and I haven't gotten laid yet. Sean would be ashamed of me.

"Wait," Paul says, sitting up. "Wait. Someone might see."

I run a hand up Paul's T-shirt and brush his nipples with my thumbs. I remember Sean's lengthy, three-page ode to the power of sensitive nipples in *A Boyhood*.

"Let them," I say.

He allows me to push him back down onto the sand. I unbutton his shorts. What a shame, to pull down his pale gray briefs and find him bare of hair. (Why, oh why, do we choose to rip out our pubes when, in the throes of adolescence, we couldn't wait for them to sprout?) I take the silly little tube in my mouth. Paul sighs.

One hand supports me over Paul; the other fetches my own cock from its mossy patch of dark hair. Paul reaches out to take it. I swat his hand away and suck on him more insistently.

His cock was warm and thick in my mouth. He groaned and placed a hand on the back of my head, urging me to take more and more into my throat. His body shivered with pleasure. In that moment, as I moved my head up and down, as I felt the cum well up inside him, I knew I had finally arrived where I belonged. A moment later, he arrived as well.

I finish myself into the sand. Paul does the same into my mouth. I look to see if anyone's on the beach around us, disappointed to find it's just Paul and me under the lifeguard stand. With the ghostly lights and the faint noises from the boardwalk, with the sound of the waves in the dark, I feel removed from the entire world.

"That was hot," he says.

Like a crab, his hand creeps along the sand and burrows underneath mine. He sighs with longing. The wood slats above our heads are warped with age. One day, I imagine a lifeguard's going to fall, dropping right through the unsteady surface of things.

Paul asks if I want to do something back in D.C. next week. Dinner somewhere?

I take my hand away from his, check to make sure my fly's zipped.

I vow, henceforth, to live by cock alone.

"No," I say.

~~⋆~~

Sebastian

The names were always the hardest part. Three weeks into the school year and I still didn't have them down. Confused Stephanie with Jasmine. Steven with Steve. AP Art History Cath with Honors English Kathy. I scrolled through the online student database during lunch, trying to memorize the plain names, the strange names, the trendy names, the foreign names. The unfortunate names, like Andrew Buzzard, a scavenger of a boy already growing bald, staring off into space instead of at the gaunt Rublev Christ looking down on our class in judgment from the smartboard.

One name I had no trouble remembering. Arthur Ayer. Seventeen years old. AP Art History, seventh period. The runt of the class-room litter, a transplant from the Philadelphia suburbs thanks to his father's new government job, finishing his final year of high school at Mortimer. Short, strange, self-assured, with purple streaks in his brown hair and a messenger bag freckled with pins and patches. A smiley face. A Spartan helmet. A half-eaten hot-dog. A rainbow flag.

It felt good to begin the steady rhythm of another school year. My English classes started with vocabulary lessons, with short sto-ries by Hawthorne and Poe. Fridays were devoted to thirty min-utes of sustained silent reading, during which students would read at their desks or on the floor from their own books. (No tablets or smartphones, I insisted. Physical books. I told them I wanted to hear the pages turning, I wanted to smell them in the air.) I took the time to read as well, wanting the students to follow my example. Periodically, I'd look up from my biographical study of Caravaggio to make sure the class was using its time wisely. As for my AP Art History unit (forty-five minutes on Mondays, ninety minutes on Wednesdays and Fridays), I considered it sacrosanct. It never got old or boring, the chronological progression from primitive cave art to the chaos of people like Malevich and De Kooning, whose disregard for form and order and meaning made my head hurt. Our class had to keep pace with other classes in the county, in the state, in the country, so we covered at least twenty different works of art each period. An entire history of human expression, distilled in time for the AP exam in late April.

On the last Wednesday in September, our LGBT group met for the first time. I'd dismissed my class for the afternoon and was checking email, thinking no one would show. Then I looked up, saw Arthur still sitting at his desk, phone out. Everything okay, Arthur? Fine, Mr. Mote. Just waiting for the group to start. It is here, right? It is, I said. Welcome. I went over to Arthur and, for no reason, shook his tiny, hot hand. I asked how he was getting along, if he was adjusting to the pace of things here. Oh sure, he said. Not that different from Philly. Over the next few minutes, several other students arrived. I heard them clomping up the outdoor steps, felt the trailer shake with their arrival. It was Arthur who stepped in, who got up to greet the other students, to assure them they were in the right space. There were six of them that first afternoon, Arthur the only senior. All we did was sit and talk. I laid the ground rules for the group, emphasized the safety of these walls, reminded them that, first and foremost, we helped each other here. I told them about my summer, they told me about theirs. Arthur threw ideas out for social media pages, for a charter, for a bake sale. I watched him move effortlessly among the students, listened to him talk as if he'd been at this school his entire life. The uncanny confidence he took in his own body, his own identity, only heightened the awkwardness of the other kids in the room. It brought into relief my own high school days, an adolescence spent hovering below the surface of the social waters, too quiet to be popular—or to be bullied. Of course, I didn't need peers to bully me at that age. I had myself: a bully I couldn't escape; a bully I slept with, showered with, ate meals with. A bully who was less a person and more a heavy wool blanket, thick and itchy, suppressing feelings I wanted to feel but also keeping them safe from daylight. Watching Arthur move about the room, watching the others gravitate toward him, I felt a profound sense of loss for my own boyhood. To have been out, to have been comfortable with myself as a teenager, to have talked freely about my identity. God, how that would have changed things! How much more powerful, how much less brooding, I could have been! How much more proud! Only after the meeting ended, as I watched Arthur at the head of the group leaving my trailer, did I realize no one said anything about Thomas Pitt.

A few weeks later, Dani joined me on one of my regular after-school walks around Lake Mortimer. At one point, she turned to me and, wind whipping her black hair in my face, asked if I was ready to start dating again. I asked her if she knew anything about Arthur Ayer. Had him for geometry for a week, she said. Then he transferred up to trig. He's pretty astute. Scholarly. He's going to go places. He's been coming to our LGBT group meetings, I said. Pretty much taking it over from me. I just sit there now and listen to him lead. I laughed to make it seem like this didn't bother me at all, like it had been my idea from the start. For several minutes, Dani and I played soccer with a pinecone. He's just so comfortable with it, I said. With what? Himself. I mean, he practically advertises it on his messenger bag. Can you imagine seeing someone when we were in high school, walking around with pink triangles and rainbow flags and interlocked male symbols? Can you imagine what people would have done to a kid like that? What they still could do, Dani said, nodding toward the water. We made another lap around the lake in silence. Also, I said, he looks so familiar to me for some reason. But he's new this year, Dani said. I know, I said. Isn't that strange. Well, Dani said, I'm just glad you've found someone to connect with out there in Siberia.

The following Friday, during an afternoon of silent reading in my last English period of the day, my phone clucked with an incoming text. Several students looked up, disturbed from already dwindling levels of concentration. I forbade them from using their phones after class began, kept a drawer in my desk for such infractions. In the drawer, Mr. Mote, Alexander said. (Yes. Alexander. Not to be confused with Andy, that other steer of a boy.) Right, I said. In it goes. I put down my Caravaggio biography and moved to open the drawer. I looked at the screen. It was Oscar Burnham. *Sebastian, SO SORRY for the slow response. Been SUPER busy. Let me know when you plan on coming to the city again.* This in response to a voicemail I'd left over a month ago. But I had no reason to be surprised. I thought of all the times in our childhood he'd been late: coming in from recess, arriving for sleepovers at my house, on tests, showing up to games of flashlight tag. Back then I'd always given him the benefit of the doubt, however reluctantly.

I had inklings the chronic tardiness had some connection with his home life. But Oscar was a grown man. What was his excuse now? Busy like everyone in D.C. was, with their swollen social lives, their double- and triple-booked evenings that staved off the terror of being alone. Forget you, Oscar. I dropped my phone in the drawer, slammed it shut. The students looked up at me, perplexed. See, I said to them with a grin, even I have to follow the rules.

I spent the second Saturday in October, sharp with chill, working in my father's backyard as best I could while negotiating with the looseness in my right shoulder. When he'd left, he'd given me permission to fix up anything I thought needed fixing. It was a mess of a house, one he'd purchased simply because he needed somewhere to live after my mother's death and couldn't stand being in our old home. Do whatever, he told me. It could use something different. So far, all I'd done was tear up the obnoxious shrubs on either side of the front door and hire someone to cut down a large pine on the left side of the driveway, opening the front yard to more eastern light. As for the interior, I wasn't sure where to begin. Or even if I should. Jake and I had discussed redoing the living room in vibrant colors, something to add life to the off-white walls of what Jake called, with a malice I'd only caught on to after he'd left, a scholar's bachelor pad. I was content to keep my renovations outside for now, while the weather was still cooperative. My plan that day included mowing the lawn and mulching the flower beds around the front stoop and back deck. Wearing my father's sweatpants stained with grass and motor oil, I attacked the first of the six bags of mulch lying on the driveway like beached seals, disemboweling them with a shovel, thinking again of Oscar's indifference to my offer of connecting. I tossed handfuls of mulch around squares of lamb's ear, thinking what a fool I was to have even called in the first place. You just can't let go, can you, Sebastian?

At the after-school meeting last week, Arthur had told the others (apropos of what, I couldn't say) that he'd been out since he was a toddler. Probably, even, while still in utero. My mom said she'd always wanted a gay son, he told us. She had gay friends growing up. She named me after one of them who died. She says she knew I was gay before I did. There was this boy in my class I had a crush on. I said I wanted to marry him one day. My mom said, Maybe you will. The story still stung. How easy Arthur made it seem. A simple, unexceptional declaration.

And me? In the weeks after my mother died, hiding in back-corner study carrels during the day, I'd think of how desperately she'd wanted to go on a cross-country drive, all three of us. For as long as I could remember, she struggled to convince my father and me what fun it would be; my father, who despised long drives and depressing roadside motels, and me, who despised any sort of disruption in the normal order of my summer days. Her strange longing for several weeks on the road, for roundabout visits to places she'd hear about on television or read about in the *Post*, were something of a running family joke. I want to visit that old house in Winchester shaped like a hiking boot, she'd say. (Probably smells like toe jam, my father said.) I want to try the pancake challenge at that diner in Denver, how many could you eat, Sebastian? (I don't know, I said. Five?) I want to see bear cubs crossing a trail in the Smoky Mountains. (Sara, they'll eat you alive, my father said while burrowing his beard into her forearm.)

I want to stop halfway and camp in a tent for a couple nights, wouldn't that be fun, Malcolm? (My father hated camping. So did I.) She'd whine, she'd plead—but always with a smile. She'd act like it wasn't a big deal, but after she died I started to think maybe it had been. Sometimes, she'd tell us on the way to work or to run errands that she'd decided to take herself on the drive, asked my father if he would be fine eating two weeks of frozen dinners, asked me where I'd like a postcard sent from. But she never did it. She always came back to her dogs. She always came back to us. Until she didn't. Then I'd start to dream of her body, not neatly arranged inside its coffin but cracked and mangled and flung halfway out the driver's-side door. I'd lie awake at night and think, That could have been me. One day, it will be me. Several months after the funeral, I drove home to see how my father was doing. I'm thinking about moving, he said. Someplace a little farther out, a little smaller, a little quieter. It hurts to be here by myself, you know? We spent breakfast trying not to acknowledge the empty chair at the kitchen table. Then I blurted out that tortured two-word sentence. My father looked up at me. You know, he said through a mouthful of toast, if you were in your mother's village and you'd just told that to her father, he'd have taken you into the backyard and slaughtered you like a lamb. It took a moment to realize this was a joke, my father's way of saying whatever, he understood, it was fine, it wasn't his place to tell me otherwise. Or maybe he just felt he'd already lost his wife and couldn't bear to lose his son, too. We shared a quiet laugh, but I went to sleep that night thinking not of my mother's body but of my own, of the knife at my throat, the catch of serrated steel on my esophagus, my open neck pulled back by hands I'd never seen to let my dirty blood drain into the earth.

He's an Arab, Dani said. Yemeni. God, I told myself I never would and here I am, falling for a member of my own tribe. Fifth date, tomorrow afternoon. Sorry you're not the only Arab in my life anymore, Sebastian. The remains of the meal I'd cooked for us—a crockpot beef stew, a haphazard salad, baguettes, a store-bought apple tart—sat on the counter. We were on my father's couch, halfway through the second of the two bottles of red Dani had brought over. You always say that, I said. I'm just half-Arab. If that. And I meant it. Aside from my skin, my hair, what claims could I make to that community? My mother had wanted nothing to do with those old ways. She'd refused to teach me Arabic, refused to give me a name that suggested my heritage. Sebastian Allan Mote. What kind of Arab was that? I'd dated several men in the past who, intrigued by my exotic looks, ended up disappointed by how unexotic I really was. I'd been scrubbed, deliberately, of all that. My mother wanted me to be anonymous, to belong to no group or tribe. I'd like to meet him someday, I said. Maybe he can teach me how to be a better Arab. Hey, Dani said, fiddling with the stem of her wine glass. Emma told me she tried to set you up with a cousin of hers in Reston. Anything come of that? I thought of an email address to which I hadn't written, a phone number I hadn't texted. I shook my head, took a guilty gulp of wine. Surely you get lonely here, Dani said. In your dad's house, spending all your time moping. I told Dani I wasn't moping anymore, that things weren't as bleak as they'd been earlier this summer, that I'd been thinking less and less about Jake. (I didn't say I'd been thinking more and more about Arthur Ayer.) I'm trying to rebuild myself, I said. It's going to take time. I just think meeting people, just to meet them, would do you good, Dani said. Restorative, you know? I have my students, I said. Dani reached a hand across the sofa as if mine were there instead of in my lap. That's not the same, she said.

Another school week. Vocabulary lessons. The development of perspective. Act one of *Hamlet*. Emails, meetings. Another Monday, Wednesday, and Friday with Arthur, wondering where I'd seen him before, who he reminded me of. Another week of watching him live a boyhood I didn't. Interim grades, a fall pep rally. Roman copies of Greek sculptures.

Statue of a Bearded Hercules. **Unknown. 68–98 C.E.** The first butt I feel other than my own is made of stone. I'm six years old, following my parents through the cavernous belly of the Metropolitan Museum of Art. The vast space, the way it carries voices, makes me uneasy. We wander among Greek and Roman statues and sarcophagi. I think: All these statues are broken. Why doesn't someone fix them? Still, I'm captivated by the pale, cold flesh on display: the smooth muscles and powerful poses, the stubby penises with their testicles like figs. My mother draws my attention to a tall, imposing man whose head is being swallowed by a lion. That's Hercules, she says. He was an ancient hero. He killed that lion and is wearing its skin. See the paws. I stand and look with her. Then she moves on to follow my father toward a giant stone column (also broken). I walk around the statue of the ancient hero, embarrassed and entranced by marble buttocks as big as my head. I see a huge dimple in the left one, as if someone had punched it. Without another thought, I step onto the small dais where the man of marble stands and, stretching on my toes, place a hand against the concavity. I feel a shock of cold, then a growing warmth. (Whether it's my hand or the statue that's warming, I can't decide.) The museum guard barks. My father hisses. Sebastian, my mother cries, rushing over and pulling me away from the statue. No touching! Never touch! Later that night, back in our hotel, my parents already lost to sleep, I think about the marble statue of Hercules in the dark and quiet of the museum, stuck in his eternal stance, grateful for a brief moment of contact with a human hand not wielding a chisel.

I couldn't sleep, so I closed my Caravaggio biography and went out onto the back porch. I sat at the top of the stairs leading down to the lawn, beyond which stood a modest screen of slowly reddening trees. Was my sleep anxiety returning? As a child, I'd had a terror of closing my eyes at night. I'd lie in bed, staring at the ceiling, listening to the occasional car pass by or one of the dogs padding around downstairs. I'd get up, creep down to the kitchen, and stare out the window above the sink at the backs of the other houses in the neighborhood, finding comfort in whatever lights were still on, in the belief that someone else out there in the black night was awake with me. Every time Oscar came over to spend the night, he'd be the first to fall asleep, and I'd sit up on the couch and watch him, curled into a ball in his sleeping bag (which was really mine), breathing deeply, once in a while smacking his lips as if tasting something delicious in his dreams, more comfortable and calm than I'd ever seen him during the day. For a while after he moved away, I'd think of Oscar in a strange new bedroom in Ohio, sleeping just as soundly as he did here, and imagine shaking him awake and screaming for him to call or write. Now, as I sat outside an entirely different house looking upon an entirely different landscape, devoid of lights, it occurred to me that maybe all those neighbors had been asleep the whole time. Maybe they'd just forgotten to turn the lights off before bed, or left them on for security's sake. Maybe there had been no one there to give me comfort after all. Was it the people awake who mattered, or the lights? The reality of companionship, or the illusion of it?

Halfway to the sun-splashed kitchen, thinking about what needed to be done today (the grading, the lesson planning, the laundry), I realized it. Arthur. Where I'd seen him before. Not a face from last year or the year before. A face from centuries past. The random synaptic connection propelled me back into the bedroom, to the paperback biography of Caravaggio in the nightstand drawer. I sat on the edge of the bed and flipped through the glossy pages of major paintings. The saints, cupids, and martyrs. Where was it? The fortune-tellers, the giant slayers, the boys with baskets of fruit. Then I found it. Arthur Ayer, rendered in oils, staring at me from over the shoulders of a young man tuning a lute. The same half-circle eyebrows, the same thick head of brown hair (without its purple streaks), the same full lips, half-open as if prepared to interject, the same round face, the same small nose. Chin and cheeks lightly bearded with shadow. Looking at me as if I'd just yelled his name.

On Monday, before first period, I added a printout of Caravaggio's *The Musicians* to the gallery wall I'd created along one side of my trailer. When Arthur came to class that afternoon, I looked up. Yes. I was absolutely right. It was the same face and, were the body not obscured by the lute player and the male soprano, it would undoubtedly be the same body. The short legs, the small paunch of someone who spent his afternoons and evenings hunched over books instead of sprinting across sports fields. Hi, Mr. Mote, Arthur said. He dropped his messenger bag into the wire basket under his chair, stretched his legs. I saw gravel caught in the treads of his white sneakers. I was about to ask him how his weekend went, but he'd already pulled out his phone.

Mr. Matthew Ayer. It had to be him. And it was. Outgoing like his son, walking up from the cluster of uninterested parents to introduce himself to me at Mortimer's back-to-school night. I'd begun my brief introduction to AP Art History the way I always had, with the promise that my class wasn't just an excuse to stare at naked people. Mr. Ayer had laughed. Now, he seemed eager to tell me how much Arthur enjoyed the class, how much Arthur admired me. The word snagged me. *Admired*. We were halfway to the trailer door when Mr. Ayer (Call me Matt, please) paused in front of my makeshift gallery wall. He laughed again, said, Well look at that. He pointed to *The Musicians,* to the second boy from the right, and smiled. How bizarre, he said. He turned to me. Now who does that remind you of? I stared at my feet, willing my face not to blush, thinking now would be the right time for the trailer floor to finally collapse.

Our lesson that Wednesday was on Gothic architecture. I ran the students through the vocabulary of arches, ribbed vaults, buttresses, spires, cruciform interiors. Together, we read the signs hidden in allegorical murals and stained glass windows. Together, we diagrammed Notre Dame de Paris. Throughout the period, my eyes wouldn't stop moving. Arthur at his chair, Arthur against the wall. Arthur in flesh, Arthur in oil. Arthur the boy, Arthur the image.

Oscar

Two weeks now since the unlucky morning of Tuesday, October 13. Two weeks now since I was summoned by Patrick into a glass-walled conference room and unceremoniously laid off, along with two other designers, two account managers, and a copywriter. Two weeks now since that embarrassing one-on-one in Patrick's office, where I stared at a photograph of him and Lee leaping into the summer air of their wedding day while he went on about lost business, about tightening belts, about a severance package designed to be generous to employees who'd given so much time to the firm, about tapping into his connections for other senior design positions and, hey, would I be willing to work out in the suburbs?

But it doesn't matter, because he'll be here in a few days.

Sean Stokes himself.

In anticipation, I read through the emails I'd sent Sean during my first days of unemployment, when my messages grew longer, more insistent. Spare time has given me the opportunity to drink—and ramble. About my renewed hustle as a bottom-feeding freelancer, scavenging for enough jobs to help me stay in this rent-controlled (but still pricey) apartment. About theme parties in Logan and Shaw, on U Street. About the barrage of baby strollers you see everywhere in the gayborhood now, plastic and steel vehicles the size of small tanks.

Sean talks, too. About the opening night of a Keith Haring exhibit in a converted warehouse off the High Line (and the time he met Haring bussing empty glasses at Danceteria). About a reappraisal of Larry Kramer he was struggling with for a literary review (which he planned to begin by recounting the time Kramer called him "a scoundrel" at a dinner party). I know from internet sleuthing that Sean's positive, but we don't chat about that much. (*It's boring, Oscar. And it's a terrible cliché.*) I let slip that I'm estranged from my parents, but we don't speak about that much. (*It's boring, Sean. And it's a terrible cliché.*) He chides me when I ask him to remind me who Peter Hujar is, who Michel Foucault is, who James Merrill is. (*Was, Oscar. They're all dead now.*) I tease him about his Chelsea boys. He complains about his inability to settle down enough to start a new project. I complain about arguments over identity politics I've had with friends on Facebook.

I blush to read what I wrote just the other day, fresh and silly after several boots of pilsner at Topiary with Bart and his (female) cousin from Memphis. Halfway through the email, something must have happened, some switch flipped in my brain, because instead of bitching I started to wax nostalgic.

> *Whatever's keeping you up there in New York instead of coming to visit, don't forget: We've got the Washington Monument. America's proud, rigid phallus. Have you ever noticed those red lights that blink at the top, like little eyes? You don't really see them in many photographs. I think they're for pilots. I could be wrong. As a kid, I used to come into the city sometimes with my friend Sebastian. (I told you about him, remember? The one I met at the wedding?) We'd leave the city in the evening, and I'd see the monument in the rearview mirror with its blinking red lights. I had this story I'd tell Sebastian, about how the monument was really this giant robot who watched over the city, and if something terrible happened to the country, arms and legs would burst out of its sides, and those red lights would turn into laser beams.*

The Washington Monument?

Jesus, Oscar.

Should have just sent him a dick pic and called it a day.

I spent the morning after sending that email feeling foolish, vowing another one of my fasts from booze and technology that lasts all of half a day. After dinner, I hooked up with a lawyer two buildings down from mine. He wouldn't stop talking about work and so I had to say, like a character in a bad porn, "Just shut up and fuck me." While getting speared, I thought of Sean's sexual adventures, so charged with risk and rebellion. So thrilling. Compared to now, when it just feels like another chore. Like getting fucking groceries.

When I got back home, I took a shower, made myself a cheese sandwich, and went to my desk to tackle a menu design for a client. Which didn't last long, because I saw I had a response from Sean. I spent several minutes deciding whether or not to open it. Then I did.

I'm coming. I need to get away from New York for a time, clear my head. Would be nice to reconnect with you. A friend of mine offered his condo for several weeks in Logan Circle. Isaiah Moore, the poet. He mentioned a bathhouse down the street from his place. Perhaps we should meet there? No. Too tragic for you, I'm assuming. You're probably like all the boys today. Wouldn't be caught dead there. You tender, tender things. I'm aiming to get in town sometime next week. Send me your number. I'll call when I'm settled.

On Friday afternoon, I got a call from a New York area code. Accepting the call and walking to the bedroom, I stubbed my pinkie toe against the corner of my desk chair and bent over in pain.

"Fuck!"

"Oscar," Sean said. "Nice to hear you, too."

He gave me the address of one of the homes ringing Logan Circle, a Victorian I'd probably stumbled by dozens of times.

"Did you know the writer Ambrose Bierce used to live here?"

"Was he gay?"

I felt proud to have made Sean laugh so soon.

He invited me over at eight, then said he had to make a few other calls. After I hung up, I leaned against the kitchen wall to rub my toe. Then I went to the bathroom and, way too early, squeezed a dime of gel into my hand and attacked my hair. The man with the cock that launched a literary career was inviting me over to his place.

Should I?

Would I?

I vow, henceforth, to live by cock alone.

SEAN'S ALREADY POURED himself a glass of scotch and hands me one as I cross the threshold, feeling like a piece of shit with my warm bottle of white wine in its ragged paper bag. His hug isn't the tight embrace I remembered—or expected.

He leads me inside the condo, through the kitchen, and over to a pair of leather armchairs in front of tall, rounded windows that offer a lordly view down into Logan Circle. Below us, gay bocce ball teams (including Bart and Jackson's) finish up league play. I look at Sean, who's already sitting in his chair and waiting for me to take my seat across from him. In the empty armchair is a cardboard tube with a thin belt of green ribbon. I stand back, cautiously, as if it were a pipe bomb.

"Nothing serious," Sean says. "I saw it the other day and thought of you. Please. I'm not asking you to marry me."

I sit down, pop the lid of the tube, take out a rolled-up white T-shirt. The tag inside the back collar says *LGBTees*. The text on the shirtfront, at nipple level, is difficult to read. It's a screen print of sloppy script, like something from the nineteenth century. Sean has to interpret: *For Oscar Wilde, Posing Somdomite*. Huh. The shirt's a large, so it's going to hang off my bones, but I put it on anyway, over the shirt I'm already wearing. Then I sit down in the chair, curling my legs underneath me. Sean's eyes appraise me the way they did months earlier.

"Not bad," he says.

"A little big." Something in Sean's eyes shifts, so I hastily add: "Thanks for thinking of me." I look again at the curious misspelling. "I hope you got a discount. They spelled sodomite wrong."

Sean laughs and drains his glass, turns to watch the bocce players disperse down P Street in their own branded T-shirts. I watch Sean watch them in the silence of this renovated living room with its exposed brick walls, its ceiling ribbed with stained wood beams that probably serve no structural purpose whatsoever. Then Sean's face starts to do that pre-crying thing, that Jell-O quiver, and I'm caught off guard. Sean Stokes, the sexual titan who wielded his manhood like a weapon for decades, is on the edge of tears. I consider setting my glass of scotch down and slipping out the front door. It would be easy. All I'd need to say is, "It looks like you need some time alone." Then I can go and forget this ever happened. Ignore emails, phone calls. It's pretty easy to do, once you've done it for so long. But I have to go before the tears. With tears come attachment.

As if hearing my thoughts and wanting me to stay, Sean turns back to me and smiles. The tears, thankfully, decide to stay behind his eyes. I feel the guilty weight of the T-shirt on my body, this self-less gift with which my three-dollar bottle of wine can't compare. I decide to stay put.

"The slightest thing sets me off sometimes," he says. "Like them." He tosses a hand out at the disappearing bocce ball players. "I was sitting here waiting for you and watching them play down there in the dusk and I don't know. Time passes. You all have no idea how easy you have it. The other week, for instance, I found myself on another one of my long walks. I used to walk everywhere in the city. For sex, yes, but after that, just to be alone with my thoughts. I walk a lot slower now, but I can still go far. Eventually, I made my way to the Chelsea Piers. Nothing now like the way it used to be, you understand. All the gyms, the residential buildings, the skating rinks and shops and restaurants put me in a mood. They disgusted me. A landscape I used to know instinctively, and now it was all new, all strange. Not a playground for gay men anymore but for everyone. I kept walking, and then I came across a row of wheat-paste ads for an HIV preventative. You know the one. The purple pill that looks just like a vitamin. Isn't it chewable now? If not, it will be. 'Dare to Bare,' one of the ads said. Another said, 'Be Free to Have Fun.' The messages were spray-painted over a photograph of boys your age, probably younger, striking the same pose from that famous Stonewall photo. You know the one. Except all these boys weren't angry. They were smiling. They were happy. Oscar, if I could afford to lose my hands, I would have punched a hole in every single one of those posters, I was so outraged. Instead, I went home distraught, frothing at the mouth. Of course, the first thing I did when I got there is take down my Eliot. 'I grow old . . . I grow old . . . I shall wear the bottoms of my trousers rolled . . .'"

Sean gets up and comes back with the bottle of scotch. He refills our glasses, then drops back down into the leather armchair as if defeated. He smiles at me, leans over, and brushes my chin with knuckles like acorns.

"Anyway," he says. "I'm glad you found time to visit. It really is nice to see you."

"How long are you here?"

"A week. Maybe two. Not sure."

"Writing again?"

Sean stares out at the nearly empty circle. "Hoping the change of scenery will help."

Maybe it's the scotch, which I'm drinking quite fast. Maybe it's the fact that I'm already here, and I may as well. Maybe it's an easy way to thank him for the shirt. Or maybe it's just what I think I'm supposed to do. Maybe this is how we help each other. Whatever it is, I lean forward—thinking of the purple pill I swallowed that morning, of the moon of lubricated latex in my jacket pocket— and put my hand on Sean's creased green slacks, far enough above the knee so he knows what I mean. Sean turns back to me and rests a hand, heavy and warm, on mine. Instead of moving it up higher, he moves it back onto the arm of my chair. I sit back, as if it'll help hide my embarrassment.

Oscar, you fucking idiot.

"You're sweet," Sean says. "And I'm flattered. Really. But that's not what you want. You're thinking of another me. I'm a little different, now. A little softer, if you understand."

"Oh," I say.

"Don't take it personally. You're handsome. Not manicured like so many boys today. You're handsome especially because you probably think you're not. You probably think you're too skinny, you don't have any muscles. But in my youth, I would have had you against that wall over there. Or maybe you would have had me, I don't know. What do you prefer?"

"Depends on how much I've been drinking."

"Well. What I'm saying is, I don't want sex. I was just thinking you could spend time with me some afternoons and evenings while I'm here. Drinks, walks, chats. Just casual company. I know you have friends and lovers. I know you're busy. I'm not asking for all of your time, just some of it."

"Why?"

More scotch.

"When I asked you, Oscar, back at that dreary bar where we first met, if you believed in metempsychosis, in the transmigration of souls across space and time, from one body to another, I wasn't trying to be a creep. It was because you reminded me of an old friend of mine. Cal. Maybe you read about him in *The Little Deaths*?"

"Sure," I say.

(A lie, of course. I still haven't gotten to that one. Too much death, too little sex.)

"I apologize if this is scaring you, it's not meant to. Cal was angry, too. Hated the way the world treated him. We used to write letters to one another. This was something people did in the past, you realize. Write out words on paper and put them in the mail. I'd address mine to 'Angry Queen' and he'd address his to 'Sad Queen.' I even wrote to him when I got back from the bar, the night I met you. Said I thought I'd come across his reincarnation.

As you know, he's been dead for some time, so there was no one to send the letter to. I burned it in the metal wastebasket by my desk. Which is all to say that while I certainly don't believe Cal is somewhere inside you, while I have no plans to conduct some sort of exorcism, I feel there's something about you I simply have to know more about. That's the best way I can explain it right now. All I'm saying is, keep me company while I'm away from home. You've written me for months talking about what my stories mean to you. So share some of yours with me."

Sean stops talking. I stare down at the heels of my sneakers against the worn leather of the armchair. I feel his eyes on me.

"You haven't left yet," he says.

"So you want to just hang out. In exchange for this shirt?"

"That comes with no attachments, Oscar. It was me being thoughtful. And, I suppose, somewhat witty."

I look down at the gift, try and read the script upside down. I think of every time Bart's asked me (weekly, it seems) when I'll settle down, as if all he needed to do was knock me out with a dart for a chance to neuter me. I think of my friends with their smirks, their eye-rolls, their subtle slut-shaming. I think of that goddamn advertisement on the bus stop in front of my building, how it mocked me even when I left the Beardsley to head over here.

MAKE HIM YOURS FOREVER.

I vow, henceforth, to live by cock alone.

"I'm all yours," I say.

I raise my tumbler in a toast. Sean's eyes widen. He reaches for his half-empty glass and knocks it onto the hardwood floor.

"Shit," he says. He eases himself to his knees and starts picking up ice chips. I see the jagged rim of the tumbler, see star-sparkles of glass on dark wood, and reach for his hand.

"Don't touch the glass," I say.

"A towel, please. In the kitchen. If you don't mind."

I get up and do as the master orders. Coming back into the room, I stop and watch Sean search under the armchairs for glass. His face is doing that gelatin wobble again. He turns around so all I can see is the green mound of his pants seat, the white plain of his shirt back.

No.

This will not do.

You're Sean Stokes. The glorious libertine. While your friends stayed huddled in the night with their clandestine lives, you burst into the day before queerness became cool, before the glory was sucked out of it. You vowed never to conform, never to contort your life to fit the expectations of everyone else. Maybe you're ready to give up, but I won't let you.

You want stories? Fine.

For you, Sean Stokes, I'll be an open book.

THE NEXT AFTERNOON, I skip Sunday Funday with the others and return to the house in Logan Circle with a small tote bag. We walk over to the armchairs. I see a small black notebook resting on the white windowsill, pen tucked inside.

"Am I interrupting?"

"Just taking notes. What's in the bag?"

I take out a bottle of scotch, then my well-worn copies of *Ecce Homo*, *A Boyhood*, *A Manhood*, *Skin Dreams*. I set the pile of books on top of Sean's notebook. I sit in the chair opposite him, legs crossed at the ankles, arms laid neatly on the armrests. I tell Sean what I want him to do.

"You tell me one of your stories," I say. "Then I'll tell you one of mine."

He reaches for the books, takes each one and flips through the pages. Outside, someone's unleashed dog runs mad sprints around the statue of General Logan.

"So," he says. "Where shall we start?"

"The beginning," I say.

Sean opens his mouth, clears his throat, looks up at me, smiles, and says in that rough voice, "'I vow, henceforth, to live by cock alone,'" and it's like I'm hearing the words for the first time.

THREE

Skin Dreams

❧

Sebastian

Every time I went to the National Gallery of Art, I thought of the shark with the human face. Rising from the depths, monstrous. Jaws outlined with lips, eyes dotted with pupils, teeth like a greedy grin. The horned nostrils, the feathery fins. The invention of someone who'd probably never seen a shark, who'd chosen instead to cobble a demon from fantasy and conjecture.

The film screening wasn't until one that afternoon, but I arrived several hours early anyway. It was Sunday, and I wanted time to stroll through the familiar galleries as if wandering through a sacred space. I wanted time to myself, before the halls grew thick with visitors trying to take the right photographs, trying to see without seeing every piece of marble and bronze and metal, every slash of oil and charcoal and pen. I walked and thought of the times I'd come here with my parents, and of the times we'd brought Oscar with us. We'd walk the National Mall and see whatever struck our fancy that day. Brontosaur femurs and tyrannosaur teeth. The timeline of the universe with its beguiling portrait of early man staring out from the depths of the Paleolithic Era. The lunar landers like candy swaddled in foil wrappers. The pinned bugs proudly displaying their glassy wings and limbs. The posters and banners advocating for the rights of blacks, of women, of (Don't stare at it too long, Sebastian!) homosexuals. But the National Gallery of Art was my favorite. Even if we were headed somewhere else, I'd beg my parents, beg Oscar, to at least walk through it on the way. Oscar hated these diversions; over time, it became obvious just how bored he was. Rarely did he want to stop and linger. Didn't he remember this was where we'd first met? We were on hallowed ground. How could he not care? But instead of looking at the paintings and sculptures with me, Oscar would look at the other kids, the tourists, the docents leading tiny tours up grand staircases, and wait impatiently for his spaceships and sabertooth cats.

There's a young man. Copley's Brook Watson. Pale hair swept back by water, in danger of catching on sharp teeth. Body startlingly white, reclined in a classical pose belying the danger of his predicament. A nude in the American Puritan style, left leg cocked to cover the subject's modesty, undoubtedly shrunken in fear of the mouth rushing toward it.

I used to take dates with me to the National Gallery. We'd meet, always, inside the rotunda, around the fountain with its eruption of greenery, its gleeful statue of Mercury. We'd walk for an hour or so and, empowered by my love of this space, I'd lead the conversation. I'd point out things I'd learned about various pieces over the years. I'd inquire, teacherlike, about what struck my dates as beautiful, as ugly. I found it all arousing—not the tiny Greco-Roman penises or the swell of Romantic buttocks so much as the charged sexuality of the space itself, the intimacy of being in hushed rooms that required us to speak into the hollows of each other's necks, the occasional brush of hand against hand as we moved around a sculpture or through a small crowd. The last man I brought here was Jake, to see a show of Edvard Munch prints in the East Wing. We spent the afternoon walking through the galleries, complaining about the perils of serial dating, snickering at awkward tourists, making mock scream faces at one another. Once, Jake leaned in and caught me on the lips mid-scream. At the end of the evening, I was invited up to Jake's apartment. If you're lucky, he'd said over our second glass of wine, I'll show you my O face. He'd slapped his hands to his cheeks, unhinged his jaw, rolled his eyes up in his head. Later, I discovered Jake's O face was nothing like a Nordic scream. It was a hiss of pleasure through gritted teeth, a thankful release, like air let out of a bicycle tire. It was a sound I'd come to memorize. A sound I was starting to forget.

The crewmates on the rescue boat stand out against the haze of the Havana harbor. More than the two men leaning over the side (reaching, it seems, for Watson's nipple), more than the man with wind-whipped hair holding them back, more even than the Saint Michael figure on the boat's prow, harpoon at the ready, is, to me, the most important face in the entire tableau: the ginger-haired rower. He stares down from between the warrior's breeches, bored and half-awake, as if thinking, Christ, Watson, I can't believe we have to save your ass again.

I took a coffee from the cafeteria and sat outside the front steps of the museum, looking out on the lawn pockmarked with people and, beyond it, the Washington Monument. Recalling how Oscar always likened it to a robot, I sent him a last-minute text, told him where I was and what I was looking at. I wasn't expecting anything, had long given up on reconnecting. Perhaps it was just habit, or maybe I was a masochist. Maybe I just wanted him to know I still existed out there in the world. I put my phone away and thought of the day we'd joined my father on a research trip to the National Archives, a day when instead of lawn the ground in front of us had been covered with massive patchworks of color around which people stood and looked down, hands behind backs or tucked into the crooks of folded arms. As we got closer, the patches revealed themselves in greater detail: letters, words, symbols, shapes, numbers. The sky free of clouds, the great work in front of us appeared without blemish, its entirety made brilliant in the sunlight. We crossed Constitution Avenue, my father leading the way, and into the alleys of this massive grid. I caught fragments as we passed. Rainbows, hearts, crosses, Christmas trees. Stars and silhouettes. Flowers and clenched fists. Names. *Hank Moir. Bill Wolff. Michael Arroyo. Lee Peters Murdered by AIDS in 1992. Michael K. Scott Henry. Rob Burkle. Pedro Zamora. Mother.* A man in one of the white plastic alleys sobbed like an animal. Someone at the far end of the Mall screamed into a bullhorn. A mother hissed at her kids not to skip, to show respect for the dead. I recalled feeling in the presence of something serious that day, something terrifying, something sacred—even if I had no idea at the time why it should matter to someone like me. I recalled how eager Oscar was to keep moving, how an untied shoe-lace trailed behind him like a pale garden snake. I finished these thoughts, finished my coffee, then went back inside the museum to flip through expensive catalogs in the bookstore.

The Swimming Hole. **Thomas Eakins. 1884–1885.** Here, my father says, and hands me a paperback copy of *The Complete Poems* by Walt Whitman. He takes the Xeroxed pages from my hands. You might find other poems in there you like, too. My twelfth-grade English class is reading "Song of Myself." It's beautiful, I think when my teacher reads passages in class. I dwell, repeatedly, on these lines: *An unseen hand also pass'd over their bodies, / It descended tremblingly from their temples and ribs.* It's a little gay, the boy in the next row says. Let's not use that word, my teacher says (unaware, or perhaps not, that many of us use this word to describe him outside of class). But yes, Walt Whitman was a homosexual. A fact all the more obvious by the front cover of the Penguin Classics edition my father gives me. I wonder: Is this a trick? Does my father want to see how I react to these two boys on their slab of rock, one in dramatic contrapposto, the other sitting up on his side, hand raised, head turned, unable to look directly at the buttocks just within reach? I hold onto the paperback long after our class's poetry unit ends, put it on my bookshelf next to the children's encyclopedia I haven't opened in years. In my room, at night, I take the book down, foregoing the poetry in favor of the cover. The limber, perfectly proportioned body I want to hold, to slide along like a wet rock. Periodically, I lie facedown on my bed, chin hanging over the edge, the book lying on the floor a foot below me, and grind myself into the mattress as if it were that same soft body. Afterward, I linger. I imagine it's not the tired twin mattress I'm dozing against, sheets crowded with the thunderheads of old cum stains, springs exhausted from years of constant frottage. Instead, it's the standing boy's sun-warmed body. While others cavort in the stream, the boy and I are alone with one another. This, I tell Jake years later, was when I first fell in love with another guy. Wait, I say. I take it back. There was someone before that.

I found myself at the entrance to the familiar gallery where *Watson and the Shark* hung. I thought of two young boys on a school trip, of fruit rollups and the beep of a waiting school bus. Then I noticed someone else in the gallery, sitting on a bench in front of the painting. A thicket of brown hair, streaked in purple, blocking my view of Watson's fear-frozen face. The puddle of a hoodie next to a ragged messenger bag freckled with pins and patches. There was a sharp cry from a young girl in the adjoining gallery, and the boy in front of the painting looked back over his right shoulder. I was gut-punched, again, by the uncanny similarities between the boy in front of me and the boy in Caravaggio's painting, the fresh young face caught in a sublime moment of discovery. Oh hey, Mr. Mote, the boy said. Hello, Arthur, I said.

At the start of every school year, I gave my AP Art History students a simple assignment. Before Winter Break, each of them must go to an art museum, a local gallery, or an artist collaborative, and find a work that speaks to them. It could be anything. They had to take notes on the composition, the symbols, the methods, the links with previous or future styles. They had to write a two-page report. Just be there, I told them. Be with the work, in the space.

Just for ten minutes. I guarantee you'll get something out of it you wouldn't get from sitting at your desk, watching these slides.

Feeling awkward just standing there in front of Arthur, I asked if I could sit. He asked what I was doing here. Waiting for a film to start in the East Wing, I said. Arthur moved his messenger bag and hoodie to the floor, and we both looked up in silence at the Copley. I watched Arthur's eyes follow the dramatic pyramid of bodies to its apex at the base of the heroic helmsman's spear, follow the straight edge down to the hooked metal seconds away from pushing into the shark's flesh. I've always liked this painting, I whispered, taking care not to lean in too close to Arthur's neck. The first time I saw it, I tell him, I was on a field trip back in elementary school. At first, I thought it was just the shark. I loved sharks as a kid. I preferred dinosaurs, Arthur said with a smile. Well, I said, to me this particular shark was hideous in a way I'd never seen before. But the more I come by it over the years, the more I realize it's not the drama of the scene but the drama of the composition that gets me. Arthur said nothing, and I thought, You're being a fool, Sebastian. He doesn't care. Stop talking. But I didn't. I traced for Arthur the slanted triangle of the action. I used to wonder, I said, why Watson was the only one in the picture naked. I thought maybe this was just a cautionary tale against skinny-dipping. Arthur chuckled, and I wondered if I'd gone too far. I was thankful, in that moment, for the bent left leg hiding the fourteen-year-old Watson's genitals. You know, I realized something before you got here, Arthur said. He pointed. His right leg. It's missing. The shark's already bitten it off. You're right, I said. You don't really notice that at first, do you? You just think the right leg below the knee is hidden by the dark water. Of course, you look closer and it's not a shadow but blood around the bite wound. Which, when you think about it, makes this all the more intense. The shark's already attacked Watson. Now, it's coming in for the kill. I nodded up at Watson's precarious situation, then turned to Arthur. Is this the work you're using for your report? Not sure yet, Arthur said. Just taking notes. My dad went to the office today, so I asked him to drop me off here. I risked a peek at the small notebook in Arthur's lap. I saw the word *nude,* saw the phrase *George + Dragon.* An elderly couple wandered into the room, attempted to read the lengthy description at the bottom of the painting's frame, gave up, and shuffled on to another gallery. What movie? Arthur asked. Movie? Yeah. You said you came here to see a movie. Oh, I said. I rolled my shirtsleeves over my sweater, up past my elbows, and clasped my hands between my knees. (Were they shaking?) I stared at Watson's outstretched right arm so I didn't have to stare at my student. It's called *J'Accuse.* It's a silent French film about the First World War. I've seen clips but never the whole movie. I was thinking about using part of it for our film unit at the end of the year, after the exam. There was a low hum from Arthur's left leg. He pinched his phone out of his jeans. Sorry, he said. The boyfriend. Oh, I said. Well. I'll leave you two. I got to my feet and looked down into the crown of Arthur's head, its whirlpool of hair. Nice running into you, I said. Enjoy your day. Arthur didn't look up from his phone. You too, he said. See you Monday. I walked out of the gallery, turning once to look back and watch Arthur type something furiously into his phone. The boyfriend. Of course.

In line, waiting for the auditorium doors to open, it was my phone's turn to buzz. *Hey! Thanks for the invite. Got plans. Friend in from out of town. Let's catch up soon!*

In recent weeks, thoughts about Jake had dwindled, and it was only during moments like this, stuffed into a tiny theater seat and waiting for the film to start, surrounded by other people but nevertheless still alone, that I relapsed. That I picked through the past, uprooting memories and moments that now clearly foreshadowed our relationship's doom but at the time I'd just passed off as Jake being a loveable curmudgeon, a porcupine with a soft underbelly. Frowning at small children on airplanes, in shopping malls, at the National Zoo. Pondering how our lives would be different if we just got up and left to another city, Chicago, say, or San Francisco. Rambling at dinner parties about bed death and polyamory. All of which I'd ignored, unable to see then as I did now that some people could quite easily forget years of time shared with someone else, could easily discard them as if they'd been no more important than a few hours. Jake and Oscar—both of them, it struck me now, were of a pair. And I, the fool, selflessly taking care of them until, selfishly, they moved on after getting what they needed. For Jake, a chance to dabble in domesticity. For Oscar, the safety of a normal childhood. I was telling myself this gutted-out feeling was all a part of reconstructing your life after a relationship when a ratty messenger bag dropped into the empty seat at my left and, in the seat next to it, Arthur. Hey, Mr. Mote, he said. My dad's held back, and it's raining outside. I told him I ran into you here and decided to stay for a movie. He'll pick me up after. Is that cool? I adjusted myself from my Sunday-afternoon slouch and said, Of course. Arthur pulled out his phone, leaving me to sit in thrall at this preternaturally earnest boy tapping messages to a boyfriend I'd never seen and who certainly wasn't at any of the Wednesday afternoon meetings. Too good for them, perhaps? I spied a flurry of yellow faces: smiles, angel halos, winks, red-lipped pouts. I saw a lime-green text bubble that read, *Wish you were here, boo!* I listened to an elderly couple two rows down bicker about the Clintons. Well I just might not vote then, one woman said. Arthur chuckled at a video he was watching, then leaned across the seat between us and proffered his phone. Have you seen this, Mr. Mote? Raymond just sent it to me. This dog's crazy. I watched the stupid clip just to laugh and hear Arthur laugh again. Excuse me, someone standing at the end of our row said, sparking a chain reaction that forced Arthur to move his bag to the floor and flop into the seat next to me.

An hour into the film, I turned to see Arthur asleep. It took effort for me not to look away from the screen, not to watch, safe in the dark theater with its ghostly projector light, the rise and fall of Arthur's small belly, not to stare at the faint glow of the phone against his hip. It was only much later, when the dead began to rise, that I kicked Arthur's foot. Yeah, he said, sitting up, rubbing a hand over his face. Did I dare? I did. I leaned in and whispered into Arthur's neck, right where it turned into his T-shirt. You're not in class, I said. Still, I think you should be awake for this part. It's pretty iconic. And so the two of us, man and boy, teacher and student, sat and watched the corpse of a French soldier rise to his feet, surrounded by comrades who lay on the flat earth like washed-up fish. We watched this soldier, the first of his undead kind, rouse his comrades from their eternal slumber and march toward a confrontation with the living. *Mes amis, le temps est venu de savoir si nos morts ont servi à quelque chose! Allon voir au pays si con est digne de notre sacrifice: Reveillez-vous!*

We watched the shambling crew make their way along country lanes, their numbers swelling and subsiding from one shot to the next. We watched the living march in victory under the Arc de Triomphe. *Pendant que les vivants passaient musique en tête.* Arthur leaned in to me and was about to say something, then stopped and yawned into my neck before he could turn away. Sorry, he said. So this is, like, early zombie cinema? I smiled and nodded. Arthur sat back and continued to watch. Haunted by the blast of warm air on my skin, I folded my hands in my lap and sat forward. I looked back over my shoulder to watch Arthur, hand hiding the glare of his phone, quickly scroll through missed text messages. I felt distraught, disoriented, torn out of reality. Like a shell-shocked veteran of a vicious war chased by pink-tinted visions of the dead.

We stood outside, sheltered from the evening rain by the East Wing's portico, waiting for Mr. Ayer to pull up the cobblestone drive separating the museum's two wings. There's been a remake, I said. With sound. Same director, too. Arthur asked if it was any good. I told him I'd never seen it. Arthur reached for his thigh, pulled out his phone. He looked out at a bronze hatch-back flashing its lights at the corner, looking lonely in the rain. That's him, Arthur said. I don't know why he parked over there. I smiled to recall my own frustrations with Malcolm Mote's silly idiosyncrasies. I offered Arthur my umbrella, told him he could return it on Monday. I'll be fine, he said. Thanks. He pulled the purple hood over his hair, adjusted his messenger bag against his chest. Well, he said. Thanks for letting me watch the movie with you. Sorry I slept. Until Monday, I said. Arthur hustled down the stairs, sprinted toward his father's car, threw himself into the passenger seat. Why did I feel, watching him go back to his seventeen-year-old life, left behind? Take me with you, I wanted to say. Tell me more about what it's like to be you. I thought I saw the flicker of a waving hand behind tinted windows, but I wasn't sure. I watched the hatchback pull away down Pennsylvania Avenue, caught a glimpse of the familiar blue bumper sticker with the yellow equals sign, then continued standing under the portico with several other people waiting for car shares or a passing taxi. After a few minutes, I decided to go back inside the museum and wait for a lull in the rain. I turned to pull one of the thick glass doors open. It didn't give. A guard had just locked the museum behind me, and he looked at me through the glass and shrugged as if to say, Rules are rules.

Oscar

Several hours before dawn, there's an explosion across the street. The kind of boom that throws you out of bed, bare-assed, onto the floor. The kind that shrinks your balls up inside your stomach. Terrorists, you think. But no. There's no light with this explosion, no fire. Just noise, epic, like something out of the end of days.

I cling to the floor beside my bed and wait for another salvo. Nothing. Slowly, movement begins in the apartments above and around me. Doors open in the hallway, releasing the angry murmur of busy people roused unexpectedly from sleep they can't afford to miss.

Hugging the dark so as not to flash the wakening street, I creep out onto my balcony for a look. And there it is: the small construction crane that once stood tall and proud next to the skeleton of the Echo now lies like a storm-struck tree along the eastern side of Fourteenth Street.

The bulk of it, I'm sad to report, rests inside Fourteenth Street Baths: one of the last relics of old gay life in D.C., having survived the online chat rooms, the dating apps, the bars and clubs and theme parties but not, it seems, the forward march of urban development. An unimpressive one-story building scaled in blue tile and fronted with wide frosted windows, now just another wreck. Goodbye, sea-green hallways. Goodbye, empty exercise rooms. Goodbye, hiss of steam, grunt of release from behind louvered doors. Goodbye, old queens sitting naked in upholstered armchairs or lying naked on sauna benches. Goodbye, private rooms, in which I'd occasionally wait for a passing stranger, thinking of shameful pleasure but also of my father, wishing he could see his son now.

Of course, I don't tell my friends about my visits. They say I'm not allowed to go there.

Bart (holding, as always, Jackson's hand): "It's tragic."

Drew (pursing his lips and shuddering): "Dirty old men."

Tom (eternally single, probably a virgin): "Where's the love? The romance?"

Jackson (holding, as always, Bart's hand): "Why bother? It's all on your phone."

I've stopped trying to convince them about the beautiful queerness of the whole enterprise. They just don't get it.

Later, in sweatpants and a wool sweater, I sit on the balcony and listen to the peal of police and ambulance sirens grow louder, watch as the scene is cordoned off with tape, as fire trucks fill the street with their noise. I wait for bodies, for blood.

Nothing.

Bored with the scene, I go back inside.

THAT EVENING, SEAN invites me over for scotch at what we now both affectionately call the Ambrose Bierce House. It's his second week in D.C., and he has me over every few days, usually just for drinks. Once, I came over to find him stirring a pot of boiling water, and we ate spaghetti with garlic and oil in our armchairs, watching leaves drop from the trees inside Logan Circle.

Tonight, I bring Sean a fresh bottle of scotch I bought with what little money I have to spare on sundries for myself. I ask him over the slow burn in my throat—which I'm slowly getting used to—if the sound of the collapsing crane woke him up. He takes a sip of his drink and winces.

(Sorry, Sean. Bottom-shelf is all I can afford.)

"Slept through it," he says. "Only saw it on my way across town to meet a friend. What a mess."

"I still feel that noise in my bones. I mean, just imagine if that crane had fallen in a different direction. It might have been the Beardsley taking the hit, not Fourteenth Street Baths. I've been thinking about that all day."

"That's trauma for you."

We sit in our armchairs like lords while outside the window an evening boot camp performs jumping jacks and burpees in the circle. We sip our drinks. We talk, as always. Me about my life, he about his. Mostly, I try to impress him with my sexual escapades while I remain in thrall to his ancient ones. Occasionally, still, I'll ask him to read. I've grown less self-conscious about having an old man read books to me, grown more and more attached to the heavy sound of his voice. I've started to hear it everywhere, even when I'm alone. It's a voice in which I've started to think and dream.

Sean finishes a particular moment of debauchery with laughter that turns wistful when he looks back out at Logan Circle, at the fit and flabby boys exercising under the trees. He seems small tonight in his white button-up shirt with the brown slash of a coffee stain I'm not convinced he knows is there. Lost in another of his melancholy moods. To bring him back to the land of the living, I tell him about two hookups I had last weekend. A delicious shiver runs along my body as he crosses his legs, rests his chin in one hand, asks questions. I tell him everything. Where it happened, when it happened, how many times it happened. How long I lasted, how long they lasted. Who came first. Who fucked whom. Cut or uncut. Protected or bare. Spit or swallow. Kissing or no kissing. I give Sean demographics: age, race, eye color, hair color, weight, length, girth. I want the details to impress him, to keep him hooked. But as the words come out of my mouth, they start to lose what power they contained in my head. Stories that seem like such an essential part of myself, a display of my power and pride, now sound dull in Sean's company. Uninspired. The more time I spend with Sean in such concentrated doses, the more I start to worry how plain, how banal I sound to someone like him. If our storytelling is a dick-measuring contest, I'm woefully at a loss.

Still, I talk.

Still, he listens.

Occasionally, I'll come back from the bathroom to see him staring out the window, scribbling something into the notebook he always keeps on the side table.

THE FOLLOWING MORNING, after what Sean tells me is a good spell of writing, I invite him outside the Ambrose Bierce House for a walk.

It's early November. Bundled in coats, clutching coffees, I take Sean through Logan Circle and down to Lafayette Park, where we pay our respects to the ghosts of gay men who, under cover of night, still slink among the green in search of illicit, illegal sex. I ask Sean if he ever cruised here. He shakes his head. We sit on a bench near the Executive Mansion and I tell him about the building's brief rainbow makeover this past summer, about the crowds cheering outside the tall black gates.

"Must have been a sight," Sean says through a mouthful of muffin.

"I guess. I wasn't there."

We wait for a break in the wind, then get up to leave. As Sean turns to brush muffin crumbs off the bench and into the grass, I lock eyes for a moment with the nuclear war protestor squatting, eternally, under her tent of white tarp.

We break for lunch at a small bistro recommended by Sean's journalist friend. I take my phone out, and Sean and I watch videos of the High Heel Race from several weeks ago, the annual mad dash of drag queens down several blocks of Seventeenth Street to the cheers of the crowd. I complain about the breeders, there to see us minstrel for their pleasure. Afterward, we watch men come in and out of the restaurant, pick our favorite parts of their bodies as if they were rotisserie chickens. (Light meat? Dark meat? Thigh? Ass? Forearms?) I tell Sean about the game I play with myself on the Metro, where I search a crowded car for the one person for whom I'd be a slave forever.

"Slavery doesn't sound like you," Sean says. "Too much commitment."

"Har har," I say, and gently kick his ankle under the table.

Then our food arrives: chicken Caesar salads delivered by a stocky server in black shirt and slacks who I'm pretty sure I've seen in drag somewhere. While we eat, a gorgeous man comes in for what must be a business lunch. Fitted blue suit, perfect blond pompadour. I look up as he passes our table, wait for that secret glance I always think of as a holdover from days of cruising in secret. Sean's days. I get nothing. For all he knows, we're just any other two people eating lunch on a weekday in downtown D.C. Tourists, maybe. Father and son, perhaps.

"Do you miss it?" I ask.

"Miss what?"

"Your books. I mean, not the books but the things you write about. That life."

"Yes, there are some things I miss about it." He puts down his fork, wipes his mouth with a napkin. "There are things I don't miss, too."

"Like?"

Sean widens his eyes, frowns. "Really, Oscar?"

"Oh. No, of course. I get that. I just mean. I don't know what I mean. Like, if my dick were to fall off tomorrow morning in the shower, say. I don't know what I'd do with myself."

"So you think just because I've retired from that life, I should go dig a hole somewhere and lie down? While what? You shovel the dirt over my corpse?"

"I'm sorry. That's not what I meant."

Sean shrugs, leans back in his seat and opens his arms as if offering himself up to the world. "'Look upon my works, ye mighty, and despair.'" He drops his napkin on the table and excuses himself to the bathroom. The server comes by to ask if I'm still working on my salad. I tell him to take it away. God, I hate this about myself: that I can never talk clearly about what I want to talk about, that something gets lost between my brain and my mouth and so instead I just stumble through my words like some kid who's just discovered and cleaned out his father's liquor cabinet.

I sit there, alone. I debate whether or not Sean's ghosted. A minute later, I feel his hand on my shoulder and almost sigh with relief.

"I'm sorry," I say.

"Let's keep walking," he says.

Yes, I think. Walking's more productive than talking.

In silence, I lead Sean over to P Street Beach, the fat slant of grass overlooking Rock Creek where, years ago, club kids would lounge and smoke and go off into the bushes with one another. We take a series of worn wooden steps down the grassy plain and sit. Below us: the swerve of traffic and water bending toward Georgetown. Behind us: the shell of an old gay club, the first I ever went to, now a restaurant specializing in Peruvian small plates. I tell Sean about the massive warehouse of Wet, long since razed and replaced by Nationals Park, where hunks hit home runs on the same sacred earth where other hunks once played with different bats and different balls. I run Sean through the old names, the disappearing memories of earlier generations.

Hung Jury.

Best Friends.

Delta Elite.

Mr. Henry's.

B.F. Keith's Theatre.

Metropole Cinema Club.

Tracks.

LaZambra.

The Lodi.

Chaos.

Nob Hill.

The Brass Rail.

Places I only visited once, places I never got to visit. Places now just pictures in cheap history booklets.

"What a loss," I say, picking at the grass around my hips.

"You've gained a lot," Sean says. He flicks a paper cup away from us. "Our work's paying off. Don't forget that."

The afternoon skies threaten rain, so Sean invites me to an exhibit of old German woodcut prints at the National Gallery of Art. I think about the freelance work I need to finish, the job applications I need to start, but I join anyway, if only for another hour in Sean's company. I can't end this day on such a sour note.

Sean's the kind of person, as I imagined, who reads every museum label, gives every work at least two minutes of his time. I follow behind him as long as I can bear. Then, exhausted, I slip out of the exhibit and move through the rest of the museum, checking my email, checking social media, checking Cruze to see who else might be in these cavernous halls.

At one point, I find myself in front of a massive painting of an eighteenth-century shark attack, and I stop. I know this one. The goofy fish, the helpless twink. I put my phone in my pocket and sit on the bench in front of the painting, remembering another afternoon, decades ago, when I stood here with Sebastian. I'm ashamed to think of the unanswered text message buried in my phone. *Just checking in to see if you still want to catch up sometime.* Sebastian, who all those years ago came up to me and asked if I wanted to eat lunch with him. Sebastian, who on the bus ride home asked if I played Nintendo, if I liked comic books. And I remember, now, more than anything else from the subsequent years we spent together as boys, that first night, after the field trip, going home and sitting upstairs on my bed and crying while my dad yelled at something downstairs; crying not because my dad was yelling but because I felt, for the first time, seen by someone else.

"There you are."

Sean sits down next to me on the bench, but he's not looking at the painting. Now it's my turn to make that Jell-O face, to force myself not to blink because if I blink I'll start to cry.

"What's wrong?"

I shake my head, and Sean scoots closer to me, wraps an arm around my shoulder. The warmth is enough that I give in and tell him it's just the painting.

"What about it?"

"It reminds me of someone."

"Tell me."

"No one. Just an old friend from childhood. The one I told you about when I first met you. Sebastian. It's fine. It's no big deal."

"Big enough of a deal to make you cry."

"I'm not crying," I say as the first tears slither down my cheeks. *Just checking in to see if you still want to catch up sometime.* Sean laughs and grips my shoulder.

"You're alright," Sean says. "I can imagine he means a lot to you."

"It's not him. I'm not crying because of him."

"Then what is it?"

I turn to look at Sean, this man almost twice my age, and I'm laughing and crying at how ridiculous this all is, what I must look like to someone walking past this gallery. I see the genuine concern in Sean's eyes, the half-frown you'd give to a wailing baby you couldn't really do anything to help, and then I drop my head into his coat and laugh through my tears and say, "I don't want to be invisible!"

On one of the first evenings I spent with Sean at the Ambrose Bierce House, I mentioned Martin, a sporadic regular in my bed. An executive at a small event-planning team specializing in queer dance parties, sports leagues, happy hours, trivia nights, themed evenings for every sort of sub-group and fetish. The following night, after my childish breakdown at the National Gallery of Art, Martin texts and says he wants to meet up.

You host? I host?

Neither. You said you needed freelance work. May have a job for you.

We meet on Sunday morning outside Captain Dave's for their drag brunch, an event I normally stay away from but agree to come to only because Martin knows the manager and says he can get us an easy seat. Still, my heart drops in my stomach when I see the line of people stretched outside the door, when I see an entire family—father, mother, son, daughter—waiting to be let in for the next performance.

Martin takes my hand and pulls me around the line and through the crowd at the front door. "Look at this wall of vagina," he says to me, loud enough to be heard by the people around us. "You don't happen to have a stick, do you?"

We're seated over by the bar, at a small table for two, in the middle of a routine. Wearing a floral caftan, the drag queen lip-synchs, flirts, shyly pulls folded dollar bills from eager hands. A zoo of suburbanites that's commandeered three tables by the window is going, appropriately enough, apeshit. There's a husband and his wife, an older couple that has to be one of their parents. Look. There's a fucking baby in a fucking high chair. The drag queen passes by, rolls her eyes at us. Martin and I offer a limp wave of moral support. I think I see Paul, the boy from Rehoboth Beach, come downstairs to use the bathroom, and I shrink into my coffee. A girl cheers from somewhere over my shoulder, and I feel the ghost of a slap on my face.

"Guerilla warfare," Martin says from behind a mimosa. "I thought of it after what you said last time. Death of gay culture and all that. How we were losing our spaces, how we should be fighting to get them back. So I thought up an idea for a new monthly theme party. We get a bunch of guys together to drink and party specifically at straight places. Family restaurants, sports bars, chain restaurants. Here in D.C., maybe in Maryland and Virginia if we're feeling adventurous. We give them a taste of their own medicine. A reverse colonization sort of thing."

"A theme party."

"I know, like we need one more. But I sold the idea to some of the guys on the team, and they told me to explore it. See what I could come up with. So I thought: Why not go to the man who inspired me? It'll be a fun little revolution."

"A revolution."

"Yeah. Who doesn't love a party?"

I think of the last party I was at, just the other night at Empire, when I went up to this beautiful lumberjack of a man, introduced myself, asked what his name was, what he did for a living, then felt his hand on my shoulder and heard him apologize into my neck and tell me he was here with his girlfriend and she'd just gone to the bathroom. I think about Patrick's wedding, the little brat and the Becky at Poodle Beach, of all the thrill-seeking breeders sitting at the tables around us. Our tables. I think about everything I hate about the way we live now. I think about Sean, about how tired and vulnerable he seemed during our walk, possessed by an exhaustion I can't find in his books no matter how hard I look.

"Still here, Oscar?" Martin waves a hand in front of my face. "I said there's money in it for you."

I vow, henceforth, to live by cock alone.

"Yes," I say. "I'm here. I'm in."

We talk about hourly rates, expectations, deliverables. We toast with mimosas made with bottom-shelf champagne and orange juice concentrate. From the stairs leading to the all-weather roof deck, a baby screams in rage.

At home later that afternoon, fueled by indignation and a mild delusion of grandeur, I scour the internet for public-domain photographs of shirtless, hairless hunks with the requisite cobblestone abs surrounding the tiny wells of their belly buttons. I dress them in baggy camouflage pants and military-grade boots. Inside their arms and hands I place an arsenal of pistols, rifles, rocket launchers, grenades, serrated knives, hatchets. I find faces with steel jaws, steel eyes, steel intentions. I type headlines in military fonts and drop them above their heads. THIS MEANS WAR. TAKE NO PRISONERS. WE WANT YOU. BE SCENE. JOIN OR DIE. At the bottom of these mockups, above placeholders for undetermined dates and unsuspecting locations, the name Martin and I decided on: OUTRAGE. Outside, through the open windows (all this ferocious productivity makes me hot), I hear the hiss, groan, and clatter of construction workers making up for lost time on the Echo. Inside, I hunker down at my desk like some mad prophet evangelizing about the wrath of days to come. Like Sean Stokes typing away at his raunchy novels all those decades ago. It's well past midnight when I email dozens of these mockups to Martin, showing him how they'd look on Facebook and Instagram, on Cruze, hanging from the three-story brick wall outside Topiary and rotating on the television screens at Empire.

"This is awesome," Martin says the following Wednesday. "You've really put a lot of time and thought into this. You know I can only pay you for five hours, though, right? That's what we agreed on." His phone shakes in his hand. "Sorry. Have to take this."

Martin turns away and speaks softly into his phone. Instinctively, I reach for my own, and discover a text from Sean that's sat, unattended, for the past forty minutes.

Leaving tomorrow.

BACK NOW, FOR the last time, at the Ambrose Bierce House, in our opposing leather chairs turned to face the front windows, watching the passersby swaddled in thick coats. All those beautiful bodies, I think, put to bed for the winter.

Sean says he's been away from home long enough. He says he has business to attend to. He says the city's calling him back. He says, besides, his friend promised the condo to someone else. A painter.

"Out with one gay artist, in with the next," Sean says as he pours our first glasses of evening scotch. His own, I see. Not the cheap shit I gave him earlier.

"The first Outrage event's happening in December," I say. "Maybe you can come back for it? Deliver a short speech, give us your blessing. Smash a champagne bottle against a table and send us off. Maybe, I don't know, do a reading from whatever it is you've been working on. It's a new novel, isn't it? You haven't given up, have you?"

Sean smiles and stares out the window.

"I knew it. What's it about? Seriously, I won't tell."

Sean looks down at his folded hands in his lap.

"Holy shit. You're writing about me."

"Oscar."

"About the last few weeks."

"Oscar."

"That notebook you take with you everywhere."

"Oscar."

"I'm not upset. Honestly. I'm honored. Write whatever you want. I'm all yours."

"Oscar, there's no point in talking about it."

"Can I see what's in your notebook?"

"Absolutely not."

"Come on."

"Oscar, forget about the book." Sean drains the rest of his scotch. "I want you to do me a favor. I'd like you to reach out to your childhood friend. The one you cried about the other day."

"I told you, I wasn't crying about him."

"Oscar."

"Why is it so important to you?"

"Because I think it would be important to you."

"We have nothing in common. We're like parallel lines."

"Don't they say parallel lines converge at some point?"

"In infinity."

"Well. Patience is a virtue, Oscar."

"I'll think about it."

"Oscar."

"Let's just have another drink."

I get up and give us both a healthy pour, only so he'll have to sit and sip a little longer. Then I take my copy of *Skin Dreams* from the tote by my chair and toss it in his lap. He starts.

"Read me something," I say. "About the piers. I never got to go there."

Sean looks at the book in his hands as if it were an unexpected gift.

"Please," I say.

He flips through the pages. He stops. He begins to read.

"'Annoyed with Ben's cautionary tale of Carlos's murder, with his suggestion of the inherent danger in the life I was leading, I left my apartment that evening and went down to the piers. I wandered the public playgrounds where smooth boys beat off in side rooms; where, according to rumor, two men had collapsed, mid-fuck, through rotting floorboards into the Hudson. I walked through rooms that echoed with grunts and laughter and the faint lapping of river water.'"

When he hears the zipper of my jeans, he stops and looks up at me. With one hand, I start playing with myself; the other I use to prop up my chin and stare into his eyes. I expect Sean to protest, but he doesn't. I see (or think I see) something behind those eyes hard at work, already trying to set this strange moment down in words. It's like I can already read it on paper. I know he's writing about me, and the realization makes me all the more insistent. He reaches over to draw the curtains. I tell him to leave them alone. I say I don't care if anyone else can see me.

Sean continues reading.

"'The rot, the decay: I thought for a moment Ben was right. Maybe I was in danger. But I would not relent. To calm down, to admit defeat, would be to give up on life itself. In minutes, I secured the attention of a handsome man in cut-off jeans and an open leather jacket studded with military medals that looked hand-crafted, not earned. We did not hold hands. We did not share names. We did not look one another in the eye after that initial glance. I followed the man into a room damp with mildew, frosted with moonlight from an open hole at the top of one wall, below which, like the effigy of a primitive god, a giant painted cock spurted pale ropes of semen.'"

Sean reads and reads and reads, and then I'm down on the hardwood floor, nearly tripping over my dropped jeans, releasing my own pale ropes. Sean stops reading. I catch my breath and stare at my cum on the floor, that familiar gel, that salty cock-broth, that sap like onion milk I've seen thousands of times on pillows and bedsheets, on buttocks and thighs and lips and fore-heads and bellies, in napkins and paper towels, in toilet bowls and shower drains. Just when I think I'm tired of seeing it, I feel like I've discovered it again for the first time.

I roll onto my back and reach down to pull up my jeans. I pre-tend to keep my eyes closed in exhaustion, but I can see, through barely open lids, Sean in his chair, upside down, quickly write something inside his notebook. There, I think. I'll do that for the sake of your book, too. Sean stops writing, puts the notebook on the arm of his chair. He stares down at me. I stare up at him. Sean looks disheartened, not impressed.

"Let me get you a towel," he says.

"Thanks."

I wait for Sean to step into the far bedroom before reaching over, still upside down, and taking his notebook off the chair. I don't have much time, so all I can do is open to the page bookmarked by his capped pen and read, upside down, what he's just written. It takes me a second to fix the orientation of the words, to flip and reverse the letters so Sean's hasty scrawl reveals a single sentence on an otherwise blank page.

Never seen someone so melancholy over his own cum.

⇶

Sebastian

Throw key! Throw key! Me, as a boy, demanding to play catch with my father's keys. And a pest! And a pest! My mother, hissing, as she executes, one by one, flies in the sunroom. This was how I taught my English students about meter and rhythm, trochees and anapests. Then there was the simplest of all, the iamb, which I drilled into my classes by standing in front of my desk, slamming a fist into my palm, and proclaiming my right to exist in the world: I am! I am!

I was at the kitchen table sorting my way through reading responses. *Using what we've learned from our reading of William Blake's two versions of "The Chimney Sweeper," write two versions of your own short poem. Choose whatever subject interests you. Write the first poem from the perspective of innocence and the second poem from the perspective of experience.* I got a text. *Sebastian, SO SORRY I've been MIA. Really. Let's get together this weekend and finally catch up. MY TREAT.* I stared at my phone for a moment, then put it back on the table, facedown, and continued grading.

As if invigorated by the impending Winter Break just weeks away, Arthur began to arrive early to class in order to talk with me before the other students arrived. Like old friends catching up. Like colleagues. I cherished these moments: the languid chats about college visits and new movies I hadn't had time to see. I dreaded the eventual arrival of the other students, hated the moments when Arthur said, Well, and got up to go back to his desk and wait for me to pull up the first of that afternoon's artworks.

After class, Arthur came up to my desk. I was wondering if you'd write a short letter of recommendation for me, he said. The admissions office at Jefferson wrote to me. I told them I was part of the LGBT group here. They want to hear from the sponsor. I figured since you went there, it might help. A letter of recommendation, I said, mulling the words. Arthur stared at me in anticipation. I drew the tension out for another few seconds, then smiled. Of course, I said. I'd be delighted.

. . . In my admittedly short time teaching at Mortimer Secondary School, I have never met a student so curious about the world and so imbued with the passion of a scholar as Arthur Ayer. I have known this young man for less than a year, but I am convinced that his pride and confidence, his ability to stand up and lead his

peers, will take him far. More importantly, it will make him an exceptional fit for the diversity and forward-thinking mission of the Jefferson University student body. Had I only had the chance to learn and grow with a student like Arthur Ayer while I was an undergraduate there . . .

I handed Arthur the recommendation before the start of class on Monday. I'd deliberately not licked the envelope. Thanks so much, Mr. Mote, he said. Don't peek, I said. Please peek, I thought.

Another text, this time while watching television in bed. *Hey Sebastian. You around tomorrow? Interested in grabbing dinner?* I had no idea where this persistence was coming from. But I'd lost interest by now, felt a delicious sense of power in writing back, *Can't make it. Have plans.* I turned back to the television. It was a special report on radical Islamic terror, and the reporter was explaining how suspected homosexuals in a town overrun by religious fascists were executed by being thrown from rooftops. A still image showed one man in mid-drop, hands tied behind his back, face shrouded. A photograph of terrible beauty that stayed up much longer than seemed appropriate. The plummeting body framed by sandstone columns, the perspectival rush. What would Arthur think of such a thing, so far removed from his own daily experience? What about the other kids in the Wednesday group? Allison. Alex. Craig and Steph and Juan. Could they imagine a world like this, where they could be roused from bed and dragged, still sleepy-eyed, to the top of a tall building and tossed to the ground where their family, their friends (some of them, perhaps, closeted themselves) waited to clobber them with bricks should they survive the fall?

Tuesday evening. Another text. *Bear Happy Hour at Empire. Don't suppose you plan on being in the city later?*

Walking back to my trailer on Wednesday afternoon, I passed Arthur in the hall. He waved with one hand. The other was in the grip of another student. The boyfriend. Back at my desk, alone and waiting for seventh period to start, I reviewed my online dating profile, dormant for the past several years. I looked through the outdated photos I'd spent hours curating, the detailed (but not too detailed) responses to standard questions. The men I'd flagged for messaging. The men who'd flagged me back. The men who hadn't flagged me back. I thought of Arthur and his boyfriend off eating lunch somewhere, shoulder to shoulder. This is how you rebuild your life, I thought. Then I updated my credit card information and reactivated my account. I was reading the *Welcome Back!* email when Arthur came up the trailer steps.

Thursday afternoon: *Two for one drinks at the D Hotel rooftop bar Sunday PM. 2 to 5. Sunday Funday! Thoughts?*

Thursday evening: *Hey! I'm Michael. Any chance you're free to meet up after work tomorrow? Don't meant to scare you by being forward, I just think it's easier to meet in person as soon as possible. And I agree with what you wrote in your profile: Sick of games. Me too! Anyway, let me know.*

I arrived at Shelley's Tavern in downtown Fairfax twenty minutes early, ordered a beer at the bar, and stood there scrolling through Oscar's unanswered texts just because it was something to do, something to protect me from looking the way I knew I looked to everyone else: like someone waiting for a first date. I debated sending Oscar a curt text asking him to leave me alone, to let me get on with my life, then decided against it. Instead, I looked around the bar, watched the tired tech-corridor employees drinking pints under television screens, the young couple in a booth leaning into one another in serious conversation, talking as if it were effortless. I imagined Arthur walking into the bar with his boyfriend and his parents. I imagined Arthur seeing me sitting here, alone, with a near-empty glass of beer. I imagined Arthur thinking, Sad, lonely Mr. Mote. I imagined the four of them sitting at one of the far booths with sodas and fried chicken tenders while I watched from the bar like some forgotten figure at the back of a Bruegel canvas. Twenty minutes passed, and I waited twenty minutes more for Michael to show. I checked my phone for text messages, pulled up my dating profile to see if I'd gotten a late-afternoon email from him. Several guys over at the far end of the bar burst out laughing at something on one of the televisions. I began to mull on the futility of the whole enterprise, the prospect of having to explain myself, from the beginning, to a stranger. Where I grew up, where I worked, where I went to college, what I thought about the traffic here. My father the professor, my mother the corpse. The bartender came up and asked if I wanted another beer. I think I'll close my tab, I said. I should get going. The bartender gave me a knowing look, as if she'd seen all this before and would see much more of it to come. I paid my bill and hurried out, thinking that now, of course, when I'd made the decision to leave, Michael would show up. But he didn't.

When I got home, I sat at the kitchen table and thought about hitting something. Instead, I took out my phone and texted Oscar. *Sounds great, I'll see you there!*

Sunday afternoon, and I was already resentful from being unable to find street parking and having to pay ten dollars at a small lot seven blocks north of the D Hotel. I walked down Fourteenth Street in the cold, passing bars and restaurants and art galleries and loft-style apartments I'd never known existed. I passed the boarded-up windows of what, if memory served, had been the city's last gay bathhouse, now looking crumbled and ragged like a half-eaten cake, blocked by chain-link fencing and hip-high barricades. A sign over the front door read GOODBYE, THANK YOU FOR 32 GREAT YEARS!

The elevator to the roof of the D Hotel was packed with men and mirrors. To avoid looking at these fascinating creatures with whom I felt I shared nothing, I stared instead at the elevator buttons. Above them: a haphazardly taped flier on which a shirtless stud in an Uncle Sam hat and tailcoat raised a finger and commanded me to BE SCENE.

And there he was. Oscar Burnham, alone at a small table in the corner, looking ragged with his wild hair, with his beaten-up paperback book, with his ratty cardigan draped over a baggy shirt. There you are, Oscar said, getting up to give me a hug. I took the seat across from him, and we both just looked at each other over the table. So, he said. So, I said. Listen, he said. I'm really sorry it took so long for us to get together. Really. You know how it is, everyone in this city's so busy. You know what that used to be like. A waiter brought Oscar what looked like scotch, asked me what I was drinking. House red, I said. Raucous laughter from the crowded bar. I thought you'd be over there with everyone else, I said. Wanted to do some reading while I waited for you, Oscar said. He pushed his book toward me. *Skin Dreams*. I picked it up and thumbed through it. Never read it, I said. I thought back to a search through crowded bookshelves with Jake, then quickly pushed the memory away. Fun fact, Oscar said, leaning in as if planning murder, tapping a long finger on the book's front cover (intertwined legs: one pair hairy, one pair smooth). I know him. Yeah? No joke, Oscar said. Met him right after that wedding last summer, over at the Attic. He was just sitting there in a corner by himself. We emailed for a while, and he actually came to visit. Just went back a couple weeks ago. Oscar looked at the book in my hands as if longing for its safe return. I heard all he does is write about sex, I said. Pretty much, Oscar said. It's great. What a life he had. Has. Just open to a random page. Read what you find. Ninety-nine percent chance there's cock in it. I declined, handed the book back to Oscar. I took a sip of wine and studied Oscar in his silly shirt. *For Oscar Wilde, Posing Somdomite*. Two tables over, a waiter popped a champagne cork and five men cheered. I watched Oscar study them, watched him spin his book around on the smooth tabletop, lost in thought. I asked Oscar if he was dating Sean, and Oscar laughed. God no, he said. I don't do long distance. I don't even date outside Northwest. We just talk, share stories. Oscar paused, as if debating something, then said with a smile, He's writing a book about me. I said, A book? Supposedly. That's what he told me before he left. I put my wine glass down and sat back in my chair, looking at Oscar and wondering what such a book would be like. And you, Oscar said. Still getting over your ex? I'm putting myself back out there, I said. How's that going for you? Seeing a moment to elevate the conversation, I took out my phone and showed Oscar the dating profiles I'd flagged. Oscar took my phone from my hand. Seen him on Cruze, he said.

And him. And him. Exasperated, he gave the phone back to me. Whining for husbands by day, begging to be fucked by night, he said, then cackled as if sharing a joke with some invisible person sitting next to us. I continued to drink my wine and let Oscar commandeer the conversation, going on about Sean Stokes, about halcyon days at the Piers and the Pines, about the complex mathematics behind how many lovers he'd had over the decades, about his vow to live according to the needs of his penis. Oscar kept referring to us—me, himself, Sean, everyone—as fags. I thought about telling him to stop using that horrible word but decided it wasn't worth the battle. Instead, I told Oscar about a conference in New York City in February, about my father snowbound in the mountains. I was going to tell him about Arthur, but something perked Oscar's attention. New York? He smiled, then said, Think you can relay a message for me? Never mind. I don't even know where exactly he lives. Isn't that strange.

We had just finished our second round of drinks when Oscar placed his hand palm-down on the table as if preparing to deliver an important address. Alright. We need food. Let me get this, I said, reaching for the bill. Well thanks, Oscar said. He looked down at his phone while I paid. Still taking care of Oscar, after all these years. I realized we'd been sitting here for almost two hours and hadn't said a word about our childhoods, our shared past. All we'd talked about, mostly, was Sean Stokes. How anticlimactic this all was. I felt as if I were just another in a long line of men waiting to take their seat in front of Oscar, no more or less important to him than anyone else in this rooftop bar shielded against the weather by white plastic tents and black heat lamps. Follow me, Oscar said. On our way out, he waved and smiled at several people. Who's this, someone asked of me. I tensed, ready to introduce myself. Oscar said, Just an old friend from elementary school. On the elevator ride down, just the two of us, I debated going home. Then I saw Oscar's reflection wave at me, make silly faces, play with the distortions of his body in the glass, and I thought, There you are. So I joined in, and we laughed. Tipsy, we moved around the elevator, making ourselves tall and short, skinny and fat. Counting our doppelgangers in the mirrored walls.

Oscar led me down the street to a small restaurant redolent of pork and bourbon, the walls armored in thick wood planks, the ceiling in tin. He slid into the booth across from me, took his phone out, placed it faceup on the table. I ordered the salmon, Oscar a steak salad. Our food arrived, we started to eat, and then Oscar suddenly put his fork down. I want to ask you something, he said. What do you want to ask me, I said through a mouthful of flaky pink flesh. Look, Oscar said. We're both adults, right? We go way back, right? I tried not to frown. If you have to ask the questions, I thought, the answers are no. What I mean is, we're not boys anymore. So I was wondering. Oscar paused, smiled like a devil. Any interest in going back to my place after this? Having sex? I almost drowned in my water glass. You're insane, I said with a laugh. Just like that? I thought it would be a novel experience, Oscar said. You're single. I'm perpetually single. I mean, really. Why are we bothering to get together after all these years when everything was just fine? To catch up, I said. To maybe become friends again. Come on, Oscar said. He tapped my leg with one of his sneakers. I think you're just as curious as I am. Admit it. I sat there, overcome by the realization that yes, this was a terrible mistake after all. I should have just let Oscar flit by at the wedding,

I never should have come up to him at that college party. It was useless trying to recapture the past. It's just sex, Oscar said. I'm on the pill, too, so you don't have to worry about AIDS this time. He snickered, and I wanted to shatter his shin under the table with my boot. I was eleven years old, I said. My voice rose. I didn't know anything about all that. Jesus, Oscar. What's your deal? He sighed and scraped the remains of his salad to the edge of his plate. Okay, he said. Forget it. Just kidding. I didn't realize it would be such a big ask. Well it is, I said. It's completely inappropriate. And if we're bringing up the past, you already had your chance, right? At Jefferson, when you turned me down. I had to fight the urge to close my hand into a fist, to keep from slamming it on the table. Oscar laughed. I turned you down because you were shit-faced, he said. I'm pretty sure we were all shit-faced, I said. But we weren't all desperate, Oscar said. I stared at Oscar, enraged. Were my cheeks burning? Around us, the air smelled faintly of charred flesh. Oscar raised his hands in mock surrender. Anyway, sorry I asked, he said. Seriously. We went back to our meals, and I was thankful for the cutting, the chewing, the swallowing, the wiping, the entire procedure that kept us both occupied, kept us both quiet. Then the bill arrived. We split it. All this way for thirty seconds in an empty elevator, I thought.

Look, Oscar said outside the restaurant. I'm sorry about that. Really. I didn't mean to be presumptuous. I just thought it would be fun. It's fine, I said. (It wasn't.) It's no big deal, I said. (It was.) We shared a pathetic hug, then I watched Oscar, phone in palm, walk back up Fourteenth Street, past the wreckage of the Fourteenth Street Baths. I remember how despondent I'd felt when Oscar had left me, alone and rejected, for Ohio. How embarrassed I'd felt ten years later when he'd left me, alone and rejected, on the Jefferson lawn. Now, watching him turn the corner and move out of sight, I felt strangely satisfied with my refusal of Oscar's casual, awkward proposition. Vindicated. Now you're the one rejected, I thought. Now you're the one slinking off with no pride.

In bed that night, bored and angry and sad, I began to masturbate. At first, I just went through the motions. Then, like something forcing itself to be born, I thought of Oscar, and my fantasy took on the feel of vengeance for countless wrongs both real and imagined. I kept asking my phantom Oscar if this is what he wanted, if this was like something out of one of those books he wouldn't shut up about, if I'd be reading about this very moment in a couple years written down in purple prose. As I came, I thought of someone else: a painted face, spider-cracked by the passage of time, soft and secretive, open mouth like a gasp of shock. Was it curious? Was it judging me? I wasn't sure, but the horror of being seen like this was enough to drop me out of my silly fantasy and back onto the reality of my four-poster bed: the violently rumpled down comforter, the bunched-up pillow I'd been humping, the gobbet of semen puddled in my red palm.

Oscar

And so the revolution begins, the first shot fired at Winston's, that unassuming Connecticut Avenue bro-magnet infamous for its generous pours and its raucous din of straight-boy babble. By my best (admittedly drunk) count, there are forty or fifty of us at the inaugural Outrage assault. The posters taped to the back doors of bathroom stalls and elevators, the signs wheat-pasted onto the wooden walls of curbside construction sites, the viral messages on social media, the email blasts, the shout-outs by drag queens and deejays—it's working. We're here: the bears and cubs and otters, the short and tall and toned and average, the white and black and brown, the whole glorious fucking rainbow ready to give these breeders a taste of their own medicine. Eyeing-down the confused frat boys until they shy away, avoiding the Beckys pleasantly surprised to see their gays in this most unassuming of places.

To celebrate, I go home with a young politico newly arrived from Florida. I'd caught this duckling staring at me from near the bar where he'd been sitting with two girls. Stout and unassuming, his full beard and hairy forearms promising more fur that had yet to be revealed, looking confused, as if this were the last place on earth he expected to see us. Who knows? He might not even have been one of us. Nevertheless, I got him to take me back to the Columbia Heights apartment he shared with his two friends. Drunk and tired, we collapsed head-to-foot halfway through mutual blowjobs, one of his hairy calves slung across my neck and prompting a brief nightmare of strangulation.

Walking home in the morning through the early December chill, chest puffed out like a proud cock, head held high, set apart from the other people making their gloomy winter walks of shame, I send Sean a text.

Outrage = SUCCESS!

"It was spectacular," I tell him later that day during our weekly phone chat. "Seriously. You should have seen their faces. They were stunned. Remember that story you told me a while back, about writing the word *MURDERER* in fake blood on the front door of that doctor's office who said you were sick in the head? I imagine his face was like theirs."

"Oscar. Those are two completely different things."

"I guess."

"Did your friend Sebastian show up?"

"No."

"That's a shame. Still no word?"

"Nothing."

Nothing from Sebastian since our dinner, despite my invitation to join us at the Outrage party on the heels of yet another apology. Perhaps I'd been a little too insistent on meeting up with him after Sean left, maybe even a little too desperate given the months we'd spent trying and failing to connect. Not perhaps. Definitely. Then there was the sex. Sean needed it for his book, I imagined, and I failed to deliver.

"I took a page from you," I said when I broke the news to him about that Sunday. "I thought I'd be up front with it. Just ask. I think I was a bit too forward for Sebastian's tastes."

During the next several minutes, I regale Sean with the story of last night's hookup, embellishing it as much as possible, working hard to transform a drunken morning into a spectacle of sex worthy of one of his early novels. Midway through my story, he coughs. It sounds like he's eating something. Crackers? Nuts?

LATER, IN THE shower, scratching shampoo into my hair, I start to think about Sebastian. Admittedly less morose the other week than at Patrick's wedding. A glow about him, too, like he'd recently met someone. Strange, considering how sad his social life seemed. Such a plain boy. Reminds me of all the people in the stock photos I work with, acting happy, acting shocked, acting in love. All of them dull, all of them sapped of any real spirit. And the hair. Still shackled to that same boring part. Should I have reached across the table and destroyed it like I used to? I wonder if that would have turned him on.

It had been the same back at that spring lawn party at Jefferson, the first time I'd seen him since we were kids. It was a few weeks after I'd been informally, unceremoniously disowned by my father, after he agreed to finish paying for college and then send me on my merry, sinful way. So, frustrated and abandoned, I did what all frustrated and abandoned young gays do: something dramatic, something clichéd. As soon as I got back to Adams (my father's alma mater, an hour east of Jefferson), I took my roommate's electric shears and dragged them through my hair. I gathered the clippings onto a copy of the student newspaper I'd spread over the bathroom floor and tossed them out our third-story window. I don't know what I was thinking. I suppose I imagined the wind carrying my shorn locks throughout the small campus, into the mountains, perhaps even all the way back to my parents' front door in Yoder. But the wind was still that day, so my hair just dropped, without drama, into the boxwoods surrounding our apartment building.

The rest of that day, I sat at my computer in gay chat rooms, telling random strangers what I'd just done, running my hands along the bristled dome of my skull, rapidly, as if trying to start a fire. I kept staring at myself in the mirror, surprised at how alien I looked, how free I felt.

The following Saturday, I didn't think twice when some classmates invited me on a night-jaunt to Jefferson, whose Queer Student Organization (like everything else, ten-thousand tiers above ours), was holding a spring lawn party. We arrived in town in the early evening and pregamed with wine coolers and watery beers at someone's off-campus apartment. Around nine, we stumbled down East Main Street to the senior dorms lining either side of the university's historic quadrangle. There were fewer people than I'd expected. Instead of the mob of wild and crazy outcasts like myself, there were just a few small clusters hanging around the portico outside someone's dorm room, the boys in polos and pressed khakis and the girls in floral-print skirts. I was expecting a rave, and instead I got a garden party. We helped ourselves to what we could siphon from a dying keg but mostly made do with the bottles of peach schnapps we'd pulled from the pantry before walking over.

Soon enough, surfing a wave of tipsiness and reeling from the rejection of someone who wasn't thrilled when I said I wasn't particularly interested in marriage rights and I just wanted to fuck in peace, I found myself cornered against one of the portico's columns by a stocky guy. Eerily familiar, as if dropped from a dream into this moonlit spring evening. He kept looking at me, waiting for me to do or say something. (What it was, I had no idea.)

His smile dipped into a frown.

"You don't remember me," he said.

But I did, sort of. It's just that through the haze of schnapps I wasn't making the connection he expected me to make. Then he moved back into the light and I saw the part and then, only then, did I realize who it was. Only then did I dig out the boyish face from the padding of weight.

Little Sebastian Mote. All grown up. And, sadly, not my type. Too soft when what I craved at the time, what I searched for on

AOL and in the rec center showers, were hard bodies. Flawless, as if carved from marble.

"Ah," I said. "What are you doing here?"

"Um. I go to school here."

"No, I mean here."

"I joined last year."

I opened my mouth to ask if he was gay, then caught myself. Still.

Sebastian Mote.

Did I ever suspect? Confronted with this grown man I'd last seen several feet shorter, I felt like the guy in that movie who realizes he's been dead the whole time and, recycling through the entire film, all the little clues suddenly make sense to him. Not the dick touching, so much. Chalk that up to being bored, dumb boys discovering what they could do with the meat between their legs. (I recall now, still standing under lukewarm water in my shower, what Sean told me once over scotch, quoting Voltaire: "Once a scientist, twice a sodomite.") No. Other things. How he'd look at me, intently, over pizza in his family's sunroom. How he'd watch me sometimes in his basement, at night, when he thought my eyes were closed. How, during one of the rare games of football we played with other neighborhood boys, he'd take a strange delight in tackling me so that, even after I dropped the ball, he wouldn't let go until we'd both fallen to the ground and one of the other kids yelled "Make out!" and he'd pull away from me in fear. How, for no reason I could understand, he seemed so intent on making sure I was having fun. Still. He'd walked normal, talked normal, acted normal. Whereas I had no straight-boy camouflage to hide behind. My limbs, my voice—it was clear, even then, something was off with me. My father knew. Had Sebastian? Well. He did now.

So we played a polite game of catch-up, pausing every now and then out of respect for the passage of time, for our shared identities, for the dumb coincidence ("serendipity," Sebastian called it) of running into one another here of all places. Sebastian's face was lit with happiness and alcohol. He asked me when I knew, if my family knew, if I had a boyfriend. Unsteady on his sneakered feet, he seemed insistent on an answer to this last one. But I didn't really want to talk about any of that.

Soon enough, Sebastian and I had exhausted our conversation and just watched several guys dance inside the dorm room to a new Madonna song that lifted the beat from an old ABBA track. I drained the last drops from my plastic cup, stared out at the swatch of manicured lawn descending down to East Main Street.

Someone's cigarette smoke kept blowing in our faces, so we moved a little farther down the portico, into the shadows. Then I felt Sebastian's hand slide along the top of my shorn head.

"What made you do this?"

"Time for a change," I said. Then, because it was better than awkward silence, I caved and told Sebastian the story of my exile, about the 1998 car accident outside Avon from which Harrison Burnham emerged unscathed and born again, about my foolish belief that my father's love for his only begotten son could transcend his love for God's.

"I'm not surprised," he said. "Your father wasn't very nice."

"No. No, he was not."

"I remember once I asked my parents if we could adopt you. Because you spent so much time at our house."

"What did they say?"

"No, of course."

"Oh."

I felt strange standing here while he touched my head as if I were some amateur Buddha, so I reached out and ruffled the part in his hair, asked if he remembered that. Which I shouldn't have done because, as if I'd triggered some emotional failsafe inside his chest, Sebastian pushed me with his body deeper into the shadows, against a brick wall. His breath was sweet with the schnapps I'd shared with him, his lips surprisingly dry as they searched for my own. Sebastian moaned softly. To be polite, I didn't struggle or protest. I also didn't reciprocate, just waited for the moment to pass, which it did after several seconds when Sebastian pulled away from me and sucked in breath. His eyes were closed. He was smiling.

"You never wrote when you left," he said. "You never called. And we were both the same, the whole time." This last bit came out of his mouth like the solution to some arcane riddle, as if the universe now made perfect sense—to him, at least. The same? We were nothing alike.

From down the portico, several people giggled. At him? At me? At us?

Sebastian took one of my hands and started stroking my fingers. He stared into my eyes and, his face catching light from a nearby sconce, I saw just how drunk he really was. More than drunk. Somewhat unhinged.

"I live alone," Sebastian said. "If you want to stay over. I mean, if you're not staying with other people." He leaned in for another dry kiss, and I took the moment (it was now or never) to gently (if one can ever do such a thing gently) move away. I patted Sebastian on the shoulder, though from the look on his face I may as well have kicked him in the gut.

"I think we're heading back soon. Besides, you look ready to pass out."

Sebastian looked at me, confused. Then he understood.

"Oh. Yeah. Right. I should get going. I've got a paper to work on tomorrow morning anyway. Well." He put his cup on a peeling windowsill and came at me again. I braced for impact, but instead of another kiss I was folded into a soft hug. I worried Sebastian would never let go but, a few seconds later, he did.

"I'd give you my phone number or email address," he said with a reddening face, "but we both know you probably won't call or write. Anyway. Take care of yourself."

Before I could say the same, Sebastian had turned and was stalking off, alone, down the portico, away from the party and into the night. I went to find something to drink. When I woke up the next morning, hungover, on the couch in our dorm room back at Adams, I wondered if the whole thing—Sebastian, the party, my father—hadn't just been some strange dream. Then I went to the bathroom to piss and saw my shorn head in the mirror, like a soldier ready for war. No. It had all happened. It was all happening still.

A WEEK BEFORE Christmas, we're at Empire. It's chaos. Massive fake trees with coils of disco-shiny boas and silver plastic balls that occasionally drop and roll across the dance floor. Testicular puns on banners and bar napkins. Thick crowds packed together in ugly Christmas sweaters and red suspenders. Remixed holiday music. Prefab studs dancing on raised platforms in Santa hats and elf booties. The glow of holiday lights, the glow of smart-phone screens.

I find Drew and Marcus over by the bar. Above us, anonymous text messages slowly scroll up television screens. I'd been told on the way in to text the club and my messages would show up for everyone to see. I read some of them while sipping my first scotch of the evening.

Guy in Xmas tree sweater, can I buy you a drink?

Alvin, I still miss you!!!!!!!

How does this work?

Is it true they're shutting this place down?

Anyone find keys in the bathroom?

Let's take this party onto Cruze. TimTim94.

At one point, I fire off my own flare: *I vow, henceforth, to live by cock alone.*

Some asshole responds: *See your doctor first.*

Soon the music segues into a dance version of Nat King Cole's "Mrs. Santa Claus," and the floor erupts in cheers and hoots. It's Madame Pamplemousse again, dressed in a red gown with white fur trim, pushing her way through the dance floor, sticking candy canes into mouths and down pants. A shirtless man in peppermint suspenders walks by. Drew, Marcus, and I follow him with our eyes, united in a fleeting moment of communal lust. Then I'm back to glaring at a straight couple jumping up and down and crying out for their own candy canes. I order another drink, ask the bar-tender to be generous with the bottom-shelf scotch.

"Scotch?" Drew asks. "Since when?"

"Sorry I missed your dance-party thing," Marcus says. "Mom was in town."

Someone in the crowd calls our names. I have a crazy thought: Sean? But it's Bart, dressed in a knitted mess of reindeer and polar bears. His face looks distorted, distended in the red-green-blue-white strobes.

"Guys! Guys!"

Then I see it, brilliant in the slashing lights.

"An early Christmas present," Bart says, showing us the silver band on his left hand. "Can you believe it?"

Drew and Marcus lean over to fawn, and maybe it's the music, maybe it's the crazy lights, maybe it's Madame Pamplemousse tucking a candy cane into my back pocket, or maybe it's the bear who bumps into me and apologizes for not seeing me there, but I do something silly. I start to cry.

"Honey," Bart says, pulling me into his fuzzy arms. Drew and Marcus look at me, unsure what to do. Bart pats me on the back like he's trying to burp me, steps away.

"Hey," he says. "How you doing?"

I nod and wipe my tears with my shoulders. I take deep breaths of hot dance-club air.

"Sorry," I say. "Just happy for you."

"Yeah?" Bart says.

"Yeah," I say.

He lets me go, raises his arm, and yells down the bar. "Jackson! Jack! Over here!"

Jackson comes up to us in a ridiculously large Santa hat. He wraps his arm around Bart's waist.

"Hey, Oscar," he says. "Surprised?"

"No. I mean, yes. I mean. Excuse me, guys."

In one of the bathroom's steel stalls, I sit on the closed toilet lid and hope the thump of holiday music from outside is enough to cover the sounds coming out of my mouth. In front of me, taped to the back of the stall door, is an ad for my dance party thing. BE SCENE. Sean, I think. I need to talk to Sean. But he's not here. He's out of the country, in London, through the end of January. I gave him my address and have been waiting, impatiently, for a postcard that still hasn't come.

Several minutes later, I stumble out of the stall into a group of guys pissing into a long steel trough. I avoid their looks. I focus on washing my hands, drying my eyes.

Outside the bathroom, I collide with a wall of muscle.

"Oh," the chest says. "Hello."

I look up into a face of rich brown skin, into plump lips that, in a moment of desperation, I lunge toward. The man and I kiss long and deep in the flow of people outside the bathroom door. His mouth tastes, strangely, like peach schnapps. Several guys burst out of the bathroom, pushing us off into a darkened corner. This stranger, this muscle god with his hard body, steps back from me with his hands on my shoulders. He's smiling. He looks like he could swallow me whole.

"Haven't I seen you online?"

And then I'm not crying anymore. I'm on the cusp of delirious laughter, thinking what a beautiful gift the universe has delivered to my front door. Serendipity. Just like Sebastian said all those years ago.

"It's Jerome," the stranger says.

"I don't care," I say.

FOUR

The Little Deaths

Sebastian

Amazing, how students could emerge, ex nihilo, in a school this small. That I could have passed someone countless times in hallways and have no idea he existed. Only now, in the doldrums of early January, the students still moping from a short Winter Break, had I become aware of this student's existence. Showing up outside my trailer during the Wednesday afternoon meetings, wearing a puffy jacket over a school hoodie with the initials MSS. Keeping his distance, waiting for Arthur to walk across the blacktop toward my trailer so he could point at him and mouth the word *Slut*.

That's Trent, Arthur said when I asked him one afternoon if he knew that boy, as if the answer should have been obvious. He lives in my neighborhood. We're not friends, obviously. I drew the blinds to the trailer's front window and went back to my desk. Our after-school group was discussing winter prom and plans to march in June's Capital Pride Parade with students from other district schools. At the end of the meeting, I pulled Arthur aside. Is he bullying you? You can tell me if he is. It's important I know. Arthur shrugged. He's annoying, he said. But I can take care of myself. He's just bitter Raymond's going to winter prom with me, not him. He thinks because I'm the new kid this year I'm going around stealing everyone's boyfriends. So he's gay, too, I said. He's an idiot, Arthur said. I'm here to help, I said. Oh I'm fine, Arthur said. He left the trailer. I watched him make his way across the basketball courts, face forward, swinging his messenger bag by its straps like a mace.

Over the next two weeks, our AP Art History class wound its way through the Italian Renaissance. The students endured image after image of putti and saints, of chiaroscuro suppers and depositions. There were several Caravaggio paintings. *The Calling of Saint Matthew. The Crucifixion of Saint Peter.* On a Monday toward the end of January, we discussed *The Musicians.* The image, transposed from my computer screen onto the whiteboard at the front of the class, was blown up as large as I'd ever seen it. I walked my students through the painting. I told them the central figure, the teary-eyed lute player, was a depiction of Caravaggio's muse. I told them musicologists had taken time to recreate the sheet music held by the boy with his back to the viewer. And this last figure, I said. I made circles around the cornetto player's face with my laser pointer. It's a self-portrait of Caravaggio. I paused, then said, Kind of reminds us of our friend Mr. Ayer over here, doesn't it? The eyes, the lips? I turned away from the whiteboard to look at Arthur. He stared at me as if he'd just swallowed something unpleasant. He shook his head. No, he said. I don't see it.

After class, on my way to my car, I saw Arthur standing by the flagpole looking despondent. I thought, It's that kid. Trent. He did something to you. This is where I finally come to your defense, where I save you. What's the matter, Arthur? He looked at his phone and groaned. My ride's going to be late, he said. Again. Across the parking lot, Trent stood with a couple other boys, monstrous in his baggy coat, his thick black jeans, his tanned construction boots. Receding hairline, double chin, flat nose. The face of a pugilist. From the far side of the school came the violent crack of jackhammers. Here, I said. I'll give you a ride home.

Arthur guided me to one of the newer developments in town, a cluster of build-by-number homes owned mostly by city commuters like Arthur's father. The house was at the base of a narrow cul-de-sac. Red Christmas lights framed the upper right-hand corner window, where a small rainbow flag was taped to a pane of glass. I didn't realize you lived so close, I said as the car idled beneath us. I'm over in Driftwood Court, the older homes. It's my father's house, actually. I'm taking care of it while he's away. I bike around there sometimes, Arthur said. You never say hi, I said, feigning hurt. Arthur smiled. That's because I'm usually there visiting Raymond. He lives in that neighborhood. Oh, I said. Arthur gathered his messenger bag under his arms and undid his seatbelt. The phone in his hip pocket buzzed. Raymond, I guessed. See you Monday, Arthur said. He stopped halfway out the passenger door. Oh, I didn't tell you. Jefferson—I got in. Fantastic, I said, restraining myself from patting him on the back or ruffling his hair the way you would an obedient dog. So thanks again for your recommendation. My pleasure, I said. That's what I'm here for. Just remember they're taking you because of you, not because of what I said about you. Yeah, Arthur said. I guess. He turned and walked up the driveway. I watched him key in a code for the garage door, watched him disappear into the rising darkness, watched the garage door descend. At a first-floor bay window, Arthur looked out and waved at me. I quickly reversed, fast enough so the front of my car dragged on the dip at the bottom of the driveway.

In early February, leaving my classes with a five-hour film adaptation of *Hamlet* and the final two episodes of John Berger's *Ways of Seeing*, I joined a team of teachers from other districts for an AP conference in New York City. I was, admittedly, thankful for the brief respite from Mortimer. I was also worried about Arthur, about the squat bully I couldn't help but notice following him around, calling him names. I wondered if I should have declined the invitation, if I was somehow shirking my duty by going away. I worried something terrible would happen while I was gone.

The conference was spread over Thursday and Friday and ended promptly at three each afternoon. I passed on networking, passed on happy hours and dinner invitations, and instead spent my afternoons and evenings wandering alone through the delicious winter chill of Central Park, watching steam rise from the carriage horses' angry nostrils, admiring the joggers dashing past slowly melting hillocks of dirty snow. Compelled by history, by a sense of duty, I went to visit the Stonewall Inn, thinking I'd take some pictures to show the after-school group when I got back. It was dusk as I walked down Christopher Street. I saw the thick neon lines spelling out the bar's name in its small square window. Inside, it was dark. I stepped closer, saw the typed sign on the door. CLOSED! CRACKED PIPES. WATER LEAK. COME BACK TOMORROW. SORRY! A group of young men pushed past me to cluster in front of the neon sign. One of them raised a selfie stick, and they all gaped in mock awe. I walked over to a bench across the street and watched the pilgrims come and go, excited to arrive but disappointed to find the doors closed to them. I tried to feel some sense of mystery, of awe, of connection. I recalled Philip Larkin's line about a serious house on serious earth. All I could think of, though, all I could see, was the present. The commuters, the tourists, the pigeons. Four children scampered around George Segal's plaster sculptures, giggling to themselves. Life, I thought. I watched one boy brace himself against one of the statues and dig into his runny nose. Then, as if summoned by an invisible voice, he rushed to the other side of the small park, drumming his hands along the iron posts.

Back in my hotel for the night, inspired by the anonymity of the city, by its great swell of people, by the feeling I'd slipped out of the constraints of my normal time and place, I downloaded Cruze. Just to see how the other half lived. I spent five minutes in the bathroom trying to take a decent profile picture, raising my phone for a more slimming angle, maneuvering my stance to block out awkward cameos by a shower curtain or the curve of a toilet bowl. I made myself taller by two inches, lighter by twenty pounds. Lying on my bed and re-reading *Crime and Punishment* in anticipation of my English classes' next unit, I was bombarded by vibrations. Most of the messages were worthless. Dull introductions, simple interrogations, unsolicited private pictures (soft, hard, long, small, cut, uncut). I amused myself for several minutes talking about the weather with a furry butt, about presidential primaries with a pair of cobalt eyes. Too fearful to meet any of these strangers but thrilled, nevertheless, by the attention. By the feeling, however brief, of being desired. I left the app on silent while I slept, woke up in the morning to more faces, more messages. Enough to drive one mad. How on earth did someone like Oscar stand it?

The next evening, halfway through dinner at a dumpling shop on Mott Street Dani had recommended, I heard the sound of another incoming message. I put down *Crime and Punishment* and saw, staring out at me, a simple portrait. One of the men I'd been sitting near during an afternoon workshop on digital learning tools. RICHARD, his name tag had read. ANDREWS HIGH SCHOOL, ANN ARBOR. *Hey,* his message said. *You're in the AP conference. I was sitting a few rows across from you. I'm Rich.* I wrote: *Hi, Rich. I'm Sebastian. How's it going?* Three minutes later: *Good. Glad all the boredom is over with.* Me: *Agreed. Nice to get away from students, though.* Rich: *Agreed. You leaving town tonight?* Me: *Saturday evening.* Another five minutes passed. I was handed a small fortune cookie and the bill. Rich: *Out with friends now. Staying at the hotel, though. Are you?* Me: *Yeah.* Rich: *Around later?*

I got back to the hotel a little before ten, ordered a glass of wine at the bar, and spent several minutes adjusting my posture on the barstool. Twenty minutes later, Rich arrived, looking harried and tipsy but, thankfully, still as handsome as I remembered from my shy glances earlier in the day. Over the speakers, Rod Stewart commanded our hearts to be free tonight. We ordered several glasses of wine and talked about our lives, our students. Then Rich's hand was on my knee. We started to whisper, as if talking in an art museum. Rich's breath could sterilize medical instruments, but it was also warm and sweet against my face. My eyes roved more freely over Rich's body, imagining what was hidden beneath the wool sweater, the collared shirt, the khaki pants. Rich made a joke about dandruff, and I took the opportunity to slip my fingers into his black curls and pretend to hunt for an elusive flake. I like your hair, I said. My Jew fro, Rich said. He touched my hair, gently. The part's cute, he said. He drained his glass. I drained my glass. So, Rich said.

And then we were in the elevator and Rich was dropping his head into my neck and I was lifting his chin up and guiding his thin lips to my own. The first man I'd kissed since Jake. It felt as if someone had twisted a closed valve in my body, releasing pent-up pressure; I almost expected to hear the hiss of escaping steam from my ears and nostrils. Rich started sucking on my tongue, more forcefully than I would have liked. He was definitely drunk. Then again, so was I. One of Rich's long-fingered hands clasped the back of my neck, tried to push my face deeper into his mouth, and I had a brief feeling of drowning. I felt the thunder of rushing blood in my head, in my belly, in my crotch. I didn't think of Jake or of Oscar but of Rich as his own person, unencumbered by the men from my past. I thought: I'm doing it, I'm doing it, I'm doing it.

And then we were in my hotel room, collapsing on the bed in a frenzy of fumbling hands, stubborn buttons, catching zippers. The first man to touch my nipples, my belly, my thighs since Jake. I pulled back the covers. Rich pulled down his pants, revealing a pair of briefs with a dancing menagerie of anthropomorphic dogs, snakes, bears, cats. Rich saw me looking and asked if I was a fan of the show. I shook my head. Never seen it, I said. Naked now except for my own boring white boxer briefs, I slipped my body alongside Rich's. The feel of warm flesh against mine, the anticipation of sex already announcing itself in our underwear, reminded me of that sweet, sad piece by David Wojnarowicz. One I'd never be able to show my students. The buck-toothed, school-age boy announcing his simple, earnest desire to place his naked body on the naked body of another boy.

And then I awoke from a dream in which I walked along a shoreline cluttered with broken shells, and it was early morning and the space in bed next to me was empty. The covers were pulled taut over the pillow. Nothing to suggest any of it ever happened except a pair of cartoon underwear, neatly folded next to the television and topped with a note that read, *You're sweet. Best of luck with everything! Watch this show!* I imagined Arthur walking into my room and seeing me lying here, seduced and abandoned. I imagined Oscar beside him. I imagined them giggling.

Waiting for the Metropolitan Museum of Art to open, I wandered through Central Park, preferring the anonymity of the winding paths to the public pastures and plazas. I passed through a tight stone arch and into a dense copse of woods. In front of me, a sign read, THE RAMBLE: A PLACE WHERE THE RELATIONSHIP BETWEEN ANIMALS, BIRDS, PLANTS, AND THE ENVIRONMENT IS PROTECTED. I continued through the cold, along the paved trail, peering occasionally through the web of trees. I wanted, for just a moment, to see and hear ghosts. The rustle of shrubbery, the whispers, the wild abandon of a space that, according to the sign I'd just passed, was now among the top bird-watching locations in the nation. Today, there were no ghosts. Or birds. Only the scattering squirrels and, from far off, the crack of laughter. I imagined more Segal sculptures here, among the naked trees and dead leaves, necking and stroking, sucking and fucking, shaking hands and slinking back to private, shameful lives.

I'd made it across the park to Fifth Avenue, five blocks down from the museum, when Dani called. Just wanted to let you know your favorite pupil won't be there when you get back on Monday, she said. My first thought was of a purple lily pad floating in a still lake. My God, I said. What happened? Suspended, Dani said. Three days. There was a fight on Friday at lunch, outside the cafeteria, by the student art gallery. A fight, I said. Right, Dani said. Arthur and this other senior. Short little kid. Trevor? Trent, I said. I pressed her for details. As Dani told it, Arthur had been sitting against the wall, eating his lunch with Raymond. Then Trent came up to them, and he and Arthur exchanged words. Arthur ignored him, but Trent kept talking louder and louder, saying something about dirty pictures. Dirty pictures, I said. Right, Dani said. That's how Nate tells it. He was on cafeteria duty and said he was going to give it another minute to die down on its own. Then there's this crash and he turns to see Arthur, you wouldn't believe it, on top of Trent. Nate said he had to pry Arthur's hands off the other boy's throat. Anyway, how's your trip? Did you get those dumplings? Did you get in touch with my friend, George?

Inside the museum, I meandered among the Greek and Roman statues, the marble men and women in states of triumph, repose, passion, collapse. I stared down Carpeaux's *Ugolino*, unable to turn away from the count's mad face, his gripping toes, the beautiful slump of his dead son. I visited the gift shop and pored over glossy new catalogs I didn't need.

Portrait of a Man (Self Portrait?). **Jan van Eyck. 1433.** My junior year at Jefferson, yawning through *Flemish Masters II* (8:00 a.m., Silas Hall), I think about what I'll wear when I meet up later that evening with Bryan. We're going to see a play directed by Bryan's friend. I'm intimidated by the way Bryan, a journalism student from New Jersey, adopted from South Korea at age five, moves through campus. Calm. Confident. Assured of himself and his identity in a way that seems impossible to me who, at twenty, remains unsure of my station in the world, who hasn't come out to his parents, who's merely made out with several closeted guys, even masturbated with one in the gym shower just last month (an act that repulsed me for its animal baseness, the grunt and release, then the quiet return to different planes of existence). But this. This is a date. An activity. Possibly a meal after. Possibly a late-night walk along the train tracks that cut through the southern corner of the university. And possibly. At the front of the sloped lecture hall, the professor pulls up a portrait I've seen countless times in my other art history classes: the stern face, the wrinkles along the eyes, the cleft of cheekbone suggesting the skull hidden underneath richly painted flesh. That evening, after hamburgers, Bryan and I walk not to the train tracks but back to his off-campus apartment, where I'm penetrated for the first time. Bryan's barely inside me before I ask him to stop. The dull pain, the sense of claustrophobia in my own body, is too much to bear. Bryan sighs and flops backward on the bed, rolls up the lube-slick condom and tosses it across the room. I wait in terror for the smell of shit. To compensate for my poor performance, I crawl over and begin to run my mouth up and down Bryan's wilting erection. I adjust myself on my forearms and, as I do, notice Bryan's flannel bedsheets, squares of red as deep as the chaperon I saw that morning piled on Jan van Eyck's head. Afterward, there's no mistaking the silence, the lingering smoke of disappointment. Mouth still salty, I stare at the poster for *2001: A Space Odyssey* tacked above Bryan's desk. I read the tagline over and over: AN EPIC DRAMA OF ADVENTURE AND EXPLORATION. I really just wanted to be inside you, Bryan says. Then: Maybe you should try exploring that part of yourself a little more? Maybe you're right, I say. I look away from the poster to my fingers against red flannel. I think, I do what I can.

In the American Wing, I followed a striking young man in tortoiseshell glasses past colonial furniture, Tiffany windows, Winslow Homer seascapes. As if what? As if I would dare to say something? Hey. Hi there. How's it going? Our footsteps like heartbeats on the gleaming wood floor.

I made my way to Gallery 621, my movements slow, reverential. This was the real reason, the only reason, I'd come. Past the inattentive visitors, I saw the painting, quaint in its simple wood frame, smaller than I imagined. I sat on the bench in front of it, unsure what to do. I tried to block out the whispers, the sneaker squeaks. Even now, in front of the painting, I delayed. Admiring the folds of the lute player's crimson cloak and the water beading from the marbles of his eyes. Tracing the curves of the boy with his back to the viewer, trying to create in my mind an entire face from the glimpse of cheek, nose, eye, and ear Caravaggio allowed me. Then, finally, I moved my gaze to the cornetto player. I stared directly at him. I thought of Arthur's fight, how it had all happened without me. I felt disappointed, embarrassed I hadn't been there for him, not so much to help perhaps as to witness the moment, the act of righteous violence. Arthur, triumphant, on top of that little toad. I continued to stare at the painting. There was a mystery now, a danger in that toothless mouth, in the half-hidden cornetto. I thought: Dirty pictures? What's that about? My hip pocket buzzed, reminding me I needed to get over to Penn Station. My right foot, I discovered, had fallen asleep, so that when I got up to go there was a precarious second where I feared I would topple headfirst into the Caravaggio, my head hitting the wall through the torn canvas, my hands clutching the wood frame and snapping it as I slid down the wall onto the floor, bringing the whole mess on top of me. I stood as still as I could, waited for the throb in my foot and ankle to fade. Then I left Gallery 621, slowly, as if stepping on spring ice.

⤚✦

Oscar

The week of the Great Betrayal starts on Monday, March 14, in a used bookstore off Dupont Circle. Walking home from a client meeting, I find a paperback of *The Little Deaths* sitting, thick and foreboding, in the display window surrounded by several other brick-sized books. EPIC READS, the handwritten sign hanging above them says. God knows how many hands have held it before. And now, with the exchange of seven dollars (plus tax), it's in mine.

I go home and text Sean a picture of the book on my coffee table, next to a glass of scotch. As if what? As if he'll respond? It's been weeks with no texts, no calls, no emails. No out-of-office message for the desperate young queer idolizing the king of hedonism. Sean Stokes has, like a ghost, vanished. Maybe it's just something writers do. So, while I wait for a response I know won't come, navigating in my mind that fine line between concern for Sean's wellbeing and stalking, thinking maybe this is what it will take for Sean to emerge from whatever writing hibernation he's in, I start reading.

The epigraph: *And out of this worldwide festival of death, this ugly rutting fever that inflames the rainy evening sky all around— will love someday rise up out of this, too?* It's from Sean's favorite book, *The Magic Mountain*, which he told me he first read as a teenager and makes a point of revisiting every year. (I tried visiting it for the first time a while back and got five pages in before taking it downstairs to the free library in the Beardsley's laundry room.)

The chapter titles: Names. Some of them real, some of them fake. Some of them lovers, some of them friends. Some of them neither. All of them lost during the AIDS years, the plague I dodged like a bullet for no reason other than the dumb luck of when I was born.

Ryan, 31.
Joshua, 40.
Alexander, 19.
Abdul, 18.
Evan, 36.
Robert, 33.
Philippe, 29.
Bruce, 22.

Abe, 35.
Javier, 22.
August, 45.

Sex? Not in these 788 pages. Just hospital visits, deathbed vigils, austere funerals and wakes, clandestine goodbyes behind the backs of family members, unattended (and therefore imagined) burials in a potter's field outside the Bronx. This is a whole different author. This is a whole different book. To be honest, it's quite a downer.

THE NEXT MORNING, while boiling eggs and settling in to tackle a morning's worth of email campaigns for an educational tech company and an email blast for this week's Outrage event at an oyster bar in Takoma Park, my phone goes off. It's not Sean but a number I almost don't recognize at first, mostly because my family and I hardly speak since they bankrolled my exile; my conversations with my father nonexistent, my conversations with my mother reduced to Christmas cards, occasional emails, and two-minute phone chats about my father's health. Last year, I got a $25 gift card to Walmart. This is what passes for progress in my family.

I answer the phone with one word: "Hello."

My mother responds with two: "He's gone."

Harrison, 63.

Two years ago, you see, Harrison Burnham began to get confused. He'd complain of headaches and vertigo. More and more frequently, his hands would shake, he'd have quiet chats with the corners of rooms and barely-touched dinner plates. My mother would come downstairs in the middle of the night to find him staring at the backyard, silent and confused, an empty glass in his hand and an open container of apple juice on the counter. When he collapsed in the supermarket shopping for nacho fixings, he was bullied into seeing a doctor. The specialists who poked and prodded his body—if there's any justice in this world, there was a rectal exam—were clueless. A latent effect, perhaps, of the car accident he'd been in all those years ago, when he'd refused medical attention because he'd found Jesus among the shattered glass and spare change littering the roof of his overturned Chevy Blazer. Ten months ago, after he started progressively fading, my father used his disability payments to remove himself to an assisted living facility across town, too proud to suffer in front of his wife. While there'd been no expectation of his death, a nurse, my mother told me in her clipped voice, had come in with dinner on Monday evening and found Harrison lying there in repose, hands at his sides. As if he'd been ready to go for days, years even.

The funeral service is scheduled for Friday. My mother asks how soon I can come home, and I want to laugh hearing that word from her lips. I tell her my financial situation and ask, without shame, if she'll pay for my flight. She agrees.

It turns out *The Little Deaths* is even heavier reading thirty thousand feet above the ground, in economy seating, with my ears refusing to pop. But I keep trying, if only so I can tell Sean when he reappears that I finally read it.

Here's the book now, swaddled like a newborn in the winter coat on my lap. I pick it up again, open to a random chapter (*Tad*, 23), and then the pilot's voice interrupts to say we've started our final descent through the Wednesday morning clouds into the Cleveland area. I pull up the window shade and there it is: the land that spat me eastward all those years ago, now slurping me back, slowly, the same way other boys would dangle their drool, precariously, over my face during the rare occasions they trapped me, giggling, commanding me, Drink up, pussy.

It's about an hour from Cleveland Hopkins to Yoder. The heat in my rental is on full blast in a sad attempt to mitigate the freezing winter air swooping in off Lake Erie. I pick up an interstate road and watch the land in front of me slowly flatten out, as if ironed.

God, I hated them for bringing me to this uninspired wasteland. I hated the slow pace of the days here, the horrible quiet. I hated the people who seemed hearty and wholesome as if sprouted like corn or soybeans from the earth. Real America: Even back then, it scared the shit out of me. We'd barely settled in before I realized what my mother took pains to reassure me wasn't true: I didn't belong here. I was an alien. I wasn't sure where I belonged—if, indeed, I belonged anywhere at all. But I endured the days, the weeks, the months, the years. I suffered in silence through the longings I felt for the other boys I'd walk to school with, the boys whose bodies I'd spy on in gym class, the boys I'd imagine kissing by the community pool during hot summer weekends, the boys I'd follow into restrooms just to see if I could catch a glimpse of what they were holding and compare it to the insistent piece of flesh between my lanky legs. Dangerous times. A far cry from the simpler, more innocent moments I'd shared with Sebastian, when we'd talk about tits, when we'd touch one another's bodies gently, scientifically, with an innocence unspoiled by hormones, unobstructed by the wall separating boys-being-boys from boys-loving-boys. Sometimes, I'd think about calling Sebastian, or writing him a letter like I'd promised. Then I'd think: Why? What was the point? My parents wouldn't let me go back there, and I certainly didn't want Sebastian here, seeing me like this, where the taunts in school were more ferocious, had become physical. I was too busy trying to survive the present to think about the past.

Cutting across town, I savor the feeling only the prodigal child knows, returning after years to a land trapped in time but knowing he can, at any moment, choose to leave. Here are the same single-level houses with their monstrous acreage, the man-made pools in front yards frosted with ice. The signs warning of deer, of low flooding, of slow Amish buggies. The fallow fields, the strip mall with its pizza place, ice cream parlor, and salon. The Polish bakery, the Polish butcher, the Polish social club, the Polish Catholic church, the Polish graveyard. The roads etched in grids. The kids swaddled in winter clothes and clomping through muddy snow on their way home from school. The town square with its simple gazebo, the bandstand and benches empty for the season. At traffic lights, I take out my phone and photograph it all. I'll send them to Sean when I get back. I'll say, *Look what we escaped!*

I'd arranged to meet my mother and my uncle at Holly House, the assisted living facility where my father had spent his last months. I know my mother doesn't need help boxing up his belongings. She just wants me to see the space. As if it'll make me care, as if this trip will somehow end in love, in forgiveness.

Do I sign in as a family member or merely a guest of the late Harrison Henry Burnham? The receptionist shares a sympathetic look when I tell her who I am and who I'm here to see. On her computer, the Bee Gees inquire about the depth of my love. She directs me to the second floor, room 232, and gives me the elevator access code.

"Code?"

"So the residents can't use the elevator on their own. They get confused sometimes. They wander."

It's surreal, the walk toward the elevator along a hallway of diamond-stitched carpeting, past the small gift shop with its flowers and tchotchkes. *The Little Deaths* is crammed with slow walks like these, through long sterile corridors that barely mask the death lurking behind closed doors. Deaths from AIDS-related illness, deaths from mysterious faults in post-car-accident brains; it all amounts to the same thing in the end, doesn't it? One long struggle against the inevitable that's coming for us every day, that can arrive unannounced at any moment. Leaving the elevator and walking toward my father's now unoccupied room, I feel like a stranger previewing a strange land to which he's destined. I feel a chill I can't entirely blame on the winter weather.

Room 232 is empty for the moment but still marked with the name HARRY. It's barely large enough to fit a twin bed that's seen better days, a dresser underneath a windowsill littered with small potted succulents. More like a monk's cell. Along the wall next to the bed is a bulletin board decorated with postcards and holiday cards from relatives I've forgotten (and who've probably forgotten me). Below a calendar from the *Cleveland Plain-Dealer*, a hand-written note by a pastor reads TIME IS SHORT, FIRE IS HOT, JESUS IS COMING, READY OR NOT. There's a list of upcoming community activities (movie nights, lasagna suppers, dog-petting sessions) my father will, with regrets, be unable to attend.

And the body?

The stiffened corpse?

Gone. Already on ice somewhere. All I have to deal with, thankfully, is the bric-a-brac my mother and I will pile into boxes and take back to her house, where it'll languish in the basement until it's her turn to move into this waiting room, until it's my turn to come back and repeat this same ritual one last time.

I go over to my father's simple nightstand, open the only drawer. There are tissues, several pens, an open book of Sudoku puzzles filled out in my mother's steady hand, a limp copy of the New Testament inscribed with messages of support from names I don't recall. Something drops out of the book and onto my boots. A bookmark. No, a photo, one of those wallet-sized yearbook pictures my mother ordered every year. This one is from senior year. The face looking out at me may as well be the face of a stranger: black hair ironed flat into a mop, giant glasses, the phantoms of several pimples along my brow and left cheek, the same tuxedo drape worn by everyone else. You'd look at a portrait like this and think: This boy needs to get some sun. This boy needs to get a life.

Voices come down the hall. I tuck the photo somewhere deep inside Romans, put the Bible back in the drawer. I turn around, and there she is. Still petite, still unassuming, still with that long, fat coil of braided hair, now gray with age. She carries three file boxes over to the bed with the deliberate steps of someone focused solely on movement, not introspection. She moves like someone who's medicated. Behind her, bearlike in his Cleveland Browns sweater, my uncle Jason stares at the shirt peeking out from my open winter jacket, at the rainbow-lettered word QUEER.

"Oscar," he says.

"Jason," I say.

My mother puts the empty boxes on the bed, gives me a hug, steps away. "This is it," she says. "All this has to go in here, then out to Jay's car. We can sort through it later."

We pack what little there is in silence, awkwardly brushing against one another in the tight room. We wrap the framed photographs in brown paper towels from the tiny en-suite bathroom. We stack the holiday cards, the birthday cards, the postcards, the sweaters and sweatpants and underwear. My mother opens the nightstand drawer, puts the pens and puzzle book inside her shoulder bag. She takes the New Testament, looks at it, then drops it in one of the half-full boxes.

"I'll load these up," my uncle says. He takes the file boxes and leaves us alone.

My mother sits on the stripped bed and plays with the nurse's buzzer dangling from its cord connected to the wall. I stand in the opposite corner, arms folded, avoiding her eyes, looking instead at the motion detector by the door, thinking of my father making confused late-night escapes to the elevator, calling out for dead friends and relatives. Was mine one of the names he cried out?

"Good flight?"

"Yep," I say.

We listen to the noises from the hall: a nurse leading a resident into a shower, the drone of a cowboy from the television in someone's room, the giggles of someone's kids teasing the silent parrot—Sharon, according to the nameplate—in her cage outside the elevator doors. Then, just to say something, I tell my mother who I ran into recently.

"You remember the Motes, right?"

"You and that boy were inseparable."

"He still lives in the area. Teaches high school."

"I should have given his mother money for helping raise you."

"She died. When he was in college, I think. Car accident."

My mother picks at something invisible on my father's bed. She's staring off into a corner of the room, a fugue state I remember distinctly from one of the last drives we took together, the weekend I'd come home from college to come out. We'd been returning from clothes shopping at the mall in Westlake. I told her. She pulled over, slowly, to the side of the road and sat there without saying a word. I started to cry and waited for her to cry, but she just kept looking off into the distance, which made me cry even harder. Then she said, with a coldness I'll never forget, "You'll have to tell your father. Because I'm not." Did she already know what his response would be? Did she already have a vision of my exile? Did she know, in that moment, the new jeans and polos and socks in the back seat would be a parting gift to her only child?

"I bet Sebastian's married by now," my mother says. "Children?"

"No. He's like me."

"What do you—oh."

She asks more questions about him, but I shrug them off. I don't want to talk about Sebastian. I'm only here because my father is dead, and she'd asked me to come bury him. I'm only here out of duty. I'm only here to drop my father into the earth, cover him in soil, and forget about him forever.

My uncle comes back upstairs and asks my mother if she's all set.

"I think we are," my mother says.

Outside, she asks if I've had something to eat. I tell her I need to check in to the motel and get settled, I've got work to do, I'm not particularly hungry right now. I tell her and my uncle I'll see them, and everyone else, tomorrow morning.

Of course, I can't sleep, so I lie in the stiff bed in a pair of gym shorts and my Oscar Wilde T-shirt, chatting on Cruze with the gays out here, texting with Martin about T-shirt designs for upcoming Outrage events. I think about the parties I'm missing back home, the excitement happening without me.

Martin drops off for the night and the gays on Cruze see through my dodgy answers about hooking up. I'm still wide awake, and the television doesn't work, so I go over to my bag and take out *The Little Deaths*, thinking: This should do the trick.

I open the book to a page I'd dog-eared when I'd first bought it: the chapter about the death of Sean's friend, Cal. My metempsycho or whatever. I pick up where I left off.

We were told, unexpectedly, the priest had administered Cal's last rites. Against his father's will, Cal's mother begged as many of us as possible to come for a brief, quiet goodbye. Keith and Derrick and I were the last to go up. It was an otherwise peaceful November afternoon when we slipped into the ward (the attendant nurse, collaborating with Cal's mother against the hospital's wishes, was letting lovers and friends into the room). We slinked like alley cats along corridors plastered with biohazard warnings. We found room 515 and softly closed the door behind us. On the bed, trapped in a spiderweb of IV cords, was the same brittle boy we had all fallen in love with when we had first met dancing to the Pet Shop Boys at Hamilton's. His body was scrunched in on itself like a newborn bird. My sweet, angry little queen. He was staring over our shoulders at—something. We made no effort to speak to him. We were afraid forcing him to speak would be the death of him. Derrick, after a few moments, left the room, ashamed to cry in front of Cal. Keith and I remained, both on the right side of Cal's bed, our breath thick inside our medical masks. We followed Cal's gaze out the window, beyond the scrim of clouds over the Hudson, the sky lacerated with the contrails of planes taking their ignorant passengers around an ignorant world, all of them blissfully unaware of the horror happening thousands of feet below them. Another little death stacked on our shoulders. Then Cal opened his mouth and whispered. We tried to decipher what he was saying. We had only a few minutes before his mother came back. I looked at Keith, and our eyes seemed to say the same thing: I do not know how much more of this I can take. How long before I stretch my heart too thin, before it tears in my ribcage? Cal, mouthing his silent words to the outside world, was teaching me. What was he saying? Lost? Love? Life? Live? Late? I tried to think of what each word meant for him, for all of us. Keith, thinking our friend was asking for water, wet Cal's lips with a moist towel. Stop, I wanted to scream. Don't! You'll drown him!

THE VIEWING IS modest. A few family members, some aunts and uncles, cousins so young they've no idea who I could possibly be, friends from my father's church, a few lost souls trucked in from Holly House. I see them staring at me, feel them watching me while I stand next to my mother, while I shake their hands, while I thank them for their sympathies. The rumor made flesh. They're all polite in that genial Midwestern way, these people. But I can see their insincerity, their confusion, their disgust.

Good.

Be disgusted.

The feeling's mutual.

Behind me, Harrison Burnham lies in repose in his coffin, face shiny and seamless like one of the plastic comic-book action figures Sebastian and I used to play with in the sunroom of his parents' house. His hands are clasped over his crotch the way he'd often hold them in life while watching me stumble through soccer games or waiting while I got a haircut. Thick, proud hands, I recall faintly, cutting grilled chicken breasts into more manageable squares, pulling the television remote out of my hands when it was time for bed, applying bandages and ointments. Hands that also slapped and spanked, that slammed on countertops in fits of anger whose unspoken cause, I always felt, was me. They remind me, to look at them now, of another pair of hands; hands that grip glass after glass of scotch, that used to chuck me on the chin and now can't be bothered to respond to my texts and emails and calls.

"Hello, Oscar," Aunt Emma says. "How have you been?"

"Good," I say.

"Hi, Oscar," my mother's work friend, Lucy, says. "And how are things?"

"Fine," I say.

"Oscar," the pastor says. "Keeping those fools in Washington honest?"

"Trying to," I say.

Two miles south, the afternoon skies hold off on their threat of rain long enough for us to bury my father. The cemetery is a modest acre of flat land lying in the shadow of a water tower. My father's casket stands on its bier over the pit into which, once we've turned our backs, it'll be lowered. To his right, there's a bare patch of grass that, one day, will open to receive my mother, the two of them sandwiched for eternity between Michael Blaz and Peter and Janet Menkiti.

There's no space, I see, for me.

One by one, we come and drop flowers on the casket. My

mother looks at me, as I toss mine onto the pile, and smiles. Through a small gap in the fake turf by my feet, I see the grave itself, a horrible darkness, and I have to step away from the group and walk off until I find a stone bench on whose seat is engraved the words, *When someone you love becomes a memory, the memory becomes a treasure.* I pick at blades of grass around my shoes and wish I could talk to Sean.

Across from me, a small headstone reads *Alan Talbot, beloved son, 1964–1992.* Not even thirty years old. "Cancer," perhaps? A "brief illness"? Were you disowned as well, Alan Talbot, beloved son? Did you come home to die, or did they have to ship you back here? If you see my father down there, Alan Talbot, beloved son, tell him I saw the photo. Tell him I don't need his prayers. Tell him, with respect, I won't die like you, buried in shame under mounds of dirt. No. Tell him I'll die out loud. Tell him I'll die on fire.

BACK AT MY mother's for the funeral repast, standing with strangers around the kitchen with their mugs of coffee, their plates of grocery-store fried chicken and church-donated potato casseroles. My uncle, lips gleaming with grease, asks if, since I'm just standing around there, I'll take a bag of trash out back.

Outside, I find my mother smoking and worrying her braid of hair. Behind the house, the bare yard and fallow field beyond it look otherworldly, a phantom stage on which I see my father, young and alive, home from Bible study and setting up a game of cornhole. I see a little praying mantis in baggy shorts that can only be me, tossing beanbags not at the tilted wood planks but up into the air. I know what he's thinking: If he can just get the bags a little higher, just an inch or two, they won't come back down. They'll float like balloons into the clouds. They'll escape.

"Mom."

Startled, she turns around and accidentally blows smoke into my face, then waves a hand as if trying to smack some sense into me. She looks lost, as I imagine she must be. Not sad so much as shell-shocked. I realize now I know next to nothing about my mother and father's relationship, hardly ever saw them show affection in public aside from a brief shoulder pat. Like they were one another's pets. Certainly nothing like the affection I'd see between Sebastian's parents. But those memories, those intimacies, have to be in there somewhere. How else to explain the way my mother looks at me now, in the late-afternoon light, as if I were the last lingering reminder of those decades? The spoiled fruit of their loins, dropped far from the trunk of the Burnham family tree. Maybe she thinks now she can step out from the shade of Harrison's branches, pick up that abandoned apple, put it in a basket, take it home and maybe make a pie with it. Whereas I'm perfectly happy where I am, on my own, sugar-sweet and picked at by hornets.

"Mom, I think I should get going."

"What time is your flight?"

"9:30."

"That's late."

"I have to be back tonight. Work to take care of."

I stare at the grass and wonder who's been helping her mow it. Uncle Jason, most likely. Then I feel her thumb and forefinger under my chin. She lifts my head up to look her in the face and thanks me for coming all the way out here. She tells me she knows it must have been difficult. I can't look her in the eyes. I won't. Then I do, and I think: Who is this stranger? I imagine she thinks the same thing.

"You'll travel safe," she says.

"I will."

"You'll maybe come visit."

"I'll try."

God, how weary we both sound.

Minding her cigarette, I lean in for a hug. Then Uncle Jason comes out back and says Aunt Emma's not feeling well and he's taking her home and can my mother help get her into the car.

"Right there," my mother says. She kills the cigarette. "Staying out?"

"A little longer."

She follows Uncle Jason inside. The screen door smacks shut and, behind it, the kitchen door. Then it's just me and the growing dusk and the fields. The same fields through which I wasn't allowed to walk but through which I'd occasionally run, chased by words that cut through the air—*fag, homo, dick licker, butt muncher*—and, behind them, the neighborhood boys in pursuit. Look! You can see them now, like popped corn in their white and gray winter jackets, speeding up when I speed up, slowing down when I slow down, calling "Hey!" calling "Run!" calling "Come kiss my dick!" Fueled by some mysterious desire to inflict pain and trauma I'll never in all my life understand. Or forgive. And look! There's little Oscar, keeping his eyes forward, pumping his long legs, pumping his long arms, the force of his book bag slapping against his back and threatening to knock him over onto his face. Running home to be defended, to be saved by his father and mother. Oh, little Oscar, how unsafe you really are there!

HALFWAY BACK TO the airport, bothered by how quickly night has settled, by how few cars there are on the road, by the rain that's finally started to fall, I decide enough is enough. I hook up my phone to the car speakers and call Sean Stokes.

It rings. And rings.

Nothing.

I wait several miles, then try again.

It rings. And rings.

Nothing.

Several more miles.

Again.

Rings, rings.

Then a click. A voice. Not Sean's, but made just as rough by the rental's speakers.

"Bill? He left his phone here, but he's on his way back. We keep forgetting we have to cross the river to get wine. Still getting used to how things work out here."

"Hello?"

"Hello?"

"I'm not Bill."

"Oh. Shit. Sorry. This number kept coming up, so I thought it was Bill. I'm still learning everyone's names. Do you need directions?"

"Directions? Wait. Who is this?"

"I'm sorry. Sean stepped out for a moment. Who's this?"

"Oscar. I'm trying to reach Sean."

"Oh, maybe we haven't met yet. I'm Jesse. He'll be back in a minute. I can give you directions, though. Which side of the river are you coming here from?"

"I don't need directions. I just need to talk to Sean. I've been trying to reach him for weeks now."

"Oh. I can imagine. It's been a busy couple of months, what with the wedding, the move. The work never ends. Don't take it personally, though. It's still a shock to a lot of people. You should see my voice-mail in-box. I think I'll need a whole week to answer everyone's messages. God, and there's still so much to unpack here."

"Wait. Sean moved?"

"Yeah. Sudden, I know. But you'll have to come visit us sometime."

"Who?"

"Sean and I."

"You live with him?"

"Well, yeah. We bought this place. He wanted—"

There's noise from somewhere on that end of the connection. I grip the wheel and lean forward into the speakers, straining to hear faint voices through what must be a hand covering the mouthpiece of Sean's cell phone. Then it's removed, and I hear the stranger's voice again.

"—kept calling so I picked up. I don't think I've met an Oscar, have I? Anyway, here he is."

The muffled exchange of the phone, a rustling of bags that sounds like thunder inside the car. Then the familiar voice.

"Oscar. How are you?"

"What was that?"

"Wine. Having some neighbors over shortly. How are you?"

"Who was that?"

"That?" I hear Sean's breath, slow and patient. A writer trying to think of the right words. He sounds like he's preparing to deliver a eulogy. Something clatters in the background. I think I hear a knock on a distant front door.

"That was Jesse," he says. "That was my husband."

I take my foot off the gas.

"Your husband."

"Yes. I'm sorry I haven't been able to connect with you. I've been meaning to sit down and write to you. There's been, well there's been a lot going on."

"I'll say. You got married."

"Yes, I did."

"You."

"Yes. Me."

"Why the fuck would you do something like that?"

More voices, emerging into whatever space Sean's speaking to me from. I hear movement, the voices fade, and I imagine Sean carrying my voice into another room.

"Let's talk sometime tomorrow," Sean says.

"I'm busy all day."

"Next week, then? There's a lot I need to tell you."

"I'm busy then, too."

"Oscar."

"You sold out."

"Oscar."

"What a shame. What a waste."

"Oscar. I'll explain it."

"There's nothing to explain. Don't bother."

I kill the connection.

Humiliated, enraged, betrayed, I press on into the night, through the rain, until I see a sign for a rest stop and, without thinking, slip off the interstate and into the parking lot of a low building. I stop in front of two dimly lit vending machines that flank the opening to the restrooms. I get out of my car and take deep breaths of cold air, thinking if Sean were here I'd grab him by his shoulders and shriek and shake some sense into him.

What have you done?

WHAT HAVE YOU DONE?

But Sean's not here, so the only vengeance I can enact is to go into the back of the car, unzip my duffel bag, and pull out my used copy of *The Little Deaths*. I take the book over to a small culvert on the opposite side of the parking lot and pitch it into the dark. I go back to the car and take out my key. Only then, in the weak light from above the men's room, do I notice the shards of cemetery grass still stuck under my fingernails.

Sebastian

It was Arthur who started it. Who came into my trailer after class one Tuesday looking for his headphones. Who saw me sitting at my desk watching *Hiroshima Mon Amour* on the television, taking notes for our film unit but also lost in thought. Who stopped and listened with wide eyes to Georges Delerue's café waltz. Who asked if he could sit and watch for a while, he'd be quiet, he wouldn't say a word. Who asked the next day, delicately, before class, if we could watch another movie at the end of the school day because his boyfriend was tutoring freshmen and his father was having to pick him up later and later and the library got old after a while. Who asked if we could start by watching *Hiroshima Mon Amour* from the beginning.

We hadn't talked about Arthur's suspension the month before. In my head, I tried the stern words of a concerned parent, the neutral tone of a diplomatic counselor. But the only thing that felt right to say to Arthur was the one thing I couldn't say: I'm so proud of you.

Every time I heard the familiar knock on my trailer door, every time I opened it to see Arthur standing there, every time I led him into the empty classroom and cued up the television while he sat at a desk in the front row, I thought about flashlight tag, the weekend games I'd play, reluctantly, with Oscar and the small collective of neighborhood boys along Cinnamon Road and Rosemary Court. I'd watch Arthur watching our latest movie and think of fleeing forms slashed by beams of light. My favorite hiding spot had been a thick pine bush two doors down from my parents' house. I'd crawl inside, knees dirty, hands pricked by dead pine needles. I'd curl up on the open patch of earth, small but just the right size for me, and listen to the sounds of the other boys running and screaming in the night.

Watching movies with Arthur, I'd think, inevitably, of my friend Michael's mother. One time, hiding in the darkness of Michael's garage, behind the back of his mother's minivan, peering out into the world through the open garage door and afraid to make a dash for my beloved pine bush, I was startled by a sudden burst of light. Found, I thought. No. It was Michael's mother, stepping out to get another glass of wine from the box chilling in the refrigerator. Okay, she said into the darkness. Which of you is it? Possums don't wear high tops. It's me, I said. I thought: Michael's father doesn't live at home anymore, so is it still Mrs. Pound or Ms. Pound? I prepared to slink, possumlike, back out into the front yard. Off limits, Oscar, someone screamed from up by my house. Here, Michael's mother said. I've got a good hiding place. She led me through the kitchen into the living room. I'm just in here listening to music, she said. No one will find you. I sat on one of the high-backed armchairs while Michael's mother sat on the sofa facing the front yard so she could keep an eye on us. We hardly spoke, just listened to piano music from the stereo system in a teak wood cabinet topped with pictures of Michael and his sisters. Mozart, she said as if I'd asked. Piano Concerto No. 23. Beautiful, isn't it. I smiled politely. Listen, she said, hide out here as long as you'd like. And so, the rest of that summer, I did, longing for games of flashlight tag just to have the excuse to hide here, with Michael's mother, with her music. There was Wagner and Bach and Schumann. There was Couperin and Liszt and Beethoven's *Sonata Pathétique* on repeat. There was, on one occasion when Michael's mother seemed particularly distraught and her wine glass filled to the brim, Penderecki's *Threnody to the Victims of Hiroshima*. I loved this sentimental musical education, which lasted anywhere from twenty minutes to an hour, when Michael and Oscar would barge in and break the spell. Stop hiding in here, Oscar would say to me. That's cheap. Guilty, I'd go back outside with the others to endure several more rounds of flashlight tag until someone gave up in exhaustion or anger (or both) and, like seeds, we'd scatter back to our homes. What ended it all was Oscar, who asked me once, mid-game, if I went in there to have sex with Michael's mother. Oh, Kathy, Oscar mimed, pumping his hips while the other boys laughed. Oh, Kathy! Oh, Kathy! Oh, Kathy! I looked at Oscar with venomous eyes and screamed, It's not like that at all! But I stopped going inside Michael's house. Three months later, Michael and his mother and sisters moved to Atlanta.

Thursday afternoon, Arthur knocked on my trailer door, came inside, and pulled a red paper envelope out of his messenger bag. *J'Accuse,* he said. The remake. A little over an hour later, his phone buzzed. Dad's here, he said. To be continued, I said, pressing pause on the remote. Arthur waved goodbye. The trailer door shut. I took a deep breath, as if finally allowed to rise from the ocean depths for air.

The next week, before the Wednesday group meeting (the only weekday afternoon we didn't watch movies together), I gave Arthur a handwritten list of films on lined legal paper. *Jules and Jim. The 400 Blows. The Red Shoes. Faust. Metropolis. The Music Room. Ivan's Childhood. The Last Emperor. The Leopard. The Magnificent Ambersons. The Graduate.* This is a lot to watch, Arthur said. Can we get through all this? I handed the list to Arthur. You might have to watch some on your own, but we can try. Arthur gave the list back to me. Mark your favorites, he said, and we can watch those together. I did as I was asked, with joy. Arthur took the marked list back to his desk and tucked it into his messenger bag like a soldier securing his marching orders. A minute later, Steph and Juan arrived together, as they always did. While the students talked among themselves, I sat at my desk, looking periodically out the window at the early April afternoon thrumming with energy. You could sense the new leaves and flowers waiting to burst from the trees and undergrowth. You could hear the song of birds back from southern winters. You could feel the sun growing more generous with its warmth.

One day, I asked Arthur what he was reading in Mr. Watts's English class. Arthur handed me a slim paperback of Greek myths. The following afternoon, we started *Black Orpheus*. Every time Arthur came into class now, he'd cry out Orfeu! and I'd respond with Eurydice! We'd break out into private laughter while the other students in the room sat there, perplexed. That evening, turning onto my street, I saw the flash of Arthur and his boyfriend on their bikes, speeding past me toward the main road. I rolled down my window, but by the time I craned my head out to cry after him— Eurydice!—they'd rounded a bend and disappeared. It felt wrong to follow them any farther than that.

I began to stay late at work, later than usual, grading practice exams, making up for the time I lost watching films with Arthur. Cool spring air came in through the open windows of the trailer, carrying with it the call and cry of lacrosse players from the nearby fields. At half past seven, I looked up from my desk and started when I saw Arthur still sitting there. No. Not Arthur. His purple hoodie, draped on the back of a desk chair. I walked over and looked down at the garment, felt the tenderness of the trailer's floor under my feet, imagined the body, more familiar to me now in the past several weeks, fitting inside the limp sleeves. Limbs full of youth and vigor, limbs that defended their owner from bullies, limbs that curled around the waist of another boy. The Caravaggio kid and his fleshy Caravaggio body. I looked around, then tried to put the hoodie on. It was far too small. I carried the garment over to my workbag as if it were the drapery of a long-dead saint. I'd take it home, give it to Arthur the next day. No sense in some errant janitor thinking it was up for grabs.

I thought about it for the rest of the evening. While finishing up my grading. While driving home through a rain shower. While eating a sandwich in the living room and watching the television replicate the same news stories I'd seen on my computer and phone all day: a missing senior citizen in Gaithersburg; protests outside the Old Post Office with its banner reading TRUMP COMING 2016; the week's second dead celebrity. While taking my evening shower. While making my final rounds of the house, checking locks, checking lights, checking windows. While unmaking the bed. While stacking the decorative pillows in a perilous pile on the floor. Then I did it. I took the second pillow, the same one Jake used to rest his head on, and turned it so it lay on the bed like a torso. I went to the kitchen table where the hoodie lay folded and carried it—so heavy now!—into the bedroom. Then, as if dressing an infant or dying parent, I slipped the hoodie around the pillow, pulled up the zipper, and folded back the empty sleeves. I stepped back for a moment to see what I'd done, to admire this strange, limbless trunk. Then I got into bed, turned off the light, and after several moments lying still in the dark wrapped my right arm around the lower half of the pillow and pulled it into me. I took a greedy breath. A cologne I couldn't properly place, bargain-basement laundry detergent. Mild sweat. A musk like cigarette smoke. Maybe Raymond's? I thought of the boyfriend, who'd once dipped his head into a Wednesday group meeting but otherwise kept to himself, who mostly met Arthur afterward. Several times, I caught them holding hands while walking to Mr. Ayer's waiting car. This, I thought, clutching the pillow, is what it must be like for Raymond to bury his face into Arthur's head of hair, to hold his tired body, to know him in a way I never could and never would. Cutting through the shame of all this was an envy so sharp and jagged it could easily be mistaken for rage. I wanted Arthur. No. I wanted to be Arthur, because if I were Arthur, I wouldn't be myself. If I had his life, then I wouldn't have to have my own. Thinking of the two boys slumped into one another on the living room couch watching the movies I'd recommended, I clutched the pillow tighter. Outside, rain drummed against the bedroom windows like a warning.

The next afternoon, I returned the hoodie. You left this in class yesterday, I said. Without a word, Arthur shrugged the hoodie over his body. I caught a slice of belly, a thinner slice of green underwear. I was tense as I led the class through another round of practice questions and identification drills. Title the work, name the artist, date the piece, describe the style, identify the movement. I expected Arthur to sniff some lingering scent of what I'd done, expected him to get up on his desk like an Edgar Allan Poe maniac and stab me with an accusatory finger. Arthur, in his purple hoodie, stared at the front of the room with sleepy eyes. He has no idea, I thought. No idea at all. I couldn't decide whether I was more relieved or hurt by this.

Last slide, ladies and gentlemen. We were outside the cafeteria on testing day, and I had my smart tablet over my head. Several students shouted. *The Death of Socrates*! Jacques-Louis David! Then the cafeteria doors opened and my students filed in for their AP exam. Good luck, Natalie. Good luck, Taylor. Good luck, Arthur. Good luck, Mehdi. Then the doors closed and I walked back, alone, to my trailer. At my desk, I looked closer at the David painting on my tablet, at the crimson-cloaked young man handing the philosopher his deadly chalice, rosy-cheeked, pinching his eyes in what had always struck me as exasperation. (Ugh, Socrates you idiot.) Then I thought of Thomas Pitt, dead now for almost a year. Strange, how rarely we thought of Thomas anymore. He'd been lost, overlooked in the continuing onrush of life: graduation, exams and quizzes, dances, backyard joints and beers, lockers that wouldn't open, peers who wouldn't go out with you, sports leagues and chess leagues and honor societies and literary magazines, sleepy heads nodding back during class, awkward bodies and voices, rebellious haircuts. I remembered the time a cup was proffered to me, on a five-day cruise out of Baltimore a year after my mother's death. My father and my father's family were celebrating my college graduation and my decision to become a teacher, to follow in my father's footsteps. One night, unable to sleep, despondent at how no one seemed to remember someone had died, I slipped out of the room I shared with my father and went up to the main deck. We were at sea that evening, but with the moon gone we may as well have been sailing through some inky abyss. Standing against the railing, looking out into the blackness, I was overcome with suffocating dread. There was nothing, aside from the ship and its noisy passage, against which I could orient myself. There was something seductive, in that moment, about just disappearing. Dropping into the black water like a stone. My family wouldn't find me at breakfast the next day, and they'd grow concerned. They'd search for me, spread the word throughout the ship, but by then it would be too late. I'd already be long gone, dozens of nautical miles back, while the floating party continued without me. Then the moon slid out from behind a gray bouquet of clouds, and I could see the sea again. I could see the world, a world in which I continued, however stubbornly, to exist. I stepped back from the railing, went over to an empty lounge chair, and lay back to watch the moon until I fell asleep. I was late to breakfast the next morning, but no one seemed concerned. They'd gone to the buffet without me and were already halfway through their first helping.

That afternoon, we finished *L'Avventura* together. Afterward, I opened the trailer door and there was Raymond, standing outside, on his phone. Skin the color of mine. A mutt like me, whose parents, Arthur said, were from El Salvador and the Philippines. Hey boo, Raymond said. Hey you, Arthur said. Ready? Their hands sought one another's instinctively, without hesitation. I almost cried to see it. Have a good evening, boys, I said. Back by the main school building, Mr. Ayer's hatchback poked out from behind an industrial trash container. From the threshold of my trailer, I watched Arthur and Raymond walk toward it, holding hands.

Driving home on Thursday, I took the back way into my father's development. I drove slowly, thinking I wasn't going to see it. Then I did: Arthur's bike, purple and yellow equals signs wrapped around the frame, lying on the overgrown front lawn of a yellow ranch house a quarter-mile away from my father's.

This is on me, Dillon (AP Calculus) said. He placed four fresh beers on our table and passed them around. There were nine of us at Shipley's that Friday, spread out between two tables. We'd driven out to the Arlington bar after work in a coordinated effort to celebrate the end of the AP Exam period. We drank draft beers and toasted our students, our impending summers. We looked up at the bank of television screens around the crowded bar or down into our phones. I watched Dillon and Jennifer (AP U.S. History) lean into one another to speak, watched the dance of their hands just a few feet from my own, wrapped protectively around a pint glass. I was describing the plot of *Metropolis* to Brian (AP Government) when I overheard Olga (AP Spanish) say to Rachel (AP Earth Science), It sounds like you're in love with the kid. I leaned in, thinking I'd misheard her over the abnormal din of the bar. (Never this packed, Dillon had said when we'd arrived.) I mean, it's okay, Olga continued. I've been in love with several students before. It happens. They don't tell you about it, but it does. It's nothing to be ashamed of. It's not weird. It's that parental instinct, right? You see kids you're proud of, you wish they were your own, you want to take credit for the way they behave, the grades they get, the futures they have. Believe me, I've been doing this for too long. You should see the list of obsessions I've had. I guess, Rachel said, deciding whether or not to pick up a fried pickle. It's bothersome. There's got to be some psychological name for it. I leaned in and smiled. Aschenbach Syndrome, I said.

Brian excused himself to the bathroom, and I watched the crowds while the conversations continued. Rachel mentioned moving on to a beer garden down the street. Dillon said that place had been closed for years. Olga finished her drink and said her fare-wells. Brian came back to the table. Jesus, he said. Since when did Shipley's get so gay? Sorry, Sebastian. It's just I've never seen so many around. Why didn't you say something? Your gaydar must be on the fritz. Is there some party you didn't know about? I smiled at Brian with closed lips, hating as ever the way he felt entitled to joke about gay men because he had one for a cousin. I looked around, and my eyes followed a man past our table cradling several shot glasses. I looked at his shirt, thought: Did I read that right? He went over to a cluster of bar tables, downed his shot, then handed out the rest. In simple white type against black cotton was the word INVERT. And then it started to unfurl around me. The crowd. The shirts. BOYS BEWARE. BOTTOM. YES, I'M JUDGING YOU. BOTTOM. TOP. BOTTOM. VERS (KIDDING: BOTTOM). And then I saw him. Long arms poking out of a black T-shirt that read MARRIAGE = DEATH, hair pulled into a crown of short spikes. Before I could look away, Oscar caught my eye. Lacking any grace, he slid off his stool and stumbled over to our table. He dropped into the empty chair next to me and marked me on the cheek with an exaggerated, boozy kiss. Well hello there, Brian said. Reluctantly, I introduced Oscar to those coworkers who were curious. Then, when they'd gone back to their private conversations, I said to Oscar, I thought you never crossed the Potomac. The revolution knows no boundaries, he said. No straight bar is safe. Um, Dillon said. Safe from what? Oscar threw his arm around my shoulders and said, Us! I winced to be associated with his silly little party, with someone who had clearly been drinking for quite some time. More people here than we expected, Oscar said. Must have been the free T-shirts. Want one? My bag's here. Somewhere. I shook my head and thought of how to get Oscar back to his table, to his crowd, when someone called over, Oscar, get back here! You've got to hear this! Well then, Oscar said. He stared for a moment at the table, lost in our half-eaten baskets of fried pickles and wings, the incomplete rings of condensation from our pint glasses. He moved his lips as if saying something to someone who wasn't there. He looked drunk, yes—but also confused, lost. For a moment, I was genuinely concerned about him, despite what a mess he was and even how he'd acted last year at dinner. Then he pulled himself out of the booth with something that looked like renewed anger and nearly tripped on his shoes. Instinctively, I reached out to steady him. Thanks, he said. You know, we keep running into each other like this, it's only a matter of time before we rub dicks again. Parallel lines meet in infinity. He laughed, and I let go of his arm so that he stumbled back into a barrel of a man wearing a shirt that read WHAT JIMMY DIDN'T KNOW IS THAT RALPH WAS SICK. Rachel laughed. He's certainly enjoying himself, she said. I watched Oscar disappear upstairs to the covered roof deck with the rest of his party. Brian stabbed several fries into a drying puddle of ketchup and asked if that was an ex of mine. I rolled my eyes, waved the question away as if it were a persistent fly.

An hour later, our group dispersed. I cut through the rear of Shipley's to get to my car, eager for bed. I stopped to peer up into the night, separating airplane light from starlight, staring at the moon. The same one, I thought, that saved my life all those years ago. If only there'd been a moon for Thomas Pitt. If only Arthur had been around to help him. Then I heard a lurch and splatter, and I turned to see a slender shape leaning against a white truck. The shadow looked up at the sky, made movements with its mouth. I crept over, because of course it was Oscar. As if it could have been anyone else. He was staring at the stars, and I thought I saw tears in his eyes, a vulnerability that gave me permission to come closer. Oscar looked over at me. Ugh, he said, whether in sickness or recognition I couldn't tell. Maybe it was both. I think I overdid it, Oscar said. Seems so, I said. Here, lean against the truck. Take deep breaths. Good idea, Oscar said. He rocked back and forth on his heels. Don't judge me, Oscar said. I'm mourning. I asked him who he was mourning, saw deep yellow streaks of vomit cutting through the words on his shirt. My dad died, he said. I think I'm finally feeling it. Or maybe it's just all the shit I've been drinking tonight. Oscar listed a menu of cocktails, of wines, of liquors sipped from hip flasks on the Metro, of free shots handed out by the bartender—a recitation that sent him flinging forward with renewed heaving. I turned away and watched two of Oscar's black shirts cross the street toward their car. Don't judge me, Oscar kept saying. I'm not judging you, I lied. I drew Oscar away from the unfortunate pickup that had turned into his toilet bowl. I'm sorry about your father, I said. Oscar cackled, and I had to turn away from his sour breath. He was a prick, Oscar said. More heaves. He betrayed me. I looked up into the night, held Oscar's shoulders to keep him from stumbling off. I'm needed back inside, he said. I loosened my grip on Oscar's shoulders and let him go, like a father watching with wonder and fear as his child takes its first precarious steps across a room. He wasn't going to make it. I rushed over and held him against me before he fell. Whoa there, I said. I don't think that's a good idea. Here. Let me take you home. Where do you live? Oscar was sobbing now. I don't know anymore. Okay, I said. I'm not driving around pointing at apartment buildings all night. Come with me, and I'll drive you back in the morning when you're better. But my friends, Oscar said. He waved limply at the back door of Shipley's. They'll be fine without you, I said, helping Oscar into my car. They're adults. Oscar looked down at his shirt. This is so gross, he said. I helped Oscar with the seatbelt buckle. He dribbled like a baby. To think I once wanted to kiss those lips. Oscar caught my stare and groaned. Don't judge me, he said. Shut up, Oscar, I said.

Oscar

Ugh.

The time? The time. What's the time? Morning, I'm guessing. Hoping. My phone's dead, which means I may as well be, too. But if so, it's a strange sort of afterlife: a room with smooth, cream-colored walls, a small office desk, a heavy antique armoire flashing empty insides through its open doors. A window through which I can hear, faintly, a hollow sort of crash, like logs being thrown on a fire.

It's only when I get up to go look outside that I really start to feel it. My mouth a wad of cotton, my throat a boulder rolling up and down my neck, my stomach bubbling like a pot of soup. And my head.

Christ, my head.

That same hollow crash from outside the window. I pry apart two cracked blinds and see, through a dagger of morning light, Sebastian Mote dragging what look like incredibly long slats of wood from somewhere on the side of the house out into the backyard, trying his best to lay them on top of one another. I watch him drag one, two more slats of wood, and it's clear I've been looking too long because he stops after setting down the last one and turns to look at me looking at him. I drop to the floor, hide below the window, groan at the fire the sudden movement ignites in my brain, my bowels.

Okay, Oscar. You can do this. Let's try and remember how you got here.

There was Outrage. Pregaming at Martin's, gummy worms swollen with vodka. The Metro ride to Arlington with the other

Friday-evening commuters staring at us in the shirts I was handing out from a canvas bag, was demanding people put on before we arrived. (I don't see the bag here in this room. Probably lost to history now.) I remember feeling disappointed most people on the train didn't seem to care we were there. As if we were just another part of life or, even worse, not worth paying attention to. I remember the anger that came with this thought, an anger that spurred me to more and more drinking, that turned my stomach into a trash can of mixed drinks. Other things. Sebastian sitting at a table. Martin's hand on my inner thigh. Someone else's lips on mine in the bathroom. Going up on the roof deck to call Sean, then thinking better of it. No need for him anymore. I'd already wasted too much time idealizing him, honoring him, when in fact he'd turned out to be just another Judas gay who'd given up the fight. Of his surprise marriage, I knew little other than the scraps I uncovered online: Instagram photos in which he'd been tagged with several other men, younger than him but older than me, one of which was captioned "Hubby Happy Hour," all of which were marked as having been taken in New Hope, Pennsylvania. The man on his left, with fat ears and thin blond hair, I took to be Jesse, though I had no way of knowing for sure. In every photo, Sean was smiling, and I searched tirelessly for some sign of weakness in that grin, something to prove I was right and he was wrong. That he'd made a terrible mistake. What is it cops always ask hostages in movies to do? Blink twice if you're in danger? Then more memories. Standing out in the darkness, alone, looking up at the stars. Puking. Someone reaching out to me from the shadows and holding me up. Thinking: It's Sean. Thinking: It's my father. Realizing, with disappointment: It's only Sebastian.

A soft knock on the door.

"Hey. Coffee in the kitchen. Clean shirt in the bathroom. Aspirin, too."

"Okay. Thanks. I'm coming out."

DRAPED IN AN ill-fitting Jefferson University T-shirt I found waiting for me on the toilet seat in the bathroom, I move slowly, deliberately, into Sebastian's kitchen. The clock on the microwave reads 10:34, and I feel a sense of loss wondering what everyone else at last night's party is doing right now, at this moment, and how I'm out here, in a kitchen that looks eerily put together, staged as if for an open house. The curtains on the kitchen window in their blue sashes, the dish rack artfully stacked with drying plates, the tea towels hanging from the handle of the stove, the woolen mat in the center of the floor that says PLACE FEET HERE, the black hide of the refrigerator plastered with magnets of paintings and sculptures.

The mug on the counter into which I pour a steaming stream of coffee reads LOVE IS LOVE IS LOVE. Of course. I make the dumb mistake of using the coffee to sluice three aspirin down my throat, then steady myself against the kitchen sink and wait for the fire in my chest to die down. From over the counter, in the sunken living room, I see quilts stacked in a wicker basket in a corner by an empty fireplace. An antique mirror, a sofa still bearing the stripes of a recent vacuuming. It's like I've stumbled into a diorama in a natural history museum labeled *Homo americanus domesticus*. The silence in this house, the stillness, is oppressive. All it needs is the ticking of a grandfather clock to make it complete. Nothing queer about this space at all. Just plain. Ordinary. I'd scream to break the quiet, if I wasn't afraid my head would explode from the pain.

Is this what life in New Hope is like for Sean and his husband?

Out on the back porch, his morning labors apparently finished, Sebastian sits on the top step in a sweater nursing his own cup of coffee. I slip outside and stand next to him, trying to see what he sees out there along the pale green backyard. I point to the stack of wood planks, ask him if he's building an ark out here.

"Raised flower beds." He turns around and looks up at me, squinting against the sun over my shoulders, reminding me fleetingly of the boy he used to be. He points to a square patch of grass marked out with string and stakes. "One over there. Maybe a vegetable garden, too."

Feeling awkward looming over Sebastian, I sit on the top step next to him. He scoots over to give me what little more room he can. I quell a lurch in my stomach with a delicate sip of coffee.

"Lot of work for one man," I say.

"Want to help?"

"I think if I were to do any manual labor now, I'd break into pieces. Hard enough just to sit here."

"That bad?"

"That bad."

I ask the eternal question of the eternal carouser: "Did I say anything stupid last night?"

"Stupider than last time?"

"Shit. Did I ask you to hook up again?"

"No. Your dad."

"Oh."

"Sorry to hear about that."

"Would it be alright if we didn't talk about him?"

"Sure. Of course. Want something to eat?"

"Coffee's fine, thanks."

We sit there, looking out at the flat backyard, listening to the birds and the distant drone of someone's lawn tool. I think of the plot of land hundreds of miles west where my father now lies, in the dark, in the quiet, while above him cars cruise past the cemetery and boys play basketball on the courts across the street. The entire universe oblivious.

"So it's just you out here, right?"

"It is."

"Quiet?"

"Mostly. It's nice."

"Boring?"

"For you, maybe. Not me."

"Happy?"

Sebastian stares into his coffee as if waiting for the perfect response to burble to the surface. "No happier than I was before, I guess. Jake, my ex, was miserable out here. I suppose I should feel lucky I trapped him here as long as I did. Now that he's gone, though, I quite like it on my own. Everything feels a bit more under control. Maybe it's better this way. Maybe I'm stronger by myself."

I go to check the time on my phone, realize there's nothing to check.

"Hey, can I borrow your charger?"

"Of course. On my nightstand."

In the master bedroom, I find the power cord curled next to a small stack of books: dog-eared copies of *Crime and Punishment* and *King Lear* and *Pride and Prejudice* stamped with the words PROPERTY OF MSS. There's a biography of Caravaggio with its spine fractured in multiple places, an art history book the size of an infant's gravestone. On top of it—oh, boy. A hardback copy of

Tiberius at the Villa, stamped with a 40% OFF! sticker. I turn it over and see, partially masked by another sale sticker, the small square photograph of Sean Stokes, looking as he did when I first met him at the Attic. The man who wrote this tale of debauchery, now resigned to country living. I think of tossing the book into the wastebasket in the bathroom, then remember it doesn't belong to me.

I'm only human, so before I leave, I peek inside Sebastian's nightstand drawer. There's a small packet of tissues, some pens, several pennies and nickels, a slim tube of hand lotion, the remote control for the dresser-top television. No poppers, no embarrassingly large dildos, no secret perversions. So much for kinky Sebastian Mote.

Back outside, I ask Sebastian about *Tiberius at the Villa*.

"You had one of his books the last time I saw you," he says. "I don't know why, exactly, but I was killing time at the bookstore last month and saw it on the sale rack. I felt compelled to give it a try. For seven dollars, what did I have to lose?"

"And?"

Sebastian smiles into his coffee.

"It's awful," he says. "All the sex just gets old after a while. Take that out, and there's nothing left. It was really sad, too. And not deliberately sad. Not melancholy. Just, I don't know. Desperate. I feel like his heart wasn't in it. But maybe don't tell him I said that."

"We don't talk anymore." I tell Sebastian about my call with Jesse, about the mysterious new marriage, about giving Sean up for lost, betrayed by someone whose spirit I was trying to keep alive.

"You sound like you're in love," Sebastian says.

"Impossible. It's not love. More like respect. Or envy, maybe. That he had this glorious life, you know? Living at a time where being queer was still strange. Where you could feel like you were living rebelliously. Dangerously, even. Like you were getting away with murder. Now it's just so normal."

"A lot of people were very unhappy, you know. A lot of people died."

"I know. I know. I'm not an idiot. Still. All that pain and suffering for this? For wedding cakes? For everyone to love us? To become like everyone else? It just doesn't seem right. And what makes it worse is I know I'm the minority here. Like those body parts you don't need but are still there. Vestigial limbs."

"Oscar the tailbone."

"Hah."

"Oscar the appendix."

"Still got mine."

"Oscar the wisdom tooth that needs pulling before it rots in his mouth."

"Okay, okay. Anyway. I should probably go call a car. You've got a garden to build, and I need to go home and sleep. For the next forty years."

"I'll drive you to the Metro, at least. It's not that far. Your shirt's on top of the laundry. Just stuff it in a plastic bag. They're hanging in a sock on the back of the door."

A sock on the back of the door.

Of course, Sebastian.

On my way to get my phone, I'm felled by a sudden surge of nausea that sends me instead to the bathroom, where I hang my head over the toilet bowl and wait impatiently for something, anything, to come up. Sebastian calls from the living room and says he'll be out by the car. What a strange sleepover, compared to the ones we used to have. Like the one time we forced ourselves to stay up all night long, as if that was the very definition of manhood. We must have been nine or ten. We sat on the couch, not watching television but each other, smacking the other's bare thigh if we caught his eyelids drooping. We made it successfully to breakfast, then went out to Sebastian's front yard to pitch racquetballs against the garage door. In minutes, we'd both passed out in the grass.

I wash my face, run damp hands through the mess of my hair. Grabbing my phone from Sebastian's bedroom, I see Martin's texts from last night.

Leaving for Metro in 10. Empire?

Josh and I are splitting a cab share, you in?

You're missing out on pizza.

Hope you're not dead somewhere out there.

I grab my dirty T-shirt from the laundry room and head out to the garage. Walking through the shadows I hear, faintly, the ghostly bangs of blue rubber balls against painted wood.

Then I stop.

Sebastian's not alone. He's at the bottom of the driveway, talking to a boy in a frumpy purple hoodie. On the grass next to them, a bicycle plastered with Human Rights Campaign stickers lies in a wreck. The boy's shoulders are heaving, and Sebastian has his hands on them. He's whispering something I'm too far away to hear. They hug, and Sebastian ruffles the boy's hair. I slink down the driveway, trying to make them gently aware of my presence. I hear Sebastian say, "You'll be alright. It doesn't feel like it, but you will." Then the boy turns to look at me over his right shoulder. I see a thick bush of hair flecked with faded purple, watery eyes, a runny nose, raw lips, a face with haphazard child's stubble that widens in a mixture of surprise, recognition, and what I take to be muffled fear—if only because that's what I'm feeling right now, too.

"Hold on a second," Sebastian says to the boy. Then, to me: "Sorry, Oscar. This is one of my students. I'll be just a minute."

"Wow," the boy says. "It's you."

"Um," I say. "Hi."

"You know each other," Sebastian says.

"Friends of friends," I say.

Once again, that feeling of disorientation so common to my life: seeing someone first through pictures and then—days, weeks, maybe even months later—they've come to life in front of you, stepped out of your screen and into the three-dimensional world, a blip on your social media feed now made flesh. The boy's wearing a polo underneath his hoodie, but I know exactly what he looks like without it. I know what it all looks like, because I still have some of his photos on my phone, somewhere in the labyrinthine back catalog of Cruze messages I received last summer from a flake named A.

We shake hands, the boy and I.

"Arthur," he says.

The boy's blushing, fighting to hide the connection that hangs, batlike, over our two heads. Sebastian stands beside us, useless. He's probably wondering why friends of friends have to reintroduce themselves.

"Small world," I say.

"I was just getting ready to take Oscar to the Metro," Sebastian says.

The boy wipes drying tears away with his sleeves and looks at us with suspicion, like a child who's snuck into his parents' bedroom and is sniffing out the unmistakable musk of interrupted sex.

"Oh," he says to Sebastian. "Is this your boyfriend?"

Sebastian and I look at each other. I laugh, because I know Sebastian won't.

"No," I say.

"No," Sebastian says. "Just old friends."

"Ancient," I say.

I tell Sebastian I'll wait for him in the car.

Once inside, I take a few deep breaths and pull out my phone to look busy. A high-schooler. Jesus. He said he was twenty-one. He said his name was Aaron. He said he lived in D.C. He stood me up. Why, because it was past his bedtime?

I think: Wait until Sean hears about this. Then I catch myself.

Through the rearview mirror, I watch Sebastian and the boy continue to talk. They're not. No. Impossible. Twice while Sebastian speaks, the boy turns to look at me. Then Sebastian pats the boy's shoulders again, and the boy picks up his bike, wipes his face with his sleeves, and slowly pedals down the street. Sebastian stands at the end of the driveway and watches the boy for what seems longer than necessary. Then he turns to look at me looking at him.

UNEXPECTED TRAFFIC, AS expected, strikes again. It's already taken fifteen minutes just to get out of the hills and onto Interstate 66. Then, once again, we're stuck. I bring down the passenger-side window and stick my head out into the air, look up and down the road. We're not going anywhere anytime soon.

"Shit," Sebastian says through his teeth.

It's his first word since getting in the car.

We inch forward along the road, my fragile stomach bracing itself for every stop and start, Sebastian flipping through radio stations with seemingly no intention of ever stopping. Taylor Swift. Donald Trump. Drake. Bernie Sanders. Peter Bjorn and John. Hillary Clinton. Finally, Sebastian settles on some piece of classical music.

I ask what all that back there was about.

"A student. I told you."

"Well, yeah. But what was he doing in your driveway?"

Sebastian goes to switch lanes, realizes he can't make it, groans. "His boyfriend lives in my neighborhood. They just broke up this morning. Had a fight, sounds like. He was biking around for a while, crying. He saw me when I came out to the car. He's pretty upset. I told him he should go home and talk to his parents."

"Plenty more rainbow fish in the sea." I think of some of the messages we once shared. The photos. "How old is he, exactly?"

"Seventeen."

Shit.

"I feel awful he's hurting," Sebastian said.

"Can you imagine us like that, at seventeen? Crying to teachers about boyfriends? Having boyfriends?"

"It's different now."

"Well, good for him."

Sebastian stares off into traffic. We stay silent until we approach a green sign that says it's two miles to the Metro station. Sebastian grips his hands tighter on the wheel. It looks like something's boiling behind his eyes.

"How do you know each other, Oscar?"

Great.

"Him? Oh, it's nothing. It's silly."

"Friends of friends, you said."

Oh, man.

"Yeah."

"What does that mean?"

Shit.

"Nothing."

"No, seriously. I want to know. Where did you meet him?"

Here we go.

"Well. Actually. If you must know. He messaged me earlier this summer. On Cruze. At that wedding we were at, if you can believe it."

Sebastian laughs. "Cruze? No. No, I don't think so. He's not the type."

"Well he was that night. We chatted. He sent me messages, some pictures. He told me he was a freshman in college. We were supposed to meet up."

"But?"

"But he chickened out. Never showed. Now I know why. That's it. Nothing else. I moved on."

"Pictures," Sebastian says, as if it's the first time he's ever heard the word.

"Yeah. That's how I recognized him. That's how he recognized me."

"Wait. You sent him pictures back? What kind of pictures?"

"Are you serious about this?"

"I just. I just don't think he'd do something like that. He's different. It must be someone else. You must be mixing him up with someone else. God knows you go through them." Without warning, the passenger-side window starts to come up, giving me barely enough time to pull my arm in. "Let's keep the window closed," Sebastian says without looking at me.

I take my phone and cradle it in my palm, carefully, like a

loaded gun, mulling over Sebastian's unsubtle slut-shaming, over how close I just came to being mangled.

"I can show you the photos if you'd like," I say.

"No!"

I can't tell if Sebastian's yelling at me or the lime-green motorcycle winding its way between tight spaces in traffic.

We inch along. Up ahead, I can make out the red-blue spangle of police lights.

"So," Sebastian says.

"So."

"Did you have sex with him?"

"Sex."

"Yeah. With Arthur. With my student. Did you have sex with him?"

"What did I just tell you a minute ago?"

"Why don't I believe you?" Sebastian scoffs, closes his eyes, shakes his head. Another minute of silence, then: "I should have just left you in that parking lot."

"What?"

"You looked like a sick dog out there, you know? Like one of my mom's old dogs. Barfing your brains out. Crying. You're thirty-five years old. And now you're hooking up with kids."

"I told you, I—" But what's the use?

Up ahead, another green sign. One mile to go.

"Look," I say. "It's obvious you don't want me in this car, and I don't want to be here with you. Just pull over onto the shoulder. Right here. I'll walk the rest of the way. It's not far."

"I'm not pulling over here, Oscar. There's nowhere for me to turn around."

"Oh, for fuck's sake."

I open the door and get out. All I hear is Sebastian say my name, and then I'm gone, heading down the shoulder toward the Metro station. I turn around, watch Sebastian struggle to close the passenger-side door. A gap in traffic opens up in front of Sebastian's car; the driver behind him lays on the horn. Sebastian, straining for the door handle, looks out at me (and my middle finger) with revulsion and rage.

GIVEN THE TALL grass and the uneven embankment, it takes twenty minutes to hike up to the station. Making matters worse, trains are on a weekend schedule, which means my next ride back to civilization won't arrive for another eighteen minutes. I take the stairs up to the platform, ignoring the looks of the museum-bound families and the weekend office workers, and find a spot on a bench toward the end of the platform. I could flag a cab or call a car, yes, but I've hardly any battery life in my phone.

And there's something important I have to do.

I sign on to Cruze. My chat history unfolds on my screen, and there, from last July, sandwiched between an invitation for sex and grilled cheese with Martin and an early-morning discussion about Republican presidential primaries, is my conversation with A. I take screen shots of several photos, drop them into a fresh text to Sebastian, and send the package on its way.

Take that.

Soon my train pulls into the station with its familiar whine and hiss and we reverse course and head east along the curve of the interstate. Once we burrow underneath Arlington and the Potomac, my stomach starts to settle and my headache starts to subside.

Then I'm back in the city. I'm safe.

Rising from the depths into daylight, I check my phone. One percent battery. Two new texts. Not from Sebastian, from Bart.

The first: *J and I are having a debate. Didn't you meet this guy once?*

The second: A link to a news item from a gay culture site. It's not long; a bulletin tucked between a reality show recap and a photo gallery of shirtless celebrities. Not even the dignity of a photo. Just one headline and four sentences.

GAY NOVELIST DIES AT 68

SEAN STOKES, the novelist who transformed his sex life into thinly disguised fiction once called pornographic by critics, died at age 68. Stokes was popular in the 1970s for his detailed exploration of gay life in novels like 1975's *A Boyhood* and its sequel, *A Manhood* (1978), as well as *Skin Dreams* (1980), *1001 Nights* (1985), and *The Little Deaths* (1994). His most recent novel, *Tiberius at the Villa* (2015), was savaged by our critic, Robert Spellman (read it here). He is survived by his husband, the poet Jesse Board.

I read the paragraph three times. Four times. I keep reading it, standing there clueless on the sidewalk. I know as soon as I stop reading, as soon as I look up from my phone, it'll be more than just words. It'll be reality.

What the fuck is going on today?

My phone buzzes in my hand. For a second, I think it's the precursor to some horrible public sorrow I can already feel at the top of my chest and the base of my throat. Not the first time I've barfed in public. But it's just a Cruze message. A profile picture, once a torso, is now a face staring at me the same way it did earlier this morning. Its age now seventeen. Its location now forty-nine miles away. Its name still A.

Hey stranger, it reads.

Then my phone goes black.

FIVE

Tiberius at the Villa

Sebastian

A hand—one I'd seen stuffed into pockets, dragged through thick hair, rubbed against exhausted late-afternoon eyes, extended to receive graded essays, wrapped around my own in thanks and farewell—holds a cock. Squat, stubby, tapering off to a red arrowhead, networked with several veins, framed by artfully manicured pubic hair. The fingers around it open as if displaying a specimen for scientific study. A small plinth of flesh, taut and turgid, bisected by an opaque text box stating the obvious: *So hard*.

I put an immediate end to our after-school movies. I blamed it on administrative work, on nonexistent family issues. You've got your list, I told Arthur. You're a scholar, and a scholar has to be comfortable pursuing his own passions. (I thought of the photos when I said this, the nudes that weren't classically composed but urgently utilitarian, that didn't celebrate the body but sold it. I regretted my choice of words.) Arthur was befuddled, but I didn't relent. I couldn't. Not because of the photos (which I'd deleted from my phone but not my mind) but because of what they meant. This boy is not the boy I thought he was.

They look, at first, like hills. An aerial shot of an alien landscape. It takes a moment for the buttocks to reveal themselves, abstracted by the angle from which they've been photographed, by the garish camera flash. Two thick gobbets of muscle and fat, freed of skinny jeans and underpants. Smooth at the crest, dark hairs guiding eyes toward a darker canyon.

I spent my afternoons at home, attacking the backyard with renewed vigor, ignoring the ever-persistent ache in my right shoulder. The labor kept me occupied, kept my mind off Arthur, off Oscar, off thoughts of the two of them together out there in the world, off feelings that something precious had been stolen from me. I told my father I was now thinking about building a fence around the house, something to keep all the deer shit away. Be my guest, my father said from his mountain retreat. But don't be afraid to hire someone if you need help. I can do this alone, I said. I scoured how-to articles online, made recursive trips to the home improvement store. I brought home as many planks of pressure-treated cedar as I could fit in my car, carried them, one by one, into the backyard, stacked them compulsively into neat piles. Then I sat in the grass and worried my mind over what to do next, over the labor of actually seeing a project through to the end. I envisioned a ranch-style fence because it was the only type of fence I could conceive of building on my own. I saw it forced together with nails that would do just as well propping up a Grunewald Christ.

Chest hair, like delicate wings, arches in flight over tiny nipples. No face, just a squat neck, the hint of a rounded cherub chin, a soft body that leads down to a waistband of Skyler Mountain briefs. The glimpse of a bathroom counter: a sink's scalloped edge, a toothpaste tube curled like a witch's nail, the corner of a damp hand towel.

One Monday after class, as I packed my bag, Arthur came into my trailer without knocking. He held up a red envelope. *Ivan's Childhood,* he said. I said nothing, just stood there looking at this boy who, in the last few weeks, had warped and melted like some abstract expressionist nightmare. I wasn't daft, I knew my students had sex lives. Still. I'd thought of Arthur as someone free of that desperate need to be desired, to be seen. Now I knew he was just like the rest of us: bent and messy. Or maybe it was something else. Maybe I felt cheated. Maybe I wanted that body for myself. Did I? God. The lecherous high school teacher—a trope as old as Socrates. None of it made any sense, and so the only solution, as I saw it, was to dig a trench between the two of us. But a trench to keep him away from me, or me away from him, I wasn't sure. You know, I said, I didn't get much sleep this weekend. Calling it an early day and going straight to bed. Arthur was relentless. What about lunch tomorrow? Watch it on your own, I said. Tell me on Wednesday what you thought of it. Arthur stuffed the envelope back into his messenger bag and skulked over to the trailer door.

Then he turned around. You're upset with me, he said. But I'm not sure why. I'm not upset, Arthur. Is it from when I stopped by your house crying? Because that's done with now, I'm over him. (I wondered: Over whom?) Arthur, I said, you should be spending more time after school with your peers anyway. I thought you were my peer, he said. I'm your teacher, I said. Oh, Arthur said.

It's a simple portrait, fleshy and alive, plucked out of a Renaissance painting. The demure eyes, the lips open in a dumb impression of seduction, revealing the darkness inside which a wet tongue waits. It takes a moment for the entirety of the photo to make itself known. The viewer has to know where to look, what to look for, to understand this simple headshot captioned with the word *Yum*. Were it a painting by some modern-day Caravaggio, hung in a small corner of some obscure art museum, the card underneath its modest frame would read *Arthur Ayer (b. 1998), Cherub with Cum*.

Arthur was now the last to arrive and the first to leave class. He was now the last to arrive and the first to leave the Wednesday group meetings. The students were making decorations for prom and signs for June's Capital Pride Parade from flimsy craft-store paperboard I'd brought in. MORTIMER SECONDARY LGBTQ STUDENTS. PROUD TO BE A MORTIMER SECONDARY STUDENT. WE LOVE ALL OUR STUDENTS. GAY IS OK AT MSS. IN MEMORY: THOMAS PITT. This last was Arthur's.

During a guest lecture on visual literacy by the digital librarian, I sat off in a corner like the class dunce and graded reading quizzes. Occasionally, I stopped to rub my sore shoulder, search my palms for splinters, look at Arthur in the second row staring at the artwork on my trailer wall. I saw the light of his phone go off in his pocket, imagined an incoming text from Oscar soliciting more pictures, more messages. I took out my phone and, under cover of graded papers, created a new Cruze profile. No name, no photograph, no stats. I found A. immediately, five feet away. I saw the small green light. I thought about typing something—*Pay attention to Ms. Edison*—when a message appeared at the top of my screen. Philip98, five miles away. *Sup*. Arthur turned his head at the sound. I flushed red, lowered the volume on my phone, logged off, and deleted the app. Arthur stared at me for another moment, then turned his attention back to Ms. Edison, who was patiently guiding the class through the last five minutes of *2001: A Space Odyssey*.

On a Friday afternoon, three weeks before senior prom, I stepped out of my trailer into a world rushing with wind. Inside my work-bag were short essays on *King Lear* and a catalog of J.M.W. Turner seascapes I intended to flip through over the weekend. I walked across the blacktop with its potholes like bullet wounds, thinking about other people's happiness. Then I saw Arthur and Raymond over by the flagpole. I stopped, slipped behind the flimsy siding of T-1, and watched. The two boys stood apart, arms crossing over their chests and dangling at their sides and crossing again, as if tempted to reach out to one another. Raymond said something and Arthur looked down, dejected. Like he's being chastised, I thought. Then it was Arthur's turn to plead what I assumed was his case. He reached out a hand to Raymond, who jerked his away. A moment later, as if realizing he'd gone too far, Raymond reached back and squeezed Arthur's forearm. Other students walked by this scene, uninterested. Arthur and Raymond spoke for another few minutes, then turned and began to walk toward the end of the school, through the faculty parking lot, past the dwindling construction, between the familiar gap in the trees that led down to Lake Mortimer. When they disappeared, I stepped out from behind the trailer and followed their footsteps until I got to my car. I opened the driver's-side door and tossed my workbag into the passenger seat, then looked up at the tree line ahead, the shrubs thick with new growth. I told myself I should go home. I told myself I should make a drink, a big one. I told myself I should grade my essays, read my book, enjoy my solitude. I told myself that wasn't my world out there beyond those trees, it was theirs. I told myself I didn't belong where they were going. I told myself to go read some Yeats instead. I looked at my bag lying in the car and thought, again, of Arthur's photographs, the secret life they briefly revealed, the body they taunted me with. I thought about the young in one another's arms, about a tattered coat upon a stick. I thought about a boyhood I never had, the warped manhood I was stuck with for the rest of my life. Then I closed the car door and walked, as if it were any other afternoon, across the faculty parking lot and toward the path leading to the lake. Just to make sure everything was okay. Just to make sure Arthur didn't need my help. Have a nice day, Mr. Mote, Corrie said as she walked past me and into a waiting van. I crossed over into the woods, and someone else called out my name. Dani. Where are you going, Sebastian? A walk, I said. Need to clear my head. With growing anxiety, I sensed the two boys getting farther and farther away. Were they even going to the lake? What if they were going somewhere else? Somewhere I wouldn't be able to find them? Dani asked if I needed company. I shook my head, said I'd call her later, then continued on the gravel path that ran for a quarter-mile along Lake Mortimer Road before it banked right and dropped down a gentle hill. At the bottom, I slowed down, then stepped off the path into the woods, creeping, wincing at the crunch of underbrush and leafmeal, watching slices of Lake Mortimer reveal themselves through the scrim of trees. I tried to look for Arthur's purple hoodie, for Raymond's navy windbreaker. I saw a woman running peaceful laps around the lake, saw a man on the far shore step out onto his back porch with his phone. I looked and looked and looked, but I couldn't see either of the boys. Then I realized the reason I couldn't see them was because they weren't walking. They were sitting, almost right below me, at the bottom of the slope on whose edge I stood, on a bench made of recycled plastic, not looking at each other but out at the rippling water. Raymond's legs swung back and forth. I couldn't see Arthur's, then realized it was because he was sitting cross-legged on the bench. I took a few tender steps forward, bracing myself against a tree trunk, extending my neck to try and hear what they were saying. I heard, faintly, Raymond's voice carried on the wind. They're not just pictures, he said. They are, Arthur said. They are just pictures. I was just fooling around. I never met anyone. I thought it was just me, Raymond said. I didn't think I'd have to share you with other people. I know I'm going to be at another school next year, but still. Arthur turned to look at Raymond. I'm sorry, he said. Maybe Trent was right about you, Raymond said. Don't say that, Arthur said. Don't say that. The afternoon jogger passed by, smiled, raised a hand in greeting. Let's just enjoy these last few months, Arthur said. Let's just enjoy prom. Please. I like you, you like me. Why can't it just be that simple? That's not what I want, Raymond said. I told you at the beginning. Arthur folded his arms and leaned forward. I watched his tiny shoulders shake. Raymond looked at Arthur, first with disappointment, then with a slowly growing sympathy like nothing I'd ever seen on a face so young. He put his hand on Arthur's purple back. Rob and Trent and Mauricio, let them go on that shitty site, he said. You're better than that. Just be here, in the real world. With me. Arthur looked up at Raymond. The boys shifted their bodies closer to one another. They started to kiss. I caught my breath, slipped back behind the tree. The private drama of two teens playing out by a lake after school—I had no reason to be here. No right. I was a wolf, a viper disrupting the natural order of this sylvan scene. No. I knew who I was. I was Giovanni the Lame and these two boys the clandestine lovers Paolo Malatesta and Francesca da Rimini, and it was a scene put down by Ingres, by Doré, by Delacroix. Me, hiding behind the arras, boiling with jealousy. Except I had no sword to unsheathe. A breeze crept through the woods and everything around me—the treetops, the surface of the lake, Arthur's hair—trembled. The boys continued to kiss, and I felt as if I were watching a film about a life that should have been mine. I felt, in that moment, duped by fate. Arthur uncrossed his legs and lay them on Raymond's lap. They stopped kissing long enough for Arthur to scoot closer, long enough for the afternoon jogger to pass. Then they continued. I watched Arthur and thought about my secret evening with that ratty purple hoodie. What I could have done with it but didn't do. The memory of that moment, not just its tragedy but its tenderness, almost made me cry. At the very least, it was enough to push me to the surface of my afternoon delusion, enough to remind me of what I must look like clinging to a tree and spying on two teenage boys, enough to make me realize I needed to leave. Now. Slowly, I pushed back from the tree and began to crabwalk up to more level terrain. Then the ground gave way beneath my feet. I slipped down the embankment not with the justified anger of a royal cuckold but the juvenile idiocy of a court jester, tumbling through the screen of shrubbery, over branches that snapped like bones, sliding the last few seconds on my stomach, feet first, the way I used to slide down carpeted basement stairs as a kid. There was an explosion of birds, the landslide rush of dead leaves and soil. My dress shirt was forced up out of my pants and into the pits of my arms. I stopped when I hit the gravel path. I lay there on my stomach, back exposed to the early May sun, face hot with shame, right hip caked in something that smelled like the feces of a wood-land animal. I felt the boys' eyes and wished the ground would just keep giving way, that it wouldn't stop until I'd been swallowed up and safely wrapped in its chilly depths. Mr. Mote, Arthur said. Whoa shit, Raymond said. I rose to my feet and tugged my shirt down over my exposed belly. I tried to act as if this were the most ordinary thing in the world, a high school teacher tumbling from the woods. Arthur and Raymond were still in one another's arms. I definitely smelled shit. I had no idea what to say and neither, it seemed, did the boys, so I walked around and sat on the corner of the bench, brushing dirt off my pant legs and shirtsleeves. The boys slid over to make room for me, or to avoid the smell. Arthur asked if I was okay. Fine, I said, tasting soil inside my lower lip. Let's go, Raymond said. He took Arthur's hand and pulled him to his feet. I looked at Arthur, who stood clutching the strap of his bag as if bracing for a reason to dive inside it. Then I realized: He knows. He knows I heard everything. He doesn't need to ask. I thought, again, of the photographs. This time, I thought of long fingers that weren't mine roving along plump inner thighs, thought of a purple hoodie tossed carelessly on strange floors. Then, because I had to say something to counteract the shame I felt, something to tip the balance of power back in my favor, I asked: Did you have sex with my friend Oscar on that site? (I regretted the word, *friend,* which I swore I'd never use again after I'd first opened those text messages in traffic weeks earlier.) Arthur became a statue, as if all the life inside him had flushed out of a pinhole in the top of his head, leaving nothing behind but this vacuous shape, this empty shell of a boy. Then I saw water behind Arthur's eyes and knew the boy was still in there. The mortification shocked me, and I wanted to reach out and grab my question and stuff it back in my dirt-filled mouth. Raymond yanked his hand out of Arthur's. You're disgusting, he said to Arthur, then turned and sprinted on the gravel path leading back to the road. I watched him go, then turned back to see Arthur shriveling next to me. His messenger bag was open in his lap, and I saw a trigonometry workbook, deodorant, a school-issued tablet, two bent sticks of unwrapped gum, a rolled-up shirt, a small baggie of pretzel rods. It was like peering at a tiny universe through a microscope. I put a hand on Arthur's shoulder and stared into the thick, eggplant-purple crop of his freshly dyed hair. I'm sorry, I said. I'm so sorry. I should not have said that. Arthur stared at me over his shoulder. He no longer looked surprised, as he did in the Caravaggio painting. He looked furious. What were you doing up there? He was yelling, his voice thick with an authority, a righteousness that frightened me. What were you doing up there? Were you spying on us? This has nothing to do with you, Mr. Mote! Nothing at all! It's none of your business what I do and with whom! Arthur stood up and threw his bag over his shoulder. Is that why you've been mad at me this whole time? Because you think I fucked your friend? I almost fell back from the force of that word coming from those lips. Arthur,

I said. I reached out for a purple sleeve, but Arthur was already walking away. Leave me alone, Mr. Mote. Oscar's right: You're crazy. Then he ran up the road. I sat by the lake, on the bench. I folded my hands between my legs to try and keep them from shaking. The jogger came by again, flushed with exertion, and slowed as she passed. Everything's fine, I said. Then, because I didn't know what else to say: My son's just upset is all. I sat there for another hour or so, staring at the water, until the jogger had left and the sky started to bruise milky-red. Then I willed my body to move, told myself I needed to get to my car, needed to get home, needed to take a shower. I made the slow, shameful walk back up the path through the woods and out into the open air along Lake Mortimer Road, where the faces behind each passing car seemed to judge me mercilessly. Back in the school parking lot, I started my car. I turned to see my workbag in the passenger seat, still there, a reminder of an entirely different life to which I could now never return.

Oscar's right: You're crazy.

That night, I couldn't sleep. I carried myself into the living room and sat down on the sofa with my copy of *Tiberius at the Villa*. I skimmed through baroque passages of Roman musicians clawing at each other's faces for the chance to spend the night in the emperor's chamber; of the Old Goat of Capri lecturing his cruel grand-nephew on the nature of power as they walked along passageways painted with obscene murals; of prepubescent boys nibbling the emperor's genitals like well-trained fish as he lay in a warm bath.

Oscar's right: You're crazy.

The words I read felt to me like an elegy, a desperate salvage attempt, the last dying gasp of someone who knows his time has come to an end and yet is driven mad by the idea of life continuing on without him. I read about elaborate banquets and seaside orgies and fantastic theatrical performances. I read a lengthy paragraph describing wine and semen stains on the emperor's tunic. I read it again. And again. And again.

Oscar's right: You're crazy.

*

Oscar

Across the street, construction on the Echo continues in earnest. Sometimes, I'll take a break from my desk to sit outside in the warming day and watch the workers crawl like ants over the building's cantilevered roof. That, or I'll stare in frustration at the new sign, put up just last week, that reads OPENING SOON! LEASE UP TODAY!

When it gets really bad, when thoughts of Sean buried in earth or dispersed into the wind start to get to me, I go to the haphazard pile on my nightstand, the Leaning Tower of Sean Stokes, and take up one of his books. I read them everywhere I can, the books. On the Metro, at bars waiting for others, on the toilet. Sometimes just sentences, sometimes a whole chapter. On nights when I can't sleep, I pour myself a generous glass of bottom-shelf scotch and read on the sofa until I wake up hours later with *Ecce Homo* or *Tiberius at the Villa* tented over my belly.

It's guilt—guilt and shame—that makes me take up these books again, that pulls me back to the delicious stories of life in bathhouses and public parks, in leather bars and basement dungeons and waterfront piers and private clubs that no longer exist. But all the perverse rebellion, the joyful queerness of it all—it's gone. The spell's broken, as if the only thing that kept this world alive for me was the existence of its creator. Now it's all just a bunch of words. Stories told by a dead man.

Still, I keep reading.

Then there's the death itself. I think about it while in the shower or at the grocery story, while watching the timer on the basement washing machine tick down to zero. Everything I know about Sean's death, let alone of his last two months as a married man, I've culled from late-night online searches, from archaeological digs into the social media posts and five-hundred-word articles of friends, students, the handful of ex-lovers still alive. I prowl for funeral photographs, for parting words from the husband, for some kind of literary appreciation or reevaluation. Nothing. And the thought of that nothing, the fearful truth that I'll never know what those last months of life were like for him, if I ever knew him at all, drives me mad. It sends me on walks over to the Ambrose Bierce House, looking now like a shuttered castle from some children's bedtime story.

It wasn't cancer. It wasn't a heart attack. It wasn't an opportunistic infection he'd kept hidden all this time. He wasn't run over in a car by a desperate john or strangled by a self-loathing lover or beaten to death by some homophobic zealot. He wasn't, as I feared in those first weeks after hearing the news, a suicide. I waited to find, somewhere in my searches, a variation on "His body was found in the Delaware River after he'd been reported missing for several days by his husband." Perhaps because I imagined that, at the end, he'd realized his mistake, realized he'd betrayed the philosophy he'd set down all those years ago in *Ecce Homo*, and he just couldn't bear the trap he'd found himself caught in. (Or maybe it's because if I were in his situation, stuck in conformity, I'd have pulled a Virginia Woolf, too.) But no. Sean Stokes, according to cryptic internet message boards, simply fell down the stairs. Five steps, to be exact. A modest tumble, but he fell the wrong way, headfirst, so that when the paramedics arrived they found a split skull, a broken neck, a vacated body.

Sometimes, at night, I imagine all that life, all that history, leaking out from a blue-black fissure in Sean's forehead. I imagine a moment, mid-slip, when Sean's ankle twisted and his body torqued and he felt the drop in front of him, the dangerous weight of gravity pulling him down to the fierce edge of the bottom stair—I imagine a moment when, instead of trying to cushion his fall, Sean just decided to drop. Gave himself permission to go while the going was good. Let all those little deaths—the dead friends, the dead career, the dead culture—embrace him. *It's okay, Sean*, those ghosts say in one voice. *You did plenty. You don't want to stay for what happens next.*

I suppose the logical way to stop dwelling over the insignificance of our lives—the eventual insignificance that came for my father, that came for Sean, that comes for countless people around the world every single minute, that one day will come for me—is sex. It worked for Sean, who even during the worst of the plague years continued to fuck with abandon. But it doesn't work for me. At least, not anymore. For the past month, my penis has hung abandoned between my legs, itself, I suppose, in a state of mourning. At Broadway sing-a-longs and Sunday afternoon tea dances my friends drag me to, I catch glimpses of myself in some distant mirror looking shell-shocked, oblivious to any flirtatious gestures sent my way.

I go home alone more often now.

Even Outrage feels like a chore. Yesterday, I forced myself off the couch and headed over to a pirate-themed bar in Rockville, paneled in wood like the belly of a galleon, dimly lit, ringed with stuffed parrots and skull-and-crossbones flags, the air reeking of used frying oil and cinnamon-sweet grog. We wanted the straight buccaneers and wenches to feel as if their ship had been unwillingly boarded, hence the T-shirts I'd had made that read ASS PIRATE. But instead of disturbing the status quo, I spent the evening tucked away in a corner of the bar, alone, ordering round after round of grog and reading through old emails from Sean. Trying not to feel trapped on a giant sinking ship.

EVER SINCE THAT first sinister text from A. last month, I'd no intention of doing anything. In fact, I did what I often do on Cruze: ignored the message. Then, a week later, he messaged me again.

Hi. Oscar. How's your night going?

I didn't respond.

The next day: *How are things?*

I didn't respond.

Two nights later: *What are you up to tonight?*

I didn't respond.

Then, a week later, different messages.

Talked to Mr. Mote lately? He alright?

I think something's wrong with Mr. Mote.

Hey, did you tell Mr. Mote how we met?

And no, I shouldn't have written back, but I was drunk and I was bored and I was sad and I was lonely and I was angry and, like every other gay man on this blessed and cursed phone app, I just couldn't help myself.

I don't talk to him anymore. We're not friends. I don't think we ever really were. In fact, I'd stay away from him. He's crazy.

?????

Yeah. Nuts.

I thought that had done the job, because I didn't hear from A. for a while. Life trudged on, with its parties, its brunches, its freelance and temp gigs, its failed job interviews, its expensive rent and utilities—just as I imagined, in the hinterlands, Sebastian's life trudged on, with what I imagined were his classes, his grading, his yardwork, his cleaning. His silly little vegetable garden. And then, having slipped shamefully away from the Outrage party that day at the pirate bar, back on my couch and flipping aimlessly through *Tiberius at the Villa*, wondering what was going through Sean's mind when he wrote about the Old Goat of Capri lounging poolside while, under the water, young boys wound around his legs and nibbled at his cock and balls, the seventeen-year-old liar reemerges and asks if I have time for "a serious chat."

Not really. Go take your boyfriend out for ice cream or something.

I don't have one anymore. He found out I was on here.

Well, I'm not taking you to prom if that's what you're asking.

Already happened. I went with friends. He wasn't there.

What does he have against Cruze?

He thinks it's for sluts. He thinks it's for sad people.

He's a piece of shit. Besides, you're on here.

Maybe I'm sad, too.

What do you have to be sad about? Someone bullying you?

No.

Parents kick you out of the house?

No.

Then there's nothing to be sad about.

I think I'm sad about Mr. Mote.

How is that ass hat?

He's gone.

Gone?

He left the school. Leave of absence, the principal told us.

Oh. Shit. Where did he go?

I don't know. I bike by his house sometimes, but I don't see anyone outside. His car's there. I'm too afraid to knock.

Like I said. Crazy.

What if he killed himself?

Sebastian? Why would he do that?

I don't know. There was a student last year who killed himself.

Sebastian likes to hide. He likes to be by himself. I wouldn't worry.

He thinks we hooked up.

What did you tell him?

I said it was none of his business.

Great. Couldn't you have just said we didn't?

I wasn't thinking. Could you call Mr. Mote for me and make sure he's okay? Maybe he'll listen to you.

I don't have time for this.

Please.

I'm sure he's fine. There's nothing to worry about.

Please.

Forget him.

PLEASE.

Wait. Are you hooking up with him?

What? No. Are you?

What? No.

OK.

And then, shocking even me, something stirs in my jean shorts. A sign of life! It's like those bells they used to set up next to Victorian gravestones, attached to strings attached to index fingers so that, with just a twitch, the accidentally buried could make a noise those up in the land of the living could hear. *Ring! Ring! Ring-ring! I'm still here! Help me!* I look down beyond my phone, beyond the book, at my lap. Yes. Something still breathes under the denim, eager to be exhumed and rejoin the horrible human world.

Do I dare?

I do. Why? Because, for some reason beyond my infantile knowledge of biology and psychology, the opportunity arouses me for the first time in what feels like forever. Because all my tests from the clinic last week came back negative. Because, at my age, Sean Stokes would have done it without a second thought. Because Sebastian Mote wouldn't dream of doing it. Because I never had sex in high school. Because, in other parts of the world, people like me are thrown off roofs and burned alive for even entertaining an idea like this. Because the rumors are getting stronger that Empire's owners might not renew their lease, that one of the last big-box gay dance clubs in the city might close its doors forever. Because my father's dead, and I'm alive. Because I vow, still and forever, to live by cock alone.

I'll reach out to him. I'll check and make sure he's alive, which he is. But what's it worth?

Are you serious?

Hey, you messaged me.
Alright.
You're coming here. I don't do the suburbs.
Fine. Saturday?
Fine.
Your place?
Public first.
How about where we were supposed to meet up last year?
No. Sad memories. And you're not 18.
Four weeks. Fine. You like museums?
Whatever.
National Gallery of Art.
OK.
1?
OK.
Then your place?
Then my place.

THE NEXT DAY, I take a break from job applications for junior design positions I'm overqualified for and text Sebastian.

FYI. Your student reached out to me. He's worried about you. Thinks you did something stupid like kill yourself. I said you were fine. You might want to let him know yourself. Bye.

Halfway through a cheese and tomato sandwich, scrubbing a spot of mayonnaise off a W-9 form I need to scan back to a client, Sebastian writes back.

WHY THE FUCK ARE YOU STILL TALKING TO HIM?

Wiping my hands, I log on to Cruze and message A.

Everything's fine. He's alive.

SATURDAY MORNING, HALF past ten. By the time I eat breakfast, take a shower, air dry, get dressed, check emails, fix my hair, and take tags off my new bargain-bin tank top, it's close to noon, and if the freelance check I've been expecting from Martin's company has arrived, I can pick it up and cash it at the bank on my way down to the Mall.

I give myself a final approving look in the mirror, then rush down to the lobby mailboxes. Inside mine is a forgettable notice for a Ward 2 community meeting, my freelance check (!!!), and a Chinese carryout menu. Stuck to the back of this is what passes for a package slip in this old building: a torn square of paper with my apartment number and the date written on it in thick strokes of magic marker.

The Eritrean woman usually behind the front desk is gone, replaced by a man I've never seen before who looks confused and distraught. I hand him my package slip, and he goes off into the back room, returning with a fat white envelope on which is written, in fanciful script, PLEASE DO NOT BEND. A small Post-it note above the return address (an apartment in Foggy Bottom) shows yesterday's date.

The man looks at me expectantly, a hand open palm-up on the counter. "The other one?"

"I'm sorry?"

"The other slip. There's another package back there that hasn't been claimed."

"There was only the one slip in my mailbox."

The man shrugs like it's no big deal and goes back into the package room. He returns with a padded envelope stamped with the words MEDIA MAIL and puts it on the desk in front of me. The note on it reads *3-20-16*. I look at the handwritten address, the handwritten name. My stomach lurches.

"This is from two months ago," I say, trying to mask my shock with indignation.

"That's strange."

"Yeah. It is."

"Must have been a mix-up. Just another reason they let go of Rita. Anyway. Better late than never, right? Sorry about that. Hope it wasn't too important."

I take the stairs back to my apartment because I can't be bothered to wait for the elevator. Inside, short of breath, legs weak, I drop my mail on the coffee table and sit on the couch. I stare at the padded yellow envelope as if it were some foundling dropped on my doorstep. I can't open it. Not now. So I start with the first package. Hurried and harried, I rip open the envelope and pluck out its insides: thick card stock, followed by an unexpected spray of rainbow glitter.

My.

Fucking.

God.

Glitter everywhere. On my hands, on my knees, on my shoes, on my coffee table, on my rug, on the rest of my mail, on the sofa. On the mysterious package from Sean Stokes. My hands and forearms sparkle. I think about how I'll have to take another shower now, how long it'll take to scrub all this off, how I'll probably find glitter in the crack of my ass.

Printed letters on the card stock proclaim IT'S HAPPENING! Below this: a blown-up photograph of Bart and Jackson looking out from the deck of the beach house in Rehoboth we rented last summer. (I remember the photograph because I took it.) Below that: a glitter-coated announcement of a late September wedding on the beach where they first met two years ago. (OFFICIAL INVITATION TO FOLLOW.)

Two years ago. The summer Bart and I shared a hotel by ourselves, when it was just the two of us. I remember drawing his attention to Jackson at the Beachcomber and agreeing to stay behind for an hour while the two of them went back to the room together. I remember flirting with this Persian man, remember being rebuffed and leaving the bar with thirty minutes left before I could go back to the room. I remember going down to the beach and sitting in the cold sand, in the dark, by myself, pitching fistfuls of sand at the black waves.

My phone buzzes.

Here early. Walking around. Meet you in the rotunda.

Now the package from Sean, the one he sent back in March when he still had a hand to write with, still had a brain with which to organize his thoughts. A package that sat, unclaimed, unacknowledged, while I carried on with my life, hating the man who'd sent it. There's no trickery in this one, no shock and awe of glitter. Just a folded letter and a small book wrapped in green tissue paper. I start with the letter because I already know what the book is going to be, and I just can't right now.

Dear Oscar,

I believe I once told you I used to write letters to my dead friend. The Angry Queen. I knew he wouldn't respond, but there was a freedom in those letters. I could write free of responsibility, free of judgment. Why bother holding anything back, if you're just speaking to the dead? So while you're still fortunate enough to be alive (oh, how fortunate you are, Oscar!), I'm writing to you now as if you weren't. I reach out to you, scotch-drunk, in the classical manner, with ink on paper, with the help of the postal service. Perhaps I still believe an envelope isn't something you can just ignore or delete, that it begs to be opened.

Where to begin, telling you what you don't want to hear? I could start with the winter afternoon I decided to give up on your book and go for a walk, but maybe I should start earlier. With you, looking miserable and invisible at the Attic, with Cal's wild hair, his ferrety eyes, his limbs made slender from sickness. His self-righteous fury. I left Washington after that first night excited, rejuvenated. I began to have heretical thoughts: What about another book? Do I still have something left to say? What could you teach me?

So I had to see you again. But the more I heard, the more I gleaned from the behaviors within your behaviors and the words underneath your words, the more I began to realize who you were. It was like watching pale apple flesh turn brown in the air. As I wrote, something in me wasn't satisfied. Then I realized the problem was you. I found myself, against my better instincts, judging you. Your contempt for others. Your ignorance of your own history. There was nothing new about you, nothing truly queer. Just spite. Just sadness. Just another Tiberius, a man at the end of his days, holing himself up in a secluded villa on a precarious cliff to hide himself from the universe that's still out there, hanging immense and black above his head. A posing sodomite.

Thinking about your life, I began to think about my own. What did it get me? Experiences, sure. Stories, yes. But here

I still am, older certainly, but no wiser than I was when I proclaimed to the world how I wanted to live. Perhaps experience without transformation isn't experience at all. It's just killing time. Then people around you start dying, and you have no choice but to transform.

One day, thinking of this, I went out into the beginning of another New York winter to a coffee shop I used to patronize decades ago, with writers whom you've never heard of and never will because they died too young. I met someone. A professor, a poet, twenty-three years my junior. On a whim, I took him to dinner. On a whim, I took him to London for a month. On a whim, I came back and burned the pages I'd written about you. On a whim, I asked him to marry me. On a whim, we left the city.

I knew you would feel betrayed, would wonder what happened to the man who lived according to the dictates of his manhood. But after so many decades of experience, Oscar, I was tired. I was so, so tired. I wanted to be a part of this new world, the one you take for granted. I wanted stability. I wanted humility. I wanted all the death, the sorrow, to be worth something. As your namesake once wrote in a letter of his own, "Where there is sorrow there is holy ground."

Maybe you see my marriage as a mistake. Maybe, in the future, I'll come to think it was. But you see, Oscar, marrying Jesse, slipping away from my past— it feels like the most rebellious act an old libertine like me could perform. It feels, perplexingly, like the queerest thing I have left in me to do.

I have no idea what you'll do with this notebook, but I couldn't burn it with everything else. If it's to be destroyed, it should be destroyed by you. These are your experiences, not mine. Will you learn anything from them? I confess, I have my doubts. I'm reminded of when I told you to reach out to your childhood friend, the one you kept ignoring. You told me you tried to sleep with him, as if that would make for a good story. As if that was the only way to connect. And I suppose I'm to blame for that. I was a terrible teacher because I wasn't clear about what I wanted. I wanted you to learn from each other. You, the angry queen. Your friend, the sad queen. Reunited at last, to give birth to some strange new beast. This, I thought, is where a book about you could possibly live. Because all that profound darkness? How invisible, how angry it makes you feel? Remember that you can't endure it alone.

Whatever you decide to do with these notes, I know what I'll do. I'll fold this letter and mail it off to you and hope you have the good sense to read it. I'll take this now-empty bottle of scotch downstairs to the trash and wake Jesse from his afternoon nap. Then we'll walk down the hill and find a bench where we can watch the river, together, until the light fades and the temperature drops and it's time for us to go back inside.

Your affectionate friend,
Sean

I read Sean's letter again. And again. And again. Then a buzz. I remember my phone, facedown on the sofa. I turn it over and see several missed messages.

Hey. Where are you?
Are you coming?

ETA?

It's now a quarter past one. How long have I been here, covered in glitter, reading this letter?

I unwrap the notebook from its tissue-paper skin. It's smaller than I remember, slightly bigger than my palm. I'm terrified of what's inside.

Two more buzzes.

Hey!

How much longer?

Annoyed, I type back: *Leave me alone.*

I pull away the elastic band keeping the notebook closed. On the inside cover is a strip of cocktail napkin from the Attic, secured with Scotch tape. On the facing page: OSCAR, FALL 2015. Then sentences and fragments and bullet points and words written on thin red lines, upside down in the margins, along rounded page corners. The familiar sentence: *Never seen someone so melancholy over his own cum.* After eight—no, nine—pages, the writing stops. The rest of the pages are blank.

Another buzz.

Fuck you, loser.

Sebastian

June 12. My T-shirt a Rorschach test of sweat. It's a lion, someone said. No, it's clearly an airplane, someone else said. Look at the wings. No, no, Dani said with the conviction of someone who's known the answer all along. They're two swords. Look. Two long, skinny swords. Dani described damp arcs of sweat meeting in the center of my breastbone. I guess, Dani's boyfriend said with a laugh from behind his red plastic cup. To me they just look like a pair of dicks. Dani slapped his arm. Marwan, she said. Stop it. I laughed and went over to the window, looked down at the crowds waiting along the parade route. The windowsills and balconies up and down the street draped in rainbows: rainbow flags, rainbow ribbons, rainbow streamers, rainbow banners, rainbow crepe paper, rainbow beads—most of it hanging limp in the thick, still summer air. People clustered inside the street-facing patios of bars and restaurants, around the stairs and front yards of townhouses, hunched alone or lingering in groups along curbs, leaning against stanchions at street intersections. I watched a mother lift her young son up into a tree, where he straddled the base of a branch and peered out through the leaves.

I understand, Principal Jones had told me weeks earlier. I'd be a liar if I said this didn't inconvenience me greatly, but I do understand. I lost a brother to depression. I take mental health very seriously here. Especially after poor Thomas Pitt. So when you come to me asking for an emergency leave of absence, I'm not just going to laugh that off, alright? I know we're all under some strain here with the packed classrooms, the construction. You've been looking pretty haggard these past few weeks. Longer than that, if I can be totally honest. I can't imagine it's easy teaching out there in that junky trailer. I also can't imagine losing you to burnout. Your class performance rates are outstanding, you've gotten us another great year of AP test scores, your pass/fail rates are impressive. So please. Go get some rest. Go take care of yourself. God knows we've got subs out there dying for the work. Principal Jones nudged over a box of tissues. I asked about the after-school group, if they would still march in the Pride Parade. Don't worry, she said. They'll march. We'll get the sponsor over from Beauregard to help with that. It's Arthur Ayer who's the president, right? (She pronounced it *ire*.) I'd say he could just take care of the whole thing himself, but you know how that would look, putting someone so young in charge of something so serious.

I spent my days alone. I tried to read but couldn't concentrate, tried to work on the fence but couldn't summon the strength. I closed the blinds, kept on only what lights I needed to get through the day. Occasionally, through an open window, I'd hear the sound of a bicycle passing by and restrain myself from rushing to the window in hopes of catching that familiar flash of purple hair, of shouting out my dumb apologies. Once, there was a knock on the door and I peeked out to see Arthur standing on the front stoop. But I couldn't move. Roiled, I thought of Oscar and Arthur messaging one another across the night, wished I could snatch at those messages like they were fireflies. Bottle them? Smash them? I wasn't sure. I lived in fear of my own arousal at something I had no business seeing. Had the two of them actually slept together, explored one another's bodies while all I'd explored was an empty jacket? It didn't matter what the truth was—the images were planted in my mind, and they were growing roots. So I flipped mindlessly through my art books, trying to replace them.

Saturn Devouring His Son. Francisco de Goya. 1819–1823. I shouldn't be looking at porn on the internet. I don't know what time my father will get home from his afternoon lectures. With every new picture I load, I think: Okay, this is the last one. While I wait for an image to appear, I click on more hyperlinks, open up new browsers. An image of two boys fellating one another on a white bedspread finally loads. This is it, I think. And I'm pleasuring myself, imagining what it would be like to take someone else's penis into my mouth, to roll it around with my tongue, to avoid scraping it with my teeth. Then the door from the garage opens. I shut off the computer monitor and freeze. Mouth agape, eyes wide. Thankful I only unzipped my fly, thankful there's a solid back to this office chair. My father asks how school was. I continue to stare. There's a moment of silence, then my father says, Oh, and walks back outside. In the blackness of the computer monitor, I see the door close, see my own shocked and distended visage. The face of someone caught in wild abandon. The face of someone putting things in his mouth he shouldn't.

Dani came over one evening, unannounced, with a bottle of wine. I'd thought about saying no, but she'd already found the bottle opener. I hadn't spoken to her in weeks, so for a while we just sat on the back porch in the dusk and cricket drone, saying nothing. I don't like seeing you like this, she said. I'm fine, I said. Bullshit, she said. Sorry I can't be the happy-go-lucky gay best friend for you, I said. Her voice turned angry for the first time. That's not how I think of you. Don't ever say that again. She leaned over, took my glass of wine away from me, tossed the merlot in an arc over the grass. Have some water, she said. Then: Listen. I want you to come to the Pride Parade with me. You remember John, the guy I tried to introduce you to last summer at the wedding. Yeah, I know how that worked out. Anyway, he invited Marwan and me to his apartment on Seventeenth Street, right on the route. You should come. I scoffed. She put her hand on my shoulder and I thought about just losing it. But my anger, my envy—which I sensed had spun out of control somewhere inside me—wouldn't let me. You need to come, she said. For your students. I can't show my face to them, I said. You have to come, she said. If it makes you feel better, you'll be watching from high up. They probably won't even see you. She patted my knee. I'll drive us, she said.

That night, I woke from a dream in which I watched Arthur and Oscar fuck. I was behind my familiar pine bush, the prickly sanctuary of my boyhood, shoving dirt and pine needles into my mouth to keep from crying out. I wasn't sure if they knew I was there behind the bush, didn't know which possibility was worse. The next day, I called Dani. All right, I said. I'm coming.

John's second-floor apartment was thick with people, with heat. Two open windows let in what little breeze there was. When the first dangerous tendrils of sweat slipped along my belly and crept into the waistband of my shorts, I excused myself, squeezing past the press of people in the kitchen, the hallway, the back bedroom. In the bathroom, I blotted my damp upper body with toilet tissue. Then I stared at myself in the mirror, looking half-mad from the heat, the part in my hair jagged, my forelocks sleek with moisture, my face bristly with stubble. A humidity-induced delirium reminding me of Courbet's self-portrait, the one I remembered now with mirth was titled *The Desperate Man*. I was drinking to stay cool, but also because it was something to do. I looked down to see I'd brought a half-empty beer bottle into the bathroom with me. There was a knock on the door. I took a final swab at my forehead and neck, snapped the faucet on and off, then opened the door, muttering apologies, and looked up to see John. Hey there, he said. Long time. Glad you could come. Thanks, I said. I slipped past John and out into the hallway. You forgot this, he called from the bathroom. I turned to see John holding out my half-empty beer bottle. If you need more, the cooler's over there. John pointed. Right where my boyfriend's standing.

Another drink.

Then it began. The apartment emptied out onto the front stoop and sidewalk, but I stayed upstairs with several others. Leaning out into the summer afternoon, I heard the blast of motorcycle exhaust, saw men and women on bikes blowing down the street, trailing massive American flags. The distant beat of a military marching band, growing in intensity until it finally passed by in regimented formation, flashing blue and silver like a school of fish caught in sunlight. Applause. Music from uncovered truck beds, from top-down convertibles, from the open windows of vans and SUVs. A chaos of noise and color. A giant wedding cake on top of which two men, in tuxedos, and two women, in gowns, pitched strings of rainbow beads at the crowds. Underneath the brides and grooms, the three-tiered contraption shook as the truck bed on which it rested rolled along uneven asphalt. Men and women on the cake's lower tiers, wearing T-shirts with the logo of a major international hotel chain, waving and dancing above a banner that read FREE TO LOVE. FREE TO MARRY. Behind the massive cake, more couples in t-shirts that said JUST MARRIED, that said LOVE IS LOVE, that said LOVE WINS. Dani called up to me from the front stoop: Come down here with the rest of us! I shook my head and said I could see everything better from up here.

More floats. Boys in cowboy hats riding a giant foil burrito. Girls tossing out Frisbees, pens, stress balls, condoms, necklaces, koozies, packs of gum—all stamped with the logos of HMOs, storage units, airlines, car dealerships, department stores, super-markets, coffee chains, fast-casual restaurants, social media net-works, internet search engines, dating apps.

Another drink.

Swimming teams, in speedos and floaties, spraying the crowd with water guns. Running groups making dangerous hundred-yard dashes between moving cars and trucks. Sports leagues play-ing with their respective balls. Politicians waving from the open tops of cars or shaking hands with the crowd. Bartenders from Empire, from the Attic, from Topiary. College students on bikes, skateboards, roller skates, Segways. Drag queens pulled down Seventeenth Street in elaborately decorated rickshaws, blowing kisses to their enraptured subjects. Oscar Burnham. I started and knocked my beer off the windowsill, where it rolled along the building's green awning before hitting Dani's shoulder and burst-ing into a spray of glass and foam at her feet. Shit, I called down. So sorry! Dani checked her bare legs for glass, then called up: Will you get down here, Sebastian? I looked back up the street, leaned farther out the window to try and find another glimpse of Oscar in his black T-shirt, frightened I'd see Arthur following dutifully in his wake. I felt a hand on my shoulder, felt myself gently pulled back into the apartment. Hey, John said. Careful.

Another drink.

Marchers and drivers slowed down, stopped to allow for some unseen recalibration blocks down the street. Below me, volunteers from local dog shelters stood in the heat with their panting charges in bright orange ADOPT ME! vests. Half a block up, students and faculty from Powhatan County Public Schools fanned themselves with signs and placards. HELENA HIGH LOVES ITS LGBTQ+ STUDENTS! LOUD AND PROUD BRUIN! GO SPARTANS! Then the parade lurched forward and the students and teachers made their way past John's apartment, amassed behind a banner proclaiming POWHATAN PRIDE. I found him. Arthur Ayer. Small rainbow flags painted on his cheeks, marching forward, smiling, calmly rotating his sign from left to right so both sides of the street could read it. IN MEMORY: THOMAS PITT. Look up, I thought as Arthur passed below me. Look up. Look up. Look up. Another awkward lurch, and the parade stopped. Arthur, I said from my perch. Then louder. Arthur! Arthur! Up here! It's me, Mr. Mote! Up here! Can you see me? I yelled and waved, fearing my words would be lost in the throb of the music. I was giddy and delirious and drunk and thinking this could very well be the last time I saw that Caravaggio face. Arthur tilted his head up, and it was enough to push tears through my eyes, enough to reinvigorate my cries. Arthur, I cried. Arthur! I'm so proud of you, Arthur! The parade shifted back into motion. Arthur stared at me with a face I realized in that moment would be forever unknown and unknowable. He smiled at me, faintly. He waved at me, faintly. Then he turned and continued down the street. I leaned out the open window as far as I dared and cried out his name one last time. Dude, careful, someone called to me from the kitchen. The parade moved forward, and so did Arthur until, finally, he was gone, out of earshot, out of sight, on his own, lost in the crowd and leaving me back here, a sobbing fool.

Another drink.

At half past eight, the parade ended. I lingered by the window and, in the growing silence that settled like a heavy cloud on the street, watched the slow dance of city custodians and street sweepers. Incredible, that so many people had crowded these streets only a short while ago. Let me guess, Dani said a little later. You're not coming out with us. I've had plenty to drink, I said. I see that, Dani said. You going to be alright to Metro home? Of course, I said. A little past nine, I followed everyone out of the apartment and almost tumbled down the narrow staircase. Hey, Dani said. Hey. Hey. She took my flushed face in her hands, stared at me like a doctor in search of possible brain damage. Then she leaned in and kissed my forehead. I love you, Sebastian Mote, she said. Now please go home. I will, I said.

I made it to Dupont Circle before I had to sit down. Out on the park's northern edge, a group of older men stood on the grass holding candles in paper cups. One of them moved his lips, and I caught the occasional name. Gus Manginello. Art Wallace. Stephen Wilson. Ron Angelino. And then I saw him again: Oscar, walking toward me. As if playing one of our childhood games of flashlight tag, I turned around, curled onto the bench, waited for him to pass. Then, after a few seconds, I got up and followed him around the circle. To what end, I had no idea. It was a compulsion I couldn't explain, as if some internal magnet the two of us shared kept pulling me closer, even against my better judgment. I had no idea what I wanted to say to Oscar, but I had to say something. Following Oscar, completely unmoored from the order of my world, I felt a passionate, almost delirious drive to grab him and shake him, to make sure he was aware of my rage, my resentment. To make sure that, wherever he went after this evening, for the rest of his life, he'd remember me. Dodging a small child, I slipped on a coil of purple beads and fell into the back of the man reading off his list of names. I braced myself against him, muttered apologies. The man turned to look at me with tired blue eyes through which, I imagined, he judged my own sorry state: drunk on beer and summer heat. I felt like we were caught in some silent conversation, each of us stunned by the effrontery of the other's presence. I wanted to apologize again, wanted to explain that I wasn't normally like this, it had been a difficult year. Then, in a thick voice holding back what I felt was immense anger, the man said, Enjoy your party.

The line for Empire wrapped around the building. Oscar and his friends stood thirty people ahead of me, underneath a massive digital clock that read 10:48. We'd been in line for almost an hour. I felt unsteady on my feet among the bursts of laughter, the streams of cigarette smoke, the faces glazed by cell-phone light, the bare limbs and loafers. Fun fact, someone near me said. This used to be a hot dog warehouse. Now it'll be condos, his companion said. What else would it be? Someone behind me said into his phone, My dating philosophy is, if it fits, I sits. I could hear the music through the brick walls, so loud it threatened to burst from the architecture and spill out into the streets. As if the club itself were aware this was its last summer of life. Farther back in line, someone shouted, What's the holdup? Eventually, we arrived at the club's thick double doors, flanked by bouncers in black who checked IDs and counted people on small hand clickers. *Click. Click. Click, click, click, click. Click.* And then I was inside, swallowed down a gullet of darkness. Up ahead, broad steps rose into a fury of color and light and motion, of rafters and exposed pipes like the ribs of a giant whale, all decorated with rainbow banners and flags. It staggered me, all these bodies—the crowds of a Bosch fantasia. I don't belong here, I thought. This was useless. Childish. I turned to leave, but the incoming press of people forced me deeper inside. I tried to look for Oscar. There was no sign of him.

Another drink.

I moved through the musk of damp bodies. Occasionally, someone put a hand on my shoulder or waist to help me on my way as I passed. Above and around me, the music shouted commands from underneath deep rhythms and beats, injunctions to get fucking crazy, to just dance, to not stop the music, to run away if you wanted to survive, to shake it off, to make it work, to give your love away, to get it on tonight, to evacuate the dance floor. I found a bare spot of wall and stood against it. I took out my phone to look busy, like I was just waiting for a friend or lover to arrive.

Another drink.

Up on the second-floor catwalk, it was a little easier to breathe. I leaned against the steel balustrade and spent the next half hour picking out an individual and following him for a few moments until switching my attention to someone else. I wondered if anyone here was doing the same to me.

Another drink.

I checked my phone. Ten after one. Down on the main stage, a drag queen named Pearl Nicholas walked three shirtless men, each of them leashed to her hand with a long velvet ribbon. I watched her painted lips follow the shape and sound of a remixed French pop song about blue, crazy love.

I heard my name from the bathrooms behind me. Sebastian! I felt like I'd just been caught breaking and entering. Sebastian! It was Oscar, looking at me not with the venom I expected but something warmer. Friendlier. He reached out to me. Let's get a drink, he said. I need to talk to you. I imagined that hand in places I'd only seen in small square photographs on my phone. Confused, I dropped my drink. Embarrassed, I turned to escape back downstairs. I tripped on someone's foot, smacked my right shoulder into a concrete pillar. Something shifted, briefly, along my bones. From behind me, over the music, I heard Oscar calling my name.

I made it as far as the parking lot next door before I had to stop, head fuzzy, stomach churning, ears ringing, shoulder aching. I found a car and held on to it to catch my breath, to slow down the rush in my gut. Across the street, a shadow moved past the curtained windows of a slender rowhome. Where are you now, Arthur? What are you doing out there in the night? But that wasn't any of my business. Right here, right now—that was the only thing I could claim as my own. And I didn't want it. I felt a rise in my stomach, a great unfurling of all those drinks, and ran over to vomit against a brick wall. Oh honey, a man said as he passed. Wiping bile off my chin with a shirtsleeve, I looked back up at the rowhome. The lights were off now.

I was thinking of sleeping right here, like this—what difference did it make?—when I heard my name over the laughter, the muted dialogue coming from the crowds leaking out of Empire. Oscar. He came into the parking lot. Hey, he said. What are you doing back here? I crouched low in the shadows, tried to keep as still as possible, hoped I wouldn't have to throw up again. Go away, I said. Leave me alone. Please. My breath became ragged, rapid as Oscar came toward me, his black shirt blending with the shadows so that it seemed I was being stalked by a disembodied head and arms. Something unreal. I just want to talk, Oscar said. Go away, I said, but he kept coming, closer and closer, and I couldn't take it, so I lunged and grabbed Oscar by his arm and dragged him down and backward onto the asphalt between two cars while he yelled, Shit, shit, shit. I locked my arm around Oscar's slim waist and turned my head away from his whipping arms, feeling like a fisherman who'd just landed a massive, squirming catch. The startling comedy of the thought loosened my grip enough so Oscar slid from my arms and crawled toward another car. He looked back, stopped. Sebastian, he said. What the fuck are you doing? Are you crazy? I am, I thought. You said it yourself. I grabbed Oscar's ankle, pulled him back to me. Stop, Oscar said. Sebastian, stop! Oscar lashed his free foot at my face but it was too late, I was on top of him, flattening him against the ground with my weight, hiding us from the street. His hands pushed up against my neck and chest and face. My god, I thought. He thinks I'm trying to kiss him. I felt like laughing. Oscar writhed beneath me, called me a drunk fuck, a motherfucker, a freak, a host of other names and insults, as if one of them held the key to releasing my hold when instead they simply tightened it. I wormed a knee up onto Oscar's sternum. My hands found their way around Oscar's neck. They squeezed. I watched Oscar's eyes widen. There, I thought. You remember me now.

Oscar

So this is what it's like to die.

Correction.

This is what it's like to be murdered.

All I'd wanted to do was apologize to Sebastian, to say nothing happened with his student and nothing ever would. I wanted to apologize for everything. And now he's on top of me, reeking of sour vomit and sweet soda, one hand on my throat, the other hovering next to my face, collapsed into a fist. I see the knuckles, can already imagine them colliding with my cheekbone and shattering it into fragments, can already imagine the pain and shame of a bent and broken nose. An entirely different sort of chin chuck. I'm trying not to think of what comes after that first hit, whether it's just a one-off pop or if there'll be more and more.

Sebastian swings his free arm upward.

Then, as if shot, he falls off me and curls over on the ground.

Lying there, gasping, coughing, I look up at the night sky in a brief moment of oxygenated euphoria, marveling at the way the blinking red dots of planes seem to skirt with skill between pinpricks of starlight. I rub my throat and chest in a silly attempt to massage more air into my lungs. Then I remember my current predicament and scramble away toward the street.

I'm about to cry out for someone, anyone out there to help but stop when I see Sebastian, on his knees, cradling his right arm against his chest, staring at the ground as if awoken from some horrible dream and trying to get his bearings in the real world. He doesn't sound like he's breathing so much as hissing. I see sweat in the faint lamplight, beading and slipping down his face.

"My arm," he says. "Oh, my arm. My arm. My arm."

He tries to get to his feet, bracing himself with his free arm against the ground, pushing up with his legs. He cries out in pain and falls back down. He lurches forward and vomits on the asphalt, following up the stream of sick with a low animal groan. He sits there, silent and still and alone in a dumb position of prayer.

He looks up, shivering with pain.

He sees me.

"Help," he says.

I'D SPENT THE day, as I'd been spending the last few weeks, with the notes; the haphazard scenes and scribblings I've been carrying with me everywhere: to coffee shops and jobs interviews, to movies and happy hours, to parties. My normal three-pat routine before leaving my apartment (phone, wallet, keys) now has a fourth pat: Sean's notebook. My notebook. I carry it around the city the way others carry toy dogs in purses or babies slung against their chests. In moments of solitude, I'll take the notebook out, the pages bent and ragged and damp. I'll read some of the things Sean wrote about me, behind my back. The terrible judgments in hurried script, as if Sean were trying to catch them before they slipped out of his mind. And the worst judgment of all, written in the center of a page, introducing the blank pages that follow it.

How to take someone like O. seriously?

I'd been reading these exact words when the Pride Parade came down P Street, where I stood on Martin's sixth-floor balcony and thought about who was more queer, us up here with our vodkas and mixers and phone apps, or them down there, waving to the crowds from their wedding cake float. I couldn't stop moving. I spent ten minutes on the balcony, five minutes on the sofa, eight minutes by the buffet table that was hardly being touched, seven chatting with a professional dog walker on the stairs leading to the second-floor landing, another twenty back on the balcony once Bart texted to tell me he was marching by with his bocce team, five in the bathroom shopping on Cruze and hiding from said professional dog walker. Three hours into the parade, I drained my vodka-soda and ghosted from the party.

I was supposed to meet Bart and a few others for dinner once they'd finished marching. To kill time, I pushed my way over to Seventeenth Street and wandered around Dupont Circle. For several minutes, I watched people mill outside an upscale diner that had recently opened in the footprint of an old florist. A gay couple, no older than me, laughed with a woman holding a toddler in her arms. I thought how this area had changed over the years, how the gayborhood had become just another neighborhood, how the same thing would happen where I lived now, how I'd be pushed further east, until finally I reached the edge of the Anacostia River and had no choice but to either turn around and blend in with everyone else or drown.

During dinner, I put up a front, acted and sounded as cheerful, as proud as I could, all the while thinking of the horrible line from Sean's notebook in my back pocket. *How to take someone like O. seriously?* Did any of my friends, with their tacos and lagers and sugar-sweet margaritas, think of me as a serious person?

Afterward, we found ourselves in line with everyone else at Empire. We danced, we drank, we mourned the thought of this place a year from now, razed to rubble. Some of us were sad. Some of us were angry. Some of us could have cared less. I looked down in disappointment at my Outrage T-shirt and shrugged my shoulders.

"Whatever," I said. "I give up."

Walking to the bathroom, a stranger patted my ass, and I checked my back pocket at the urinal to make sure Sean's notebook was still there. On my way out, I saw Sebastian. Leaning precariously against the walkway, looking at someone or something. I worried he was going to tip over and fall headfirst onto the dance floor, so I called out his name. He turned around, and in the flash of Empire's lights and the thump of its music, he looked just as lost and terrified and bewildered as me.

Sad queen. Angry queen.

I thought: I need to make this right. No. I want to make this right.

How to take someone like O. seriously?

So I reached out to Sebastian.

And he ran away.

"I'LL CALL AN ambulance," I say.

Still on his knees, hunched over, afraid to move, Sebastian shakes his head. "No ambulance. Please. I don't want to make a scene."

"Too late."

I move forward. Slowly, of course. Wary this all might be some sort of trick to get me back into his grasp, to get his hands back around my neck and this time to never let go. Within a few steps, however, I know he won't pull anything like that. He can't. Already I can see, through his T-shirt, a small knob of something that shouldn't be there, right underneath his shoulder. I kneel down next to him, watch him shiver. I start to roll up Sebastian's shirtsleeve. He hisses and grunts and soon I see that, yes, that knob is actually bone pushing up against the flesh of his upper arm, like a boil straining to burst.

"*Oof*," I say. "Okay, I'm calling an ambulance."

Sebastian cries out, and I leap back.

"No scene," he says. "No scene! No scene!"

"Well goddamn it, you can't just stay out here like this. Can you walk?"

"I can't even stand."

"I think you can."

"No, I can't."

"You can. Come on."

I slip my hands under Sebastian's good arm. Bracing him against my body and ignoring the reek of sweat, booze, and vomit, I lift him up. He cries out for me to wait, but I know if we keep waiting he'll never move. With no choice, Sebastian pushes with his knees and is quickly up, leaning against me, cradling his arm against his chest like a tyrannosaur. I watch him try to extend the arm, tentatively. He hisses again, starts to sweat again. I tell him to fucking leave it alone.

Slowly, step by miserable step, one hand holding his working arm steady and the other wrapped around his waist, I pilot Sebastian out of the shadowy parking lot and onto the sidewalk, toward Empire and then past it, through the people littered on the curb smoking and chatting and waiting for rides. I keep my eyes on our feet as we pass through them. At one point, Sebastian leans against me and dry heaves. "Don't barf on my shoes," someone says, and I snap, "He's not going to vomit, asshole. He's in shock." We turn up Georgia Avenue and head toward Howard University Hospital. A group of men watch us from a stoop across the street. One of them yells, "Get it, girl!"

Inside the emergency room, I guide Sebastian to the intake counter and wait for him to explain his situation through gritted teeth. He checks in, then I help him over to a row of tight chairs. We take our seats among the rest of the city's wounded. Sebastian coughs. He readjusts his body in the small chair, hisses again.

"Stop moving so much," I say.

Sebastian closes his eyes, breathes, sweats. I stare into my phone. After what feels like forever, a nurse emerges and calls Sebastian's name. I help Sebastian up and we walk toward the double doors. The nurse meets us halfway, takes over for me.

"Dislocated shoulder," the nurse says. He may as well be talking about a hangnail. "Third one tonight. Welcome to the party."

Then I watch them slip through the double doors.

Back in my seat, I replace my phone with the notebook. Just to make sure it's still with me, not lying somewhere in a parking lot for everyone to see. To pass the time, to keep away ugly thoughts of getting up and leaving Sebastian. Here's the line I can recite now by memory: *Never seen someone so melancholy over his own cum.* Here's the laundry list Sean scribbled on one page, upside down, of my *"lovers"* (I get the quote marks, Sean). A juvenile sketch of Fourteenth Street Baths, destroyed and fenced off from the public. The phrase *Watson + Shark*, underlined twice. A small shopping list: *Warren's new book, asparagus, red onion, sugar for Jesse, sea salt.* That final, judgmental line: *How to take someone like O. seriously?*

It's a good question, and I keep thinking about it until I doze off and wake at four minutes past three with the notebook open in my hands and the nurse standing over me. How long has he been here? More important: Did he read anything?

"Your boyfriend's doing fine," he says. I open my mouth to protest, but the nurse ignores me. He looks sapped of energy. "We're keeping him hydrated. He just got his X-rays, and we're going to reset his shoulder, okay? It shouldn't take much longer. But he's asking for you."

"Asking for me."

"He wants you there in the room when we fix his arm. Please follow me."

The nurse leads me down a short hallway and through a bee-hive of triage rooms, some separated by flimsy plastic curtains, others by solid doors. And there he is. Sebastian Mote. Very much alive, faceup on a hospital bed, one hand against the top of his chest, the other lying along his side and playing host to a saline drip. He's staring up at the ceiling, as if trying to peer through the floors stacked above to get a glimpse of sky. His T-shirt, cut open, hangs half inside a waste bin. When I come in, he looks at me and smiles.

"I thought you would have left me," he says. Then, to the nurse: "Alan, this is Oscar. We've been friends since elementary school. We met in front of a painting."

"Your boyfriend's a little loopy from the muscle relaxers," the nurse tells me. "And everything he's been drinking. Let's just wait for the doctor to come here so she can put your shoulder back into place, alright, Sebastian?"

I look at Sebastian. He nods in agreement. I go over to the bed and sit next to him. He tries to readjust himself into a sitting posi-tion, winces, settles for just turning his head.

"Maybe don't move so much," I say.

"I'm so sorry I tried to kill you," he says.

The nurse and I exchange looks. I shake my head dismissively, twirl an index finger against one ear.

"Mine's the same way," the nurse says. He excuses himself through the curtains.

"Hey," Sebastian says as if remembering something. "I saw a girl back there, in the hallway. While I was waiting for my X-rays."

"So you dislocate your shoulder and now you're straight."

"No. No, Oscar. You're not listening. God, you never listen to me. I was back there waiting to get my X-rays. Right? There was this girl there, sitting in a wheelchair across the hall, just like me. No one else was there. It was just the two of us waiting for the X-ray person. The radiologist. There's a lot of waiting that happens here, I've noticed. Quite a lot. And this girl. She was crying. I mean, bawling. She was drunk, too. She'd tripped down the front stairs of her apartment and cracked her elbow. She'd been waiting there for almost an hour and was looking at me as if I had all the answers. She was crying and asking me if they'd forgotten about her. And I said to her, I said, 'They haven't forgotten about you. It's not as bad as that.' I explained the word *triage* to her. I told her they were taking care of people with more serious injuries than us. People who might be minutes away from dying. I don't think that calmed her down much. I kept telling her the waiting was good, because it meant nothing serious was going to happen. We were going to live. We weren't going to die. She got mad, said they just didn't care about us. And I told her it's not that. It's just that they know we're strong enough to survive on our own. A little later, someone came and wheeled her into the radiology room. Then he brought her back out and took her somewhere. Maybe into one of these rooms."

Sebastian lays back, exhausted. I wonder if he understands how delirious he sounds. Then he turns to me and says, as if asking what I had for dinner, "Did you sleep with my student?"

How to take someone like O. seriously?

I tell him what I wanted to say back at Empire, before he ran away to prepare for my murder. I tell him about the messages on Cruze, about the arranged meeting at the National Gallery of Art, about Sean's letter, about the notebook (which I take out of my pocket and show him). I tell Sebastian nothing happened and nothing ever would. Sebastian looks back up at the ceiling and stars to cry.

I take his hand.

"Please," I say. "I want nothing to do with him."

Sebastian stops crying long enough to say, "Me neither."

The doctor sweeps into the room, followed by the nurse. I stare at the doctor's hands. They look like hands made for pulling, for shifting and bending. They look, perplexingly, both gentle and monstrous.

"Little too much partying, I hear?" She sounds like she's preparing to start a barbecue, not reset an arm. "I saw your X-rays. Congratulations. I'm going to bet you've got a big old tear in a ligament there. Probably your labrum. You'll want to have that looked at as soon as possible."

Oscar Burnham, saved by a torn ligament.

The doctor touches Sebastian's shoulder with those magnificent hands, brushes the knob of flesh that shouldn't be there. "How did this happen?"

Sebastian looks at me. I look at him.

"I fell," he says.

"So here's what's going to happen," the doctor says. "I'm going to gently manipulate your shoulder back into its socket. I'm going to do what's called an external rotation. I want you to just try and relax. Take deep breaths. If it gets too painful, let me know and we'll stop to give your muscles a chance to relax and catch up to what we're doing. Alright?"

Sebastian grits his teeth and nods. He looks at me, wild-eyed, desperate. I squeeze his hand and say it's only going to hurt for a while longer. I have no idea, of course, whether this is true. It could keep hurting for days. Weeks. It may never be completely right again.

The doctor begins to rotate Sebastian's forearm outward. I can see the pain and fear rise to the surface of Sebastian's face. He starts moaning.

"Doing great," the doctor says. "Doing great. We'll stop here for a second, then keep going."

Shortly, the doctor begins to apply downward pressure on Sebastian's forearm. I can't stop looking: at Sebastian's face collapsing in on itself, at the doctor's hands pushing slowly, at the simple watch on her wrist whose face reads 3:23, at the ragged circle of jaundiced yellow on Sebastian's wounded shoulder and the tiny red dot in the center where the muscle relaxant must have been injected. I imagine Sebastian's bones beneath his skin, shifting like continental plates back into their appropriate locations.

The doctor soothes Sebastian.

The nurse soothes Sebastian.

I soothe Sebastian.

Then there's a sound like nothing I've heard before, softer than the champagne cork pop I expected. Not quite a click, either. I wait for Sebastian to scream, but he doesn't. His moans just fall away into a long, heavy sigh of relief.

"That's it," he says. He's smiling. "It's back."

"Just hold on a moment," the doctor says. "The shoulder's a pretty weak joint to begin with. Yours is a lot weaker now." She checks to see if Sebastian has feeling in his arm, checks to see if he can manipulate his wrist, squeeze her thumb. Sebastian lifts his arm up and moves it around, lightly, hesitantly, as if he's just discovered the limb for the first time and is testing the limits of its use.

"Not too much now," the doctor says, easing Sebastian's arm into his lap. Then she slips out of the room, leaving me and the nurse to help Sebastian into a seated position, to help him ease his arm into a sling. Leaning over to tighten the loop around Sebastian's neck, I smell the salt of dried tears and sweat.

After more instructions from the nurse and the removal of the saline drip, Sebastian slides out of the bed toward the waiting room. I follow behind, ready to offer support, but Sebastian's walking on his own again. Occasionally, he looks back over his right shoulder and smiles at me.

"Thank you," he says.

He says it again.

Watching Sebastian sign his discharge papers, I'm moved to laughter by the silly paper hospital gown barely covering his upper body, the silly ID bracelet hanging from his wrist, the silly ball of cotton taped over the puncture in the crook of his arm. A nurse escorts an old man, holding his stomach, past us and toward the double doors we've just left. I wait for the man to turn around, wait to see Sean's face, wait to feel his eyes hollowing out my mind, my chest, my stomach with judgment. But Sean's not here. He's gone. It's just Sebastian and me now, checking out of the hospital, stepping out into the world and searching for a ride home.

So THIS IS what it took to get him back to my place: the offer of a shirt to replace his paper gown. I wonder what he sees in all this, the white walls with their impressionist artwork purchased on sale at home furnishing stores; the hard edges of my black desk, my black kitchen table, my black office chair; the violent red of the sofa, of the armchair toward which he shuffles and into which he drops.

"*Ow,*" Sebastian says, reaching for his shoulder.

"Hey. Be careful with that."

I hand Sebastian a glass of tap water and go to my bedroom to find him a spare shirt. I unfold the first large I find in a box of leftover Outrage T-shirts. ECCE HOMO. Somewhere in the back of my mind, I hear the ring of a tiny graveyard bell and have to sit on the bed. God, I'm exhausted.

In the living room, Sebastian's slumped in my armchair, legs spread, the paper gown hanging off his shoulders. His head leans to one side. His eyes are closed. He looks tender, sweet in some dumb way. Like a little boy. I put the T-shirt on the end table next to the armchair, snap off the overhead lights, and ease down on the adjacent sofa. I feel the pressure of Sean's notebook against my hip. I try to make out, through the dark, the steady movements of Sebastian's chest, his arm crooked in its sling. The microwave clock in the kitchen reads 3:59. I watch the numbers intently, waiting for the time to change. Then it does.

SIX

A Manhood

⟡

Sebastian

On Friday, June 17, while bodies were lowered into the soil of Orlando cemeteries and seniors at Mortimer Secondary decorated their graduation caps and gowns for Saturday's ceremony, I packed a duffel bag, locked the windows and doors, and drove seven hours south, into the North Carolina mountains, to visit my father.

You looked like one of the dogs when I saw you sitting there, my father said that evening. We were on the back porch of his rented cabin, a two-level home with quilts and framed pictures with just-folks sayings, mantel-top photographs of a traveling history professor's children and grandchildren, a wooden clock carved with deer and squirrels and hummingbirds on tree branches like some mountaineer's interpretation of Rodin's *The Gates of Hell.* The dining room was my father's ersatz study, filled with fat towers of books and file folders, a curled-up paperback of *The Birth of Tragedy,* a laptop connected to a printer on the floor, jam jars of half-finished tap water and tea. My father slept in the first-floor bedroom and gave me the entire second-floor loft, with its soft carpet and bay of windows that opened onto a small patch of lawn next to the gravel driveway. Beyond that: forest. No homes, no lights to look for in the night. That had been my first thought when I'd pulled up the drive, only to find my father out on an errand. I'd sat on the front steps and waited, staring through the trees, trying to pick out the birds whose calls I heard, the turkey I imagined shuffling through the undergrowth. Desperate to urinate, I'd walked across the lawn and into the woods, stopping where the land dipped down toward a reservoir owned by the university. Somewhere off in the green, a branch had snapped like a gunshot and I'd jumped, hitting my shoes with piss. As dusk approached, the front porch lights had come on, attracting the attention of moths and crane flies. I'd tried the front door again, as if the right grip would help it open. Then I'd heard the rattle and groan of my father's car struggling up the steep hill.

The next morning, I looked out the bedroom window and saw something small and black and furry leaning into the front door. I came downstairs to whimpering and barking, a flash of white tail. Those would be the dogs, my father said from the dining room. I asked him who they belonged to. Neighbors around the hill, he said. They let them roam outside all day. At night, they always go back to their homes. I asked if the dogs were friendly. Sure, my father said. They'll follow you everywhere.

The morning talk shows, the evening news programs, still replayed scenes from outside Pulse. Police vehicles, their red and blue lights cutting the night. Clusters of disoriented people, limp strips of yellow crime-scene tape. The club itself, squatting black and strange among the palms, like a tomb.

I spent my days walking, plunging deep into the woods, following no set path, happy to be lost for a few blissful hours. I was never alone, though. Always, there were the dogs. A black shepherd, its tangled hair matted with burrs I'd occasionally pick out. A brown-and-white border collie named Gus. A yellow Lab named Jules. A shepherd with a misshapen skull and a penchant for gnawing on his left forepaw. They followed me down to the reservoir, where I sat and read books I pilfered from my father's stacks (W. G. Sebald novels, volume four of Gibbon's *Decline and Fall of the Roman Empire*), taking big drafts of mountain air into my lungs, trying to think about nothing, watching Gus lap at the shoreline as if ashamed to steal water he knew didn't belong to him.

Some evenings, my father and I lit a fire in the bell-shaped clay chimney on the side porch. I'd watch my father's hands grab and snap kindling, tear shreds of old newspaper, strike matches. Slung back in plastic deck chairs, we'd sit in front of the fire's crack and pop, watching small flames lick out of the chimney's neck, listening to the rush of cicada song from the dark trees. I kept waiting to see my father cry. I waited for him to confess how lonely and miserable he was here. On our third night of this ritual, I finally asked him if he missed my mother. He stared into the flames in the chimney's belly, blew lightly. You know the answer to that, he said. It's just that you seem so content being up here alone, I said.

I wish I knew how to do it. My father reached over and patted my hand. I'm never really alone, he said.

The next morning, I made a goodwill trip down the mountain for groceries. Loading plastic sacks into the back of my car, I felt a looseness in my right shoulder. I looked down at the hands holding the bags, imagined the as-yet-unfixed tears in my ligaments, thought it was only a matter of time before I did something stupid and my shoulder popped out again. I'd watched videos online about how to reset your own dislocated shoulder. I thought: It looks painful, but I could do that.

Over dinner that night, I showed my father pictures of the fence-in-progress. Jesus, Seb, he said through a mouthful of grilled corn. That looks awful. Hire some help. Please.

Some days, I walked along the pothole-riddled drive that curved around the mountain and periodically branched off to rise into the trees or fall down a hill toward another cabin. Slow drivers waved to me when I moved to let them pass. College students waved at me from their porches with hands holding beer cans and cigarettes. I didn't stop to talk, just smiled back. Behind me, the dogs kept pace, ears perked, noses twitching, alert to anything that could be coming up ahead or behind.

It was still in the news. Interviews with grieving friends and family. Excerpts from wakes and funerals. Landslides of cards, flowers. Survival stories told from hospital beds. Candlelight vigils and crosses and hearts and flags. A gunman posing in a bathroom mirror as if taking a picture for a dating site. Screenshots of text messages sent by the soon-to-be-dead. Names, scrolling along the bottom of the television screen, scrawled in chalk on sidewalks, printed on the covers of newspapers and newsmagazines, recited at rallies by pop stars. An awful free-verse poem of forty-nine lines. Christopher Andrew Leinonen, 32. Akyra Monet Murray, 18. Luis S. Vielma, 22. Javier Jorge-Reyes, 40. Antonio Davon Brown, 29. Kimberly Morris, 37. Alejandro Barrios Martinez, 21. Oscar Aracena-Montero, 26.

Afraid my reception would kick out, I drove down the mountain, then parked at a gas station once I found full service on my phone. Principal Jones called at half past eleven. How are you feeling, Sebastian? Rested, I said. We talked about graduation, about the emptiness of the hallways and classrooms. Then Principal Jones said, I've got good news and bad news. My fingers drummed against the steering wheel. Across the street, cars slashed by on wet roads. I'll start with the good. I know you're concerned about how you left things last month. But now that school's done for the year, I wanted to let you know that you're needed here. We want you to come back. You're too valuable to me, Sebastian. To us. Other good news? It looks like we'll be moving some of you out of those trailers and back inside the new building. A real classroom again, Sebastian. Four solid walls, a solid door, a solid floor. Some real windows. I started to speak, but Principal Jones cut me off. Don't, she said. Don't give me an answer now. At least, not until after I've shared the bad news. They're scrapping some of our AP courses. French. Art History. I know you're predisposed to think this has something to do with you, but it doesn't. It's STEM, that's what it is. Enrollment's up, the district wants to focus on other AP classes. Computer science, calculus. So there's that. I'd need you to take on another honors English class to balance out your schedule. The district still cares about literacy, for now. And the LGBT student group. We want to keep that going, especially after. Well. Anyway. I'd need you for that, too. But take another week. I wanted to call because I'd feel awful if you came back without knowing what's changed. I thanked Principal Jones, told her I'd decide soon. Then I closed my eyes and sat in the car as the rain picked up and beaded raindrops slithered down my windshield.

That afternoon, there was a break in the rain, and I spent it outside, pushing up and over small hills, sidestepping potholes black with rainwater, comforted by the familiar sound of the dogs behind me. Too young, too healthy to be my mother's dogs, I thought. Occasionally, I tossed a twisted branch into the woods and watched one or several of them pitch forward into the bushes and return with the same stick, flecked with spittle and leafmeal. We eventually arrived at a stretch of road that curved up the woods. A voice cried out from somewhere on the mountain, and the dogs, one by one, turned and followed it. I tried calling them back, but they ignored me. The sun slipped behind another round of storm clouds. I stared ahead at the bend in the road, imagined I could see something moving behind it, could hear the slow, wet crunch of footsteps on gravel. A collective of the Pulse dead. Eyes empty. Bodies freckled by shrapnel and automatic fire. Moving toward me, unstoppable, unavoidable. In seconds, they'd turn the corner and shamble into view. I wanted desperately to run. But I couldn't move, I just stood there in the middle of the road. Then a car slowly turned the bend. I stepped aside, feeling silly, and waved at the old woman behind the steering wheel.

Out on the back porch, I read my father's earmarked copy of *The Emigrants*. Occasionally, I'd marvel at the opening in the immediate tree line, like a green picture frame cradling the distant canvas of hills and mountains, the small white square of a house poking through the trees. Then a violent noise: my phone vibrating on the glass tabletop. An email. I read the address, read the subject line. I got out of my chair and walked into the afternoon sun. I paced as I read the message, forgetting the book, the view, my father working in the living room.

Later that night, I wrote my response. I held my phone out the open loft window and hoped for a strong signal. I waited. I waited. A small blip, the word SENT. Relieved, I went into the bathroom, closed the door so my father downstairs couldn't hear me, and wept.

Dear Mr. Mote. I hope you get this email. They just gave us our Jefferson email accounts, so I'm testing mine. I got my dorm assignment the other day: Minor Hall. I think you told me once that's where you lived as a freshman? I'm on the eighth floor. I took a virtual tour, and I can see the football stadium from my room. I've been emailing back and forth with my roommate. He seems nice. He's a musician. We're planning on joining the Queer Student Organization here. I hope you're well. I'm sorry I didn't see you at graduation. I looked for you. I think I know why you left, but I hope you can tell from this email that I don't think badly of you. I forgive you. You were missed at our group. Some of us had a rough time at our last meeting, thinking about things. Remember Juan? Sophomore, hooped earrings, wore those floral-print blouses he made himself? He took it really bad. He told us he wished you'd been there to talk with. We said you'd be back in the fall. I hope that's true. If so, maybe I'll stop by. We have a reading break in October. Raymond's here, so I have to go. We're back together. We're biking over to the park. He brought sandwiches. Be well. Arthur. #WeAreOrlando.

Dear Arthur. I'm pleased to hear from you. I think you'll like living in Minor. It's close to everything you need, and it sounds like you have a much better view than I did. (I lived on the second floor.) I appreciate your forgiveness. I shouldn't have done what I did. I shouldn't have pried into your personal life. It's yours, not mine. I'm getting better now, I think. About coming back to Mortimer: a word of caution. It all changes so fast you wouldn't believe. You'll find that once you come back after having been away at college, once you see how things have started to change, to move on without you, once you see the younger kids walking along the same paths you once did, your memories will start to get mixed up. You'll start to confuse the past for the present. You'll start wishing things were, for you, the way they are instead of the way they were—which is the way they had to be to bring you to where you are now. You'll start longing for a life others have instead of the life you have. I hope that makes sense. That's why I've never been back to Jefferson since I graduated. So I say this with all the kindness and support for your future success, of which I'm certain: Don't come back. All my best, Sebastian.

The next morning, I left the house without acknowledging the dogs waiting outside to greet me. Fog occluded the view of the distant hills; what had once been a detailed landscape was now a naked canvas. I drove down the mountain to the gas-station parking lot and called Principal Jones. I'm coming back, I said.

Instead of driving back up the mountain, I headed into town, past the small strip of main street shops and on into the foothills. I passed a clapboard community church and a small graveyard behind which the mountains rose, laced with thick ribbons of mid-morning mist. The radio station, which I hadn't changed since leaving Virginia, was coming in clear here and playing Chicago's "Saturday in the Park." I followed the signs to a trail my father had recommended. I parked in the empty gravel lot, tightened the laces on my hiking boots, and set off down the sloping path and into the quiet, wet forest. Without the dogs for company, I felt estranged from the universe. There was only the crunch of wet gravel and sand under my shoes, the occasional spats of birdcall, the growing rush of water from the cascade that ran parallel to the trail. I followed the water down, stopping occasionally to admire the clumsy architecture of rocks violently wrenched from the earth, smoothed by thousands of wet years into something graceful. Hardly the Arcadian grandeur of a landscape by Cole or Bierstadt. Something average, ordinary, beautiful in its insignificance. Something one could find littered throughout the Appalachians, existing, unseen, in peace.

The murmur of conversation, the burst of laughter. Through gaps in the screen of trees above me, I saw forms coming toward the switchback. I had a horrible thought the shambling dead had followed me out here, to remind me of some secret, unspoken duty. Then the group revealed itself. Two men in khaki shorts and shirts, ankles in wool socks, feet in muddy hiking boots, faces in beards. Another man, with a torch of black hair and sticklike legs poking out of cutoff jean shorts, a wildflower tucked behind his right ear, and a small steel piercing above his right eye, who slashed at low-hanging branches with a warped piece of wood. Another man, in flip-flops and a baggy T-shirt that read WOOD-SON COLLEGE, an up-tilted safari hat. The scrabble of their foot-falls was enough to push me to the side of the trail as they passed mirthfully by. Hey, they said. The wood sprite with the pierced eyebrow smiled at me and said, with no hint of malice or irony, Cool shirt. Dumbstruck, I looked down at my chest, at the words ECCE HOMO. Thanks, I said. The wood sprite continued looking at me, walking backward while the rest of his merry band moved on. At the head of the group, the man on the right casually slipped an arm around the other's waist, hand dipping down for a light pat on one buttock. As the group turned at another switchback, the wood sprite winked, pointed at me with his wooden sword, then turned around with a fantastic leap and disappeared behind an outcropping of rock.

Tempted by the sun striking the flat rocks on my left, I slipped off the trail and onto the cascade. I felt like a child, dwarfed by the size of the stones, dipping my hand into the rills of water run-ning along and around them, skipping over small tidal pools in divots of bedrock, hunting for footholds and purchases to place my hands and heels, careful of my weak arm. I pulled myself up onto a flat rock and lay on my back. I let the sun warm my belly through Oscar Burnham's T-shirt. I listened to the nearby trickle of water.

Domestic Scene, Los Angeles. **David Hockney. 1963.** I'm the first to wake up the morning after Pride. Oscar's passed out on the couch, facedown, a foot dangling in space. I put on, carefully, the T-shirt he's set out for me, then turn on the television in hopes the noise will be enough to gently wake him. And there it is. The red breaking-news band at the bottom of the screen, the perpetual symbol of twenty-first-century dread. MASS SHOOTING IN ORLANDO NIGHTCLUB. 20 PEOPLE DEAD. I watch SWAT teams crouch behind cars, cradling rifles and submachine guns. I see limp bodies, carried by friends or splayed on the grass. I see a rose of blood blooming on a white tank top. I see social media posts: *Are those fireworks? Everyone get out of Pulse and keep running.* Then, from behind me, a groggy voice: What time is it? It's nine forty-five, I say. Are you seeing this? No, Oscar says, you're in my way. I step to one side. Jesus Christ, he says. We sit on the sofa, side by side, stunned, watching television. He keeps going back to his phone, quoting to me from his friends' social media feeds. I watch the faces on television warped by grief, by shock, by anger, by fear. Several people turn to look at the camera, at us. I pluck at Oscar's shirt, snug against my chest. I can smell the mess of last night all over my skin, vomit mixed with liquor mixed with sweat mixed with that strange hospital smell mixed with sleep. It's a massive scene, a reporter says. It just keeps getting bigger. Then, because I can't sit here and watch all this, I ask Oscar if he'd mind if I took a quick shower. Of course, he says. He walks me into the bathroom, hands me a fresh towel, and, even though I don't ask, helps me out of the T-shirt. Left is cold, right is warm, he says as he draws back the shower curtain. We stand there for a moment on the tile, me half-naked, he half-drawn to the television voices in the living room. If you need something, he says. He pulls the hollow bathroom door behind him until there's just a sliver of an opening left. I make the water as hot as I can bear, undress, step under the hiss, and close my eyes. I experiment with my right arm, see how high I can lift it. When it starts to tremble,

I tuck it back against my chest. The water, the heat, the steam, is mesmerizing, and I'm halfway between wakefulness and sleep, holding myself against the shower wall with my strong arm, forgetting about what's going on in the living room, thinking about finally going to visit my father, when I hear the shower curtain pull back on metal rings and turn around to see Oscar standing outside the tub. I can't be out there with all that, he says. It's not his nakedness I notice but his face, as weak and torn as I imagine the ligaments of my shoulder must be. The face of a boy I used to know, a man I'm not sure I understand but with whom I feel (and perhaps always will) a strange sort of kinship, a living intimacy brought into relief by the dead intimacy of bloody bodies on bloody dance floors and in bloody bathrooms, and instead of covering myself, instead of saying, Wait a second, or, I'm in here, I reach out a soapy hand and lead Oscar into the water with me and our lips find one another's lips and our hands find one another's backs and our feet are squeaking against the tub and he tastes like soap and with the suds and the water and the fear it doesn't take long for either of us, it's an afterthought, it's not the point, it's what happens after that's the point, when we each shrink back into the other's hand and we tremble with the shared knowledge that, once we step back out of the water and into the world, the moment will be over but not just yet, not just yet, and we rest our faces in the wet hollows between the other's neck and shoulder, our kisses now just simple breaths, and we're standing there in the spray from the shower as the warmth slowly dies away and we're waiting for it to become too cold to tolerate anymore and I'm thinking, as I know he must be thinking, I don't know who I am or what I'm doing or where I'm going but at least I know I'm alive.

I sat up in the sun and watched leaves make lazy circles in a small pool past my feet. I took out my phone and scrolled down until I found it. The five-letter name, the ten-digit number. From somewhere farther down the cascade came the sound of laughter, faint splashing. I tapped DELETE. Then I retied my hiking shoes, staggered to my feet on stiff legs, and started making my way up the rocks and back to my car.

At a certain point, the landscape became too scattered, too slippery, so I had to pick my way through the rhododendrons and back onto the trail. I was pulling twigs out of the treads of my shoes when I saw the same hikers I'd seen earlier, now ascending the path toward me. The two lovers with linked hands. The man in the safari hat on his phone. The wood sprite with the walking stick seeing me and saying, We meet again. Are you a student here? No, I said. My father teaches here, I'm just visiting. The safari hat: What's he teach? History, I said. Sorry, he said, I do physics. The lovers looked at me and smiled. I'm Adrian, one said. Pete, the other said. Ben, safari hat said. George, the wood sprite said, extending a hand. I took it, said, I'm Sebastian. He should come to our party, Pete said to Adrian. It's not a party, George said. It's my house and my rules and I hate parties, so it's not a party. We're just having a few people over to hang out. Nothing exciting. But yeah, if you want, you should come. I don't really know you guys, I said. We don't know you either, George said. Isn't that what it's about? Above us, the sun slipped behind clouds. We should go, Ben said. Rain soon. George asked me if I was staying out here. For a little longer, I said. Come with us, Pete said. You'll get to know us, we'll get to know you, and then you can decide if you want to come to the party. It's not a party, George mouthed to me while shaking his head. Think I'll keep to myself today, I said. George frowned. No worries, Adrian said. He turned and started walking. Pete followed. Then Ben. Nice to meet you, George said. He crouched to pick something out of his shoelaces, then hopped to his feet and ran to catch up with his friends. Somewhere behind the cloud cover, the sky groaned. I looked up, felt the temperature drop. Ahead, the others were already ascending the hill. George turned to look at me. Sunlight flashed off his eyebrow piercing. I called out for him to wait up.

Oscar

At the door, I say goodbye to the hookup from last night's candlelight vigil in the park, watch him walk down the Saturday-morning hallway with his sandals slapping against his heels until he turns the corner toward the elevator and disappears, go into the bathroom to take a shower, scramble some eggs, microwave left-over coffee, and, because there's no time like the present, because I can't keep putting it off any longer, I go to the bedroom, take the small black notebook from my nightstand drawer, flip through it one last time (*How to take someone like O. seriously?*), drop it on top of a nest of pages from last week's *Dagger* in the wastebasket beside my desk, take out the batteries from the smoke detector, grab vodka and matches from the kitchen, come back and light the whole thing on fire.

It's not the conflagration I expect. No *fwomp!*, no burst of light along the walls. Just a disappointing *pop* and *snap*, faint heat that starts to lick at my knees once the flames get going. I watch the notebook, damp with Aristocrat, buckle and retreat into itself. I wait for a feeling of release, of liberation, of closure.

Something reeks.

I pick up the plastic wastebasket, careful of the flames, and discover the bottom starting to melt. Rushing into the kitchen, I put the whole hot mess in the sink and start running the tap. I let the faucet go for several minutes, long after the flames die. I dump the soggy contents out into the sink and toss the disfigured wastebasket on the floor. I stare at the mess in the sink, the pile of black mush on top of half-eaten eggs, as if trying to read tea leaves. But I can't read anything. It all just looks and smells like shit.

THREE HOURS LATER, in the back of a stranger's car taking me through the city, I think of what Sean wrote in *Ecce Homo* about the old Freudians he was forced to sit with as a child: "Death-driven, they called me. To which I say: Very well, then. Onward into death!"

I'm not heading toward death, not today. Just suburban Maryland. Still, the Pulse dead are everywhere, bearing down on us. You can't not think of their fate—of yours—whenever you step outside. Every dropped beer bottle's an unpinned grenade rolling under Topiary's patio bar. Every scream's the battle cry of some jihadi blowing himself up in line outside Empire. Social media profiles covered in rainbow ribbons on black backgrounds, shirts that read WE ARE ORLANDO and LOVE TRUMPS HATE. This is the gayborhood, circa July 2016: caught between a mass murder and a presidential election.

Windows down, the car moves through the city, past the giant bulge of Nationals Park, past the skeletons of apartment towers, past the yellow and green necks of construction cranes, across the Anacostia River, south along the eastern rim of Bolling Air Force Base and the proto-Vegas glitz of National Harbor. Already, I feel the day beginning its slow bake, and I'm hoping it's cooler in Fort Washington, down by the water at Patrick's house, where I've been invited to a Sunday afternoon barbecue and fundraiser. One more party before it's time to go back to work.

That's right.

Monday morning, I'll take a bus over to the second floor of an office building north of Union Station and start my new job. Oscar Burnham, the new mid-level graphic designer at the D.C. offices of Boone + Baine, a boutique marketing firm helping legacy businesses, major airlines, grocery stores, lobbying firms, trade associations, and the rare multinational organization speak directly to us queers. Laundry detergent. Hardware stores. Hotel chains. Banks and storage centers and tourism boards. Pills to counteract the belly bloat of HIV medication. Mine will be the hands that select the stock art, that manipulate the coloring, the sizing, the positioning of bodies. Mine will be the pair of eyes that help approve projects for printing, for distribution in high-traffic points across the region. Proof positive we arrived at equality years ago when we became just another demographic to be marketed to.

I have Patrick to thank for the opportunity. He called me the Monday after Orlando and said he hadn't given up on me, he knew Boone + Baine's creative director from college, he'd shared my portfolio and told her to imagine how I could put my talents to good use helping our community.

And really, what choice do I have? With little savings left, with no other leads, there's nothing left for me to do but defect. Beggars, choosers, and all that. But if selling out brought Sean several months of contentment, maybe it can do the same for me. Maybe it's the queerest thing I have left to do.

We pull into the driveway of the happy couple's happy estate and the air's still thick with heat. Through a fence of trees I spot the single-level stretch of wood, stone, and glass horizontals. I put my phone into the small drawstring bag I brought with me, wedge it down into what little space isn't occupied by my wallet and keys, by a slim tube of sunscreen, by my worn paperbacks of Sean's novels. I'd planned on burning these as well, but given the debacle with the notebook, I don't think it's wise to destroy my entire apartment complex just to make an obvious point about letting go. I could've taken them to the library in the laundry room, yes, but I don't want these books anywhere near me. So instead I'm bringing them out here as a silly sort of thank-you gift to Patrick.

Thought you might like these, I'll say.

Thanks, he'll say. How soon do you need them back?

Keep them, I'll say. Give them to someone else when you're done.

I ring the doorbell and wait. Across the street, two boys in bright blue bike helmets make lazy laps in someone's driveway. A massive wolf of a dog plods by, sniffing at the ghost of urinations past, leading along a woman in bright green sunglasses. "I know he's a beast," she says as she passes by and I step back. "He's harmless."

No one answers the door, so I follow the hum of music along a cobblestone path that wraps around the side of the house and leads into the backyard. There are already people here, standing in packs along the wide deck, sitting in the iron chairs and benches under the trees, hanging out by the fire pit. Patrick comes out of the group, wearing floral swim trunks and boat shoes. His tropical shirt strains against his new belly.

"Oscar. You made it."

We hug, and he leads me to the outdoor bar to make a mimosa, a screwdriver, my choice. I shrug out of the drawstring straps, open the top.

"I've got something—"

Lee yells for Patrick from the kitchen.

"Hold that thought," Patrick says, then jogs toward the house.

I put the bag back on my shoulders, slop some orange juice and champagne into a plastic flute, meander over to the stone embankment overlooking the dock. I watch two sleek day-cruisers—*Shahdaroba*, *Happy Hours*—bump hulls with three orange kayaks. Then I turn away from the water and insert myself into a conversation with friends of friends of someone here. One of them, a ginger wearing a shirt that reads I'M WITH HER, goes on about how he knew someone who dated one of the Pulse victims.

"Just one or two dates," he says between grapes. "While he was working at Disney World last year. *Pirates of the Caribbean*. A technician, not a pirate. I don't think they kept in touch, though."

"Jesus," someone else says.

We just stand there in the sun for a while, thinking about the horrible questions we want to ask but can't, the answers we're afraid to know. How did he die? What was the song, the lyric, the word playing when the bullets hit his body? Did he crawl back into the bathroom with the others? Did he slowly bleed out under the weight of strangers? Was he pulled, still breathing, from the wreckage and taken to the hospital before finally deciding it would just be easier to leave this mess of a world? We're all, in our own private ways, thinking of ourselves in those forty-nine pairs of shoes, thinking of serendipitous run-ins not with Mr. Right or Mr. Right Now but with an explosion, with gunfire. Thinking of ourselves caught at the wrong party, at the wrong time. Born a little too early, or a little too late.

Over the ginger's shoulder, there's a folding table draped in black linen, a giant plastic barrel littered with bills and checks. Next to it, someone has blown up, laminated, and cardboard-backed a *Time* magazine cover with its roll call of the dead in white type on black, with its blood-red headline, *Why Did They Die?* I scan some of the names.

Luis Daniel Conde, 39.
Franky Jimmy DeJesús Velasquez, 50.
Peter O. Gonzalez-Cruz, 22.
Amanda Alvear, 25.

I excuse myself, step over to the table, take out a five-dollar bill, and drop it inside the plastic barrel. It's all the cash I have. Surely enough to keep the dead off my back at least for a few hours. I go back to the group, and someone else excuses himself to drop money into the barrel. Then someone else does the same.

A little after noon, Patrick and Lee, the lords of Fort Washington, stand on the deck and call us forward. They thank us for the donations, destined for the coffers of a national anti-hate foundation run by one of Lee's real estate clients.

Patrick says he'll take whoever's interested out for a boat ride.

"Oscar," he says a few minutes later, face masked by giant sunglasses, heavy hand on my shoulder. "You're in the first wave. Come on." Again, I remove my drawstring bag, but he's already moving past me down the slope of grass toward the dock, giving off an easy sort of power with his now-open shirt, his baggy swim shorts, a confident swagger that's annoying and, strangely, admirable. Is that what power looks like?

He calls back: "Grab that cooler of beer by the table, will you?"

So here I am, sitting in *Happy Hours* as it moves down a quiet inlet of the Potomac. Ship's manifest: Five souls. Patrick and two others up front, taking turns piloting the boat; me in the back on a slippery plastic seat around a small table, across from a bulky, baby-faced man wearing a T-shirt with a rainbow ribbon and a small plastic bracelet on which is hollowed out the word ORLANDO.

"I read that one," he says. "I was going to see him read last summer, but I got sick and couldn't make it."

I look down at the copy of *Ecce Homo* I took out of my bag and must have been rolling aimlessly into a tube. Fine, I'd thought while stepping into the boat. I can't burn these, I can't give them away, so I'll drop them into the water.

"I knew him," I said. "In person."

"No shit. Was he as much of a freak in real life?"

"You'd be surprised. He was pretty conventional."

"Huh."

We make our way into the main branch of the river. When the man turns away, I toss *Ecce Homo* over my shoulder and into the water. I do the same with *Skin Dreams*, then have to stop with my sad water burial when the man looks back in my direction.

We move out among the other party boats and day cruisers, the Jet Skis flashing along the river like water spiders. I feel the thrum of the engine under my feet, hear tinny music from passing boats. We toast cruisers and kayakers with our beers.

Several Jet Skis slash close by, and Patrick curses as he maneuvers *Happy Hours* away from their reckless wake. We pass under the Woodrow Wilson Memorial Bridge, stretched above us like a giant aqueduct, and eventually come to an idle just below the tip of Hains Point. We crack open more beers, listen to Patrick bemoan the responsibility of boat ownership: the cost of winter storage, the labor of cleaning sludge off its white hides, the obligation to take it out as often as possible to make sure everything's working properly. While he talks, I lean over the side of the boat and, behind everyone's backs, dip *A Manhood* into the water and let it go.

"Sometimes I think it's just not worth it," Patrick says. "Too much responsibility."

"I think it's cool," someone says.

"Hold on to it," the man across from me says. He reaches for another beer. "Something you can do with the twins when they get older."

"Twins?" I ask.

Surely he means twinks. But no, Patrick grins and then for the next few minutes everyone's talking about David and Daniel, the two boys waiting patiently in a surrogate's belly to be brought back to their destiny on a grand waterfront estate. Everyone's gushing and cooing about the quality of Maryland private schools, about the cost of day care, about matching sailor suits. They may as well be speaking Martian. Someone passes around Patrick's phone so we can see an early sonogram. I hold the phone politely for a moment. Nothing but a mass of gray and black and white, like static on an old television screen. If there's a person in there, let alone two, I can't see it at all.

I feel the old spite return.

"Sure you want to do that?" The man across from me nods at my hand, still floating in the water, fingers adapted to the cold. "You know what they dump in here, right?" Then, to the rest of the boat: "Fifty bucks to the first person who spots a floating corpse."

"What if it's just a limb?" someone says.

"How much for a syringe?" Patrick says.

On the radio, Katy Perry's telling me I'm a firework, but really I'm just claustrophobic now and desperate to get away from everyone, desperate to get back on land where I can make some pathetic excuse to call a car and go home, desperate to get away from the talk of Potomac trash and consumer-rated cribs and gender-neutral toys and the summer heat and the diamond-shimmer of light on the water's surface and the man across the table from me asking how many books are in my bag and the slow roll of the idling boat and the distant drone of speedboats and Jet Skis and the dirty-white gull swooping past us on its flight to the Virginia shoreline and the weight of the water-beaded beer can Patrick tosses in my lap before telling me to smile and relax and letting everyone know it's time to go back.

Happy Hours growls to life. We pass again under the shadows of the Woodrow Wilson Memorial Bridge. A few minutes later, the man across from me gets out of his seat, belly fat corkscrewed as he turns and points out a riverside mansion behind a fence of manicured shrubbery. He salutes the house as we cruise by.

I ask what that was about.

"Wait," the man says, affronted. "You don't know who lives there? That's Warren Cook's house. Well, one of them. There's also the Rehoboth beach house, the U Street condos, the bungalow in Cleveland Park. I think he owns one of those old houses on

Logan Circle, too. Owns pretty much all the gay bars and clubs here. Well, the ones still left. Mandel's. The Attic. Anna's Bistro. Empire. Fourteenth Street Baths, rest in peace. Every vodka soda, every plate of wings, every martini—all ends up right there."

"Take my money," someone screams, holding his wallet out in the air.

"So that's the asshole selling Empire for condos," I say. "Real pillar of the community."

"He's a Trump donor," Patrick says. "No, seriously. It's common knowledge."

"There's equality for you," I say, reaching into my bag to take out *A Boyhood*, not caring what anyone thinks of my public littering. "You can be a fag and still have the freedom to be a fucking idiot."

"Don't use that word," the man across from me says. "Really."

"Guys, guys," Patrick calls from his captain's chair. "Over there. On the right. That's the house Lee and I were thinking of getting originally. They outbid us."

Everyone on the boat stands up and moves toward the bow, leaving me alone on the stern, sitting on my knees on the plastic bench cushions with *A Boyhood* in my hands. Patrick speeds up, and suddenly there's a rocking as *Happy Hours* collides with the passing wake of another boat. I see a flash of bikini tops and swim trunks. Everyone's up at the front of *Happy Hours* looking at a riverfront home in the distance I can't see. I turn to look back at the receding city, at the faint sliver of the Washington Monument, and then there's a loud scream from the direction of the bow as the same Jet Skis return, four of them, sweeping dangerously close. Patrick tells us to hold on, then speeds up. Someone shouts in glee. Patrick yells, "Fucking drunks!" Someone pitches an empty can of beer at the pilot of the second Jet Ski, right at his red trucker hat. He misses.

And me?

Caught off guard by the sudden swerve, in the middle of getting to my feet, halfway out over the water with my center of gravity thrown off, I slip backward against the lip of the starboard side, too tall to balance myself properly. I feel the wind against my bare legs, a hollow rush, no time to say anything, noiselessly pulled along by the unbending laws of physics. Then a smack, a cold embrace, and a strange—and strangely delicious—moment when I realize, with clarity all the more shocking for its obviousness, that I've fallen into the Potomac River. An upward rush, and I'm rising to the surface, into the sun and the air, in the dying wakes left by *Happy Hours* and the Jet Skis, each continuing on its respective path: one leading downriver to Fort Washington, the other upriver toward the city.

I tread water, thankful in this embarrassing moment for the length of my arms and legs. I think of the fat motor attached to the back of *Happy Hours*, think of how close I just came to being decapitated by powerful blades. Little waves slap my chin like flirtatious reprimands.

Someone comes out onto the back porch of a house on the far shoreline, white shirt flapping beneath a cap of thick white hair. I open my mouth to get his attention and immediately receive a refreshing mouthful of river water, ingesting who knows what. Oblivious to my struggle, thinking I'm just another insignificant speck lost in the glimmer of the river's surface (a discarded life vest, a fugitive duck), the man goes back inside, leaving me out here shivering and sinking under the weight of my T-shirt, the word OUTRAGE belling away from my body in the cold, dark water.

Then I realize I've lost my drawstring bag. Yes, the rest of Sean's books are gone. But so are my keys. My wallet. My phone. Everything I can use to verify my existence now rests at the bottom of the Potomac. And with it: the numbers, the names.

Bart.

Martin.

Patrick.

My mother.

Sebastian.

WHEN I GOT out of the shower the morning of June 13, several minutes after Sebastian, I was still thinking of those two very different pulses—dance music, automatic fire—and feeling sick to my stomach. I was still thinking of sitting in the emergency-room waiting area while, more than a thousand miles away, emergency rooms had no idea of the bodies coming their way. The horrible juxtaposition of time and place that sent me, naked and bewildered, into the bathroom in the first place, not really conscious of what I was doing, shocked when Sebastian, soap-slick, extended a hand and pulled me into his arms instead of simply closing the shower curtain.

After, in the living room, Sebastian was dressed and sitting on the sofa, balling up his paper hospital gown in one hand while the television news cobbled together a timeline of events. I wasn't sure what to do or say, so I just sat down next to him as if the last thirty minutes hadn't happened, as if they'd just been a fantasy. Then I asked Sebastian if he wanted to get breakfast. He looked at me, smiled with closed lips, and said he'd already called himself a car. It was then I understood that what had happened back under the stream of city water wasn't the beginning of something but an ending. I was about to make some silly comment about our adventures in our childhood basements, about fencing with our adolescent boners. Something to lighten the strange, silent moment. But I felt it would be the wrong thing to say.

Sebastian's phone rang. We jumped.

On the elevator ride to the lobby, we didn't talk, didn't hold hands. Outside the front doors, a Mazda with Maryland plates idled. People passed by with dogs and farmer's market satchels as if nothing had happened, as if the ground hadn't crumbled beneath all of us. Sebastian went over to the car. Without warning, thinking of bodies saturated with the blood of strangers, thinking of the horrible intimacy of it all, I reached out and pulled him into a hug.

"Careful," he said. "Shoulder." Then he slipped his good arm around my waist and we were standing again, as we'd been back in the shower, breathing into one another's necks, clothed this time, not in water now but sunlight. I could still smell soap—my soap—on his body.

Sebastian let go.

I offered to help him into the car.

"I can take it from here," he said.

"Okay," I said.

The car pulled up to the corner of my block and waited to turn. I raised my arm in farewell, expected a window to roll down, an arm to reach out and return my gesture. When nothing happened, I panicked and ran across the street and up to the car. I knocked on the window, watched Sebastian scoot over and roll it down.

"Hey," he said.

"Hey," I said. "When will I see you again?"

Sebastian sat there, caught between sunlight and shadow.

"Let's try another ten years," he said. I couldn't tell if he meant it as a joke or a prophecy. He smiled. "Will you remember me then?"

The stoplight turned green.

"I think so," I said. "Yes."

A car behind us honked.

"Gotta go, guys," the driver said.

Sebastian's car turned and headed down Fourteenth Street. I stood there on the corner next to the bus shelter with its horrible MAKE HIM YOURS FOREVER advertisement until the car disappeared from view, until all I had left was my imagination, following the car on past the churches, the offices, the theaters, the museums and monuments. Past the flat patch of public ground where he'd first come up to me, where he'd first sat down with his limp paper lunch sack and asked if I was new here, where he'd first extended his hand for mine and offered to take me seriously.

Back upstairs, I cut off the television, sat down in the armchair, and started calling my friends. No one answered, so I left messages asking if they wanted to do something today. Helplessly, I scrolled through photos and videos and news stories on my phone. Already, I started to see thoughts and prayers, weeping yellow emoji and fat red hearts, rainbow flags like militant banners. Sadness and outrage. Someone posting about how his best friend always goes to Pulse on Saturdays and he still hasn't heard from her and could someone please let him know ASAP if they learn anything.

IN THE WATER, something slides past my left ankle. Seconds later, I feel it again. More insistent this time, like something trying to get my attention. Just a fish. But what if it's not? Didn't I read somewhere they've started finding bull sharks in this river?

I tread faster.

Then—yes! Look!

Happy Hours, growing larger! Coming back for me!

I hear the motor growl. I see hands wave. Patrick looks like he's laughing. The flutter against my ankle returns and I have a terrible fear that in seconds the brushing will turn into nipping, into an outright chomp, and I'm skinny enough as it is, I have no flesh to spare and I'm not ready to leave, so I raise my arms out of the water, I kick as hard as I can, I fight to keep my head, my voice, above the surface.

"Help," I cry. "Help! Help!"